HOLLOW FIRES

SAMIRA AHMED

ATOM

ATOM

First published in the United States in 2022 by Little, Brown and Company
First published in the United Kingdom in 2022 by Atom

1 3 5 7 9 10 8 6 4 2

Copyright © Samira Ahmed, 2022

Cover art copyright © 2022 by Dana Ledl. Cover design by Karina Granda.
Cover copyright © 2022 by Hachette Book Group, Inc.

Art on page 11 by Neil Swaab

The moral right of the author has been asserted.

A CIP catalogue record for this book
is available from the British Library.

ISBN: 978-0-3490-0395-5

Printed and bound in Great Britain by Clays Ltd, Elcograf S.p.A.

Papers used by Atom are from well-managed forests
and other responsible sources.

Atom
An imprint of
Little, Brown Book Group
Carmelite House
50 Victoria Embankment
London EC4Y 0DZ

An Hachette UK Company
www.hachette.co.uk

www.littlebrown.co.uk

HOLLOW
FIRES

BY
SAMIRA AHMED

To the ones we lost too soon.

Now hollow fires burn out to black,
And lights are guttering low:
Square your shoulders, lift your pack,
And leave your friends and go.
Oh never fear, man, nought's to dread,
Look not left nor right:
In all the endless road you tread
There's nothing but the night.

–A. E. Housman, from
A Shropshire Lad

~~CATALOG OF TRUTHS~~
~~TAXONOMY OF LIES~~
GLOSSARY OF INTANGIBLE THINGS

Fact: Something that has a concrete, provable existence; an actual occurrence; an objective reality.

Alternative fact: A disguised falsehood presented as true. See Orwell, George, doublethink: the simultaneous acceptance of two mutually contradictory "facts" without a sense of conflict or cognitive dissonance.

Truth: A quality or state in accordance with reality; the actual or true state or nature of a person, place, thing, or event. Fidelity. Honesty.

Lie: A false or misleading impression. A deception you tell yourself so you can sleep at night.

PART I

THE PAST IS PROLOGUE

SAFIYA

JUNE 1, 2023

Fact: The dead can't speak.

Truth: Sometimes the dead whisper to you, in the quiet: *Don't let them forget I was here once. Alive. Young. I was like you. I believed I would live forever.*

You never forget the first time you see a dead body.

It was warmish for a Chicago winter. If the temperature hovering around freezing is warm. (In Chicago, it is.) There was the sickly sweet rotting smell of leaves that had fallen from trees, mixing with mud, never totally drying up before the first snow. The odor filled the air around the sloping embankments of a crumbling stone culvert that was lined with steel. The pipe was hidden by overgrown limp grass, deep in Jackson Park, in the part where no one ever goes because there are stories of ghosts and Mothman sightings. It's not the restored part of the park—the blooming Japanese garden, the shiny metal sculpture of giant petals, the bike paths, and the Illinois prairie popping with blue cornflowers. It's the neglected area by the abandoned arched bridge that leads to nowhere. No one ever went there because there was absolutely nothing to see. Until the time there was.

The first thing I saw was a shoe.

A charcoal-colored canvas sneaker. It was damp, and there was a curved winter salt stain along its side, where the shoe had gotten wet and then dried. And another, higher water mark. Then another. Like the rings in a tree trunk that tell you how old a tree was, how long it lived before it was cut down. A passing of time. Three rings of storms. Three rings of floods. Weathering them all alone.

I remember thinking that canvas sneakers were not a good footwear choice. They weren't warm enough, even for a mild winter day. Your feet would be cold. It was too wet. *Silly Safiya. The cold and wet don't matter if you're dead.*

That's when I should've stopped. Right there. Right then. Literally. In my tracks. Called the police, moved backward and not forward into a crime scene. Would've saved me a lecture from the police. Would've saved me from the image etched forever in my mind. Would've saved me. Period.

But I didn't stop. Couldn't. I'd made a promise to a dead boy. And I was going to see it through.

I could say it was solely the hodgepodge of clues and half-baked theories that had led me there. Or my desire for justice. Or my needling curiosity that my friend Asma called nosiness. But I'm not that good a liar. There was a voice. His voice. The voice of a dead boy. I didn't want to believe it. But it was there, pulling me forward, reeling me in, asking me to find the *true* story. And to tell it.

I shined my light into the steel-lined culvert.

The shoe belonged to a body that led to a face I'll never forget.

4

When you see a dead body, you freeze, a layer of ice forming under your skin. You stare one second longer—too long—and that ice shatters, and the truth of what you're seeing cuts you in a million places. The body you're looking at was a person who lived and breathed and was part of this world. And even though your brain can't form a single clear thought, one idea burrows its way into your bones: This body—this person—is now part of you, forever. Not merely the memory of those empty, dark-brown eyes, or their crooked blue fingers, or the rigidness of their jaw, half-open in a silent scream. No. It's not what they looked like that you never forget. (Even though you never forget that, either.) It's that they never leave you. They are a part of your air. Your sweat. The blackness behind your eyes when you try to sleep. They were young. Too young. And now their too few memories are yours to protect. To hold. Their entire life was a beginning rushed to an end. They never got a middle. They never got the heart of their story.

At first you ignore it, the echo. But it never goes away. It's quieter at times. The voice. And then louder. Pleading. Plaintive. Angry. Sometimes it doesn't feel like a metaphor. Sometimes the voice sounds like your own.

I'm more than lawyers' exhibits presented at trial.

I'm more than the stenographer's click-clack.

I'm more than the sum of small facts.

I'm more than a body.

My Journalism Ethics professor tells me that I can't report on this story—I'm too close, even now, sixteen months after I found the body. He says my job is solely to find the verifiable, immutable facts. But those facts don't give you the whole story. They don't distill the truth of how it all happened, of why it was him. Of why it was me. Of what we owe the dead. Or how one death can change the way you look at the entire world.

Some facts barely scratch the surface of the truth.

Some facts obscure it.

Some facts are lies.

Some lies are necessary.

One fact that *is* the truth: Jawad Ali was fourteen years old when he was killed. And I'm the one who found him. One day he was a ninth grader. Then he was accused of being a terrorist. Then he was murdered. This isn't my story to tell, not exactly. But I'm here, trying to gather the truth, the whole truth, and nothing but the truth. Tugging at tangled threads of memory while the jury is still out. I could claim to be objective. But that would be a lie. And lies are what got us here in the first place.

October 20, 2021

MUSLIM TEEN ARRESTED ON SUSPICION OF TERRORISM FOR BRINGING HOMEMADE JET PACK TO SCHOOL

When Jawad Ali arrived at school Tuesday morning, he was excited to show off a cosplay jet pack he'd put together in an after-school class. But things didn't go exactly as he'd hoped. His English teacher mistook the costume accessory for a bomb and alerted administrators, who called the Chicago Police Department.

In the transcript of the 911 call released by the police, English teacher Patricia Jensen can be heard frantically describing Ali as "an Arab student" who was wearing "something like a suicide bomber vest."

"We'd been working on building new things from scraps and discarded items in the makerspace," Ali, the son of Iraqi refugees, told reporters after he was cleared and released from custody. "So when I finished the jet pack over the weekend, I was super excited to show it to my teachers and the other kids, even though it wasn't Halloween yet." He continued: "I'm sad my English teacher thought I'd bring a bomb to school. Maybe she thought I was a terrorist because of my religion. Or because I'm Arab American. Why couldn't she see me as a good student, though? A good kid."

Chicago Police Department spokesperson Jim Leary told reporters, "Police attempted to question the juvenile multiple times, but all he kept saying was that it wasn't real. He declined to give further details." Ali was taken into custody to ascertain that he wasn't "a sleeper, taught to blend in or distract," Leary went on to say.

Upon the teen's release, the police said he would not be charged with any crime for bringing a "suspicious object" to school.

Commander Phillip McCarthy said Ali should have been "more transparent and forthcoming" rather than repeatedly describing the device as a "jet pack." McCarthy continued: "The department is cognizant of his age and, at this time, will not be charging him with any crimes, including a possible felony count of planting a hoax bomb."

Ali is pleased he was cleared of all charges but remains suspended from school until Friday. "I don't get it," he said. "If the police cleared me, why can't I go back to school? I have an algebra test this week."

JAWAD

I made a jet pack. And they killed me for it.

It wasn't even real. It was plastic and tubes, glue and paint. I wanted to be a steampunk inventor for Halloween because I'd seen this awesome old anime called *Steamboy* about a kid who liked to tinker and create stuff, kinda like me.

In fifth grade, some of the kids started calling me Contraption Kid because I loved inventing things. Because someone gave me a stick of gum, two paper clips, and a string, and I invented a tool to sneak Starbursts out of the bowl on the attendance secretary's desk. It definitely wasn't as quick and easy as walking by and pocketing a candy when her head was turned, but it was way more fun. She only bought the original flavors. But that was fine by me because orange was my favorite anyway. I wish I could taste orange now. I wish I could taste anything.

For our elementary school engineering contest, I made a bridge out of Popsicle sticks and tape that held 150 pennies! Twenty pennies more than anyone else's. The trick was to turn the bridge upside down to hold the cup of pennies, to work against its natural bend. I got a ribbon for it and won a book about how to make cool stuff out of recyclables, called *Hey! Don't Throw It Away!* My parents were so proud. Baba always used to say that flipping your thinking was sometimes the best way to come up with an answer to a tough problem. Building that bridge was the first time I understood what he meant. My dad used to say a lot of stuff that went over my head.

Then this fall, right after I started ninth grade, the physics teacher organized an after-school club in the makerspace where we could work on our own projects. When I decided I wanted to build a jet pack for my costume, Ms. Ellis was totally into it. *Recycle! Reuse! Repurpose!* she'd always say. She knew exactly what I was doing. Saw my sketch and approved it. We'd been taking apart old electronics, like radios and TVs with dials and antennas, and Ms. Ellis said I could use any materials I could salvage. I was so excited, I took the whole project home to finish two weeks before Halloween.

My jet pack turned out so cool. I built it from two empty plastic soda bottles that I turned upside down and glued together, then linked with black plastic tubes—the stretchy kind you sometimes see on a vacuum. I added a TV knob and a dial from an old radio that had numbers from 88 to 108—its little needle was stuck on 96. Glued the whole thing to a ripped backpack I found in the trash.

I painted the pieces bronze and silver with leftover paint Baba kept in our building's basement, the same colors we used to upcycle the old pink bike our neighbor gave me when I was seven and we didn't have money to buy a new one.

I couldn't wait for Halloween to show Ms. Ellis the jet pack, so I took it in early. She loved it. "Being creative takes courage," she told me. "Never forget that." She had that look in her eyes that teachers sometimes get when you surprise them in a good way. I had the jet pack with me in English class, but when Ms. Jensen saw it, she said it looked like a bomb. I thought she was joking at first. I mean, it was painted soda bottles! I didn't even know what a real bomb looked like. But she kind of freaked out. Not the yelling kind of freaked out. The real quiet kind. The kind that's so much scarier. Her face turned gray, and she started stepping away from me. I shrugged and headed to my next class.

They walked me out the school door on a bright October day in handcuffs. Hands behind my back, like I was a criminal. I told them over and over that it was a jet pack for my Halloween costume. But it was like they didn't understand English. I was trying so hard not to cry. All I kept thinking, kept saying, was *It's not real. It's a jet pack. It's not real. It's not real. Please.* Kids were in the hallway taking pictures, livestreaming, whispering.

I thought that was the worst day of my life. Turned out, I was dead wrong.

PART II

STICKY RESIDUE

JAWAD

The news reports kept calling us Iraqis. Eye-rack-eez. That's how they said it. Like we weren't Americans at all. Like my parents and I didn't have US passports. Like my mom didn't protect them like prized possessions. But that wasn't the story the reporters wanted to tell. This was:

CHILD OF IRAQI REFUGEES ARRESTED FOR BOMB HOAX

ILLINOIS STATE SENATOR QUESTIONS LAX NATURALIZATION POLICIES IN LIGHT OF ALLEGED BOMB THREAT

POLICE: IRAQI IMMIGRANT STUDENT ARRESTED FOR HOAX BOMB HAD RECORD OF TRUANCY

In my real life, on my first day back from my three-day suspension for the "bomb hoax," someone had taped a shooting target—the kind that looks like a bull's-eye—to my locker. Then someone yelled at me. Others started yelling, too. Like a chant: *Bomb Boy. Bomb Boy. Bomb Boy.*

At that moment, right then, it felt like I was dying inside. Turns out, that's not what dying feels like at all. Dying was fast, but also slow. And cold. And hard. I barely had time to scream for help before it all ended. Before all my words were ripped away from me.

When I went back to school after the bomb hoax suspension, my parents told me I couldn't go to the after-school makerspace club anymore, at least for the rest of the quarter. Even though I'd been cleared. Even though I promised not to make anything else that could seem suspicious. When I went to tell Ms. Ellis, I thought she was going to cry.

"Don't let hate crush your creativity," she said. "Don't let them take away your shine."

I looked down at my shoes and whispered, "It's that...my parents want me home right after school from now on."

Ms. Ellis nodded her head. "I understand. I'm sorry for...everything. It will get better. I promise." She put her hands together like she was praying.

Now, even though it's too late to matter, I realize that sometimes adults—even the good ones—make promises they know aren't true. Promises made of fancy words they know they can't keep. I think they mean well. They probably think the truth is too sharp. But false hope cuts, too. At least it did when I was alive to feel things.

Ghosts don't have to go to school. I'm not saying that because it's the silver lining. It's that we don't have to go anywhere. But I visited Bethune anyway. I wasn't sure where else to go. It was the morning. First period. And I was never late to school. I guess habits stick around even when you don't need them to.

But going back to my old school, standing in the middle of the hall with everyone walking by me, almost made me feel actual pain again, like that thing when you lose an arm but feel it anyway. A phantom limb. In some ways it was barely different from when I was a real boy. No one really saw me then, either.

Except Ms. Ellis.

I thought maybe she'd be able to see me now. Hear me. She looked sad sitting there at her desk. I got kind of close to her. For a second, she stopped her grading. Almost looked up. I was so close. But then she shook her head and picked up her pen again. I think she blames herself for what happened to me, because she ran the makerspace club after school, because she encouraged me, because that was the beginning of my end. I don't blame her, though. It wasn't her fault at all. She was one of the kind adults, the ones who cared. I never told her that I knew she was on my side. That I appreciated her. Maybe she knows? I hope she knows. I hope she won't let them take away her shine, either.

Then I visited my old locker. They never reassigned it. Maybe they think it's haunted. (Spoiler: It is.) It's empty. A shell. Three days after my suspension had ended, someone duct-taped another sign to my locker: *Go home, raghead!* I peeled it off, but sticky residue from the tape is *still* there. That stripe of tacky gunk outlasted me.

SAFIYA

JANUARY 18, 2022

Fact: Seeing is believing.

Truth: Sometimes looks can be deceiving. Sometimes your brain tricks you by showing you what you *want* to see, even if it's not real.

I didn't see it until they took the boy away...took Jawad's body and loaded it into the back of an ambulance.

When they turned it over—turned him over—I noticed how gentle they were. The rubber-gloved hands of the EMTs worked in unison, like a machine, but softly, with their voices hushed, making no unnecessary sounds. As if he could feel the pressure on his cold, bruised skin; as if his ears could be damaged from loud noises. Even still, when they moved him from the culvert to the stretcher, his body landed on the vinyl green pad with a quiet thud. I cringed.

Right before they covered his body with a gray blanket—the kind they'd wrapped around my shoulders because I couldn't stop shivering—I saw a tiny glint of silver and blue dangling from his belt loop, a flash in the cold sun. A flicker of something vaguely familiar, a dulled hook snagging at a wisp of childhood memories. I shook my head and closed my eyes, in case I'd imagined it, but when I opened them, it was still there: a key chain, a small silver hand of Fatima, a blue and white stone at its center. A promise of protection.

JAWAD

The police never gave me my jet pack back. Guess they destroyed it to make sure it wasn't a bomb. It meant I didn't have a costume for Halloween, which was okay because I didn't feel much like dressing up anymore. A couple weeks after I got back from suspension, things finally started quieting down. "Bomb Boy" stuck, but mostly life was getting back to normal. My parents even said I could maybe go back to makerspace club after winter break.

That's when I started getting the texts. I ignored them. I'd gotten real good at ignoring things I didn't want to see or hear. I never told my parents. I didn't want to worry them even more. I was trying to be a good son. They both seemed so tired after my arrest. Even their bodies moved slower, like they were kind of broken. Like they got old overnight.

I guess I should have told them about the texts. I guess I should've told someone. But it was easier to pretend that nothing was happening. That everything was okay. All I needed to do, I thought, was keep my head down. Keep my eyes on my own paper. Keep my mouth shut. *Disappear*. I tried to make myself invisible. Turned out I was too good at it. Turned out vanishing was my superpower.

I died clutching my key chain. That silver hand of Fatima I'd held on to for so many years and always had with me. I thought about the last time I needed it, when I was a real boy.

Now all I am is a whisper in the dark to a girl who doesn't want to believe in ghosts. How do I get Safiya to believe in me? I need someone to believe in me.

State's Exhibit 1

Text messages sent to Jawad Ali, Nov 8–11, 2021, via Burner app

Stare into the abyss, and the abyss stares back

This is the way the Bomb Boy ends. This is the way the Bomb Boy ends. Not with a bang but a whimper ☠️

Nobody is more inferior than those who insist on being equal 🙊

Bomb Boy. Bomb Boy. Tick Tick Tick Tick... 💣

If you want me to believe in your Redeemer, you're going to have to look a lot more redeemed

SAFIYA

JANUARY 3, 2022

Fact: There are no monsters under your bed at night.

Truth: The monsters are all walking around in the daylight.

No one wanted to talk about the letter our mosque got the week before Christmas. No one, not even my parents, wanted to consider it a real threat. But "threat" was the only way to describe it:

> *Dear Muslim Scum,*
>
> *We will be coming to your mosque. It will be a massacre on a scale never seen. Christchurch will pale in comparison. You can pray all you want to your God.*
> > *But God is Dead.*

Everyone wanted us to go around like it was a regular December. Fa la friggin' la. Deck the halls. Down the eggnog. Fire up the TV yule log. A normal winter break—for Muslims whose mosque had been sent a letter about a possible mass shooting. Nothing to see there, I guess. The note had been postmarked on December 16 in London. *London.* Why the hell would anyone in England want to threaten a small community mosque on the South Side of Chicago? How did they even know we existed? The police gave us extra patrols at Jummah after the community pushed for it, but generally the police department was treating the letter like a prank.

All the adults kept saying we shouldn't let *them* scare us. Ummm? Why not? It was scary. I panicked when I first heard about the note. A massacre worse than Christchurch? Over fifty people were killed there! Our mosque was basically a neighborhood storefront. Even for Eid we probably didn't get more than fifty or seventy-five people for prayers. Why target us?

My parents kept reminding me that we'd seen worse. They remembered 9/11. I didn't, so I wasn't around to witness that fallout. But I was here for the first Muslim ban. And the second. And America's ongoing, relentless wars in the Middle East that started before I was born and that, honestly, I've never been able to fully distinguish or understand. One giant, endless conflict with a lot of nameless dead civilians. Killed by drones, which somehow made Americans feel less responsible, because drones aren't people. But only a person can issue a kill command.

Was it comforting for my parents and the aunties and uncles to know we'd been through worse? Maybe there was some twisted adult logic to that, but it didn't exactly feel like a warm blanket on a cold night.

That was the first week of winter break, and it was quiet after. I started thinking that maybe my mom was right: *It will pass, beta. Anonymous haters are all bark and no bite.* Aside from the weirdness of her casually dropping "haters" into the conversation, I started to forget, too.

The first day back at school was an unusually mild one for a January in Chicago. The sun warmed my face as I walked through the neighborhood, dodging the drips of awning icicle melt. It was a winter day with a hint of spring, of bright, new things; but every Chicagoan knew not to be duped by the false promise of a sunny day.

This was it—the final push to graduation. I'd applied early admission to college and gotten in, but there were still five months between me and the cap and gown. Until I could be rid of DuSable and most of all Dr. Hardy, our principal, who'd planted a target on my back after my very first op-ed in sophomore year, which said the school admin gave special privileges to varsity athletes. *Duh.* Reporting the obvious truth had landed me on his crap list.

I got to school early, so I planted myself on *my* bench across the street, readjusted my black wool beanie over my ears, uncapped the mitts of my fingerless gloves, and pressed PLAY on my phone's Voice Memos app. I'd done exactly zero schoolwork over the break, and my next Be the Change column was due Wednesday. I couldn't show up to journalism class with nothing.

BEGIN RECORDING.

> *DuSable Prep isn't the most privileged place in the world, but you can see it from here. It's mostly limousine liberal, faux*

woke privilege that prides itself on voting the right way. But it's one of those "celebrate diversity on paper, not necessarily in the admissions policy" situations, because for all the recognition of Day of the Dead and Lunar New Year and the Jewish High Holidays and even Eid, less than ten percent of the student body is Black, indigenous, or people of color (BIPOC!), which doesn't even come close to repping Chicago as it actually is. Ironic, since the school's named after a Black Haitian man who was the first non-Native settler of Chicago. The diversity numbers are even more abysmal for faculty, the administration, and the board of directors (which is all white this year). Sure, we have our annual MLK celebration, where we hear three minutes of the "I Have a Dream" speech and get some rah! rah! talks about diversity, equity, and inclusion from the administration and listen to the mostly white choir singing "We Shall Overcome" with no sense of irony. But do we ever read the full text of Dr. King's "Letter from a Birmingham Jail" when he calls out white moderates? No.

Before break, the Spectator had published an open letter from the Organization of BIPOC Students that called on the administration to address racial, religious, and identity-based biases at school, especially in light of a racist anti-Black meme that had been posted on the school's Facebook page. This, after the administration claimed it wasn't the school's responsibility, because it was a public page and the meme had only been posted as a comment from an unknown source. But it also stayed up for two days before they took it down because "free speech." And remember when the *assistant principal told upset students in his office that they*

needed to be "civil" and "make an appointment" if they

wanted a dialog—

PAUSE RECORDING.

"Safiya! Hey!"

I turned my head toward the alarmingly cute boy who was jogging up to me.

"You planning on skipping school on the first day back from break?" Richard Reynolds hovered above me, his pale-blue eyes sparkling in the winter sun. The space between us warmed, like his smile could thaw the coldest winter freeze.

"Ha! Me? As if. We were lab partners for a whole semester. Did you not pay attention at all?" I grinned.

"Oh, I paid attention," he said.

The way he looked at me when he said that—like I was the only interesting person on earth—made the tips of my fingers tingle. We'd known each other since I started at DuSable, but it wasn't until chemistry class last semester that I started to consider him more than a rich, preppy athlete. I began to look at him as a *hot*, rich, preppy athlete. One that was kinda sweet and funny. And fun to talk to. Someone who didn't overshare but truly listened and paid attention to other people, unlike so many popular guys at our school who couldn't shut up about themselves. But he was definitely not someone to crush on. One-hundred-percent, absolutely not crushworthy. Nope. This hard-boiled, tough-as-nails investigative journalist was not susceptible to his incredibly cute dimples. Or to his low voice that made you lean eagerly toward him when he spoke, like he was about to share a dazzling secret.

"Did you do anything fun over break?" he asked, knocking me out of my ridiculous heart-eyed reverie.

"Worked at the store. Watched a lot of holiday rom-coms. Too much hot cocoa. Tried to teach myself how to crochet a scarf." *God.* I sounded like a middle-aged lady with a lot of cats and embroidered pillows. Could I be any more of a dork?

Richard tried to suppress a smile.

"What?" I said, my defenses rising.

"Nothing. It's…kinda cute. Do you have fuzzy slippers, too?"

"Shut up." I gently nudged the toe of his boot with my worn Docs. I scooched over on the bench so he could join me.

"What about you? Were you jet-setting somewhere?"

"The only interesting thing I did was watch a bunch of movies suggested by our esteemed editor in chief."

I bit my lower lip for a second. I'd recommended some of my favorite journalism movies, like the total nerd I am, and he'd actually watched them? He *had* been listening when I was going on and on in chem lab about being a journalist.

"Seriously?" I said.

"What? I have layers." He grinned. "I can spend hours watching movies that have zero action, confusing plotlines, and a lot of talking with furrowed brows."

I laughed, doing my best imitation of that journalist-at-work look. "Which ones did you pick?"

"*Shattered Glass* and *All the President's Men*. Oh! And *Almost Famous*. What was that one line they kept saying?"

"'It's all happening,'" Richard and I said in unison. My cheeks warmed as we locked eyes.

"Not gonna lie. I fell asleep during *All the President's Men*. But the other two at least kept me awake."

"Ha ha ha. I love both of them—they're like two sides of the same coin."

Richard scrunched his eyebrows at me. "How do you figure?"

"They're about journalists who misrepresent facts. Except in *Almost Famous*, that kid lies about his age but writes the truth and has a good heart. In *Shattered Glass*, that dude was intentionally misleading. He told lies and pretended they were facts. That's why he gets busted. Good old fact-checking."

"Whoa, that's deep. It's very 'truth will out,'" he said as he joined me on the bench.

"Look at you, dropping Shakespeare references." I smiled, glancing up at him.

"I'll have you know it wasn't merely my athletic prowess that got me into this school....It was also my dad's very large donation." He laughed.

I grinned. I liked that he could be self-deprecating.

Richard placed his palm on the bench in the space between us and scooched a little closer to me.

I tucked a long stray hair into my cap and turned to him to respond, but at that moment, a singsongy voice rang out from across the street, by the school entrance. "Richard! Richard!"

Richard looked up and waved at Dakota, a perfectly perky junior he'd gone to a couple dances with. She beckoned him over with a wave of her hand and a tilt of her head.

He turned back to me and rolled his eyes. "Sorry. I gotta give her something. Winter Ball committee stuff. You'll keep schooling me on these movies later?"

"Count on it," I said, making a finger gun with my right hand and clicking my tongue. Ugh. I was the worst at this. Whatever *this* was.

I watched him jog toward the school. Dakota looped her arm through his as they walked in. I sighed and turned back to my phone. I listened to what I'd recorded so far. I wasn't sure how I wanted to finish the column. I always included an ask, one way students could "be the change." But my thoughts were disorganized. Half angst-steam ahead, half thinking about Richard's pillowy lips.

I sighed. *Again.* So much sighing, and the semester hadn't even technically begun.

I dropped my phone into my bag and watched the students amass on the stone steps that led to the large red doors of our turreted main building. Especially on misty, gloomy days, DuSable Prep looked like a spooky British boarding school without the verdant rolling hills or accents. We didn't have ghosts, but that didn't mean we weren't haunted. Everyone is haunted by something.

There was always post-holiday chaos on the first day back from break—students swapping stories about where they went skiing or snorkeling—but now there was a gaggle of students all staring down at their phones. Statue-like. Cold. Unmoving. This was not normal.

My first thought: school shooting. Or that some new, vaccine-resistant virus mutation had been found in Europe and was sweeping the continent. It was hard to know if my worst-case-scenario thinking was the world's fault or mine. Probably both. As I reached into my bag to snag my phone and see what the trash fire/horror show of the day was, I saw Asma waving wildly at me and running across the street, her long black hair in loose waves that framed her deep brown skin and killer contoured cheekbones. Unlike my nonexistent makeup, hers was impeccable, as always, but it couldn't hide the wide-eyed look of panic on her face.

"What are you doing? How are you not in journalism already?" she yelled as she neared the bench.

"And a very happy New Year to you, too!" I said. She and her family had been in Paris for the holidays. I was helping my parents in their desi grocery shop. Asma and I might have been a couple of the only desi Muslims in our class, but we occupied different stratospheres. Still, we'd had each other's backs since she caught Paula Ryan trying to clandestinely spit in my soup during our first year at DuSable—because why not prank the scholarship kid? Asma proceeded to "accidentally" knock the soup into Paula's lap. Paula was furious, but Asma didn't even catch detention. That girl could out-bargain the Angel of Death.

"Your phone must be blowing up. Have you even looked at the *Spectator* site?"

"No. Why would I? We're not posting new stories until later. Speaking of which, did you write—"

"We've been hacked."

I rolled my eyes. "What? Some sophomore post a picture of their butt or something? I swear, if—"

"Safiya. Stop talking for a second. You need to look at it." Asma shoved her phone in my face.

I glanced at the screen. My jaw dropped.

BE THE CHANGE

BY ~~SAFIYA MIRZA~~ GHOST SKIN

This is a disruption in your regularly programmed lefty brainwashing at this snowflake school. You need to wake up from the SJW-forced curriculum being crammed down your throats and realize this school is where free speech goes to die. Everyone is protected at this school. Except the pure, the alphas, who deserve to rule. Time to take this school back from the fawning beta multiculturalists and those who want to open the nation's floodgates to illegals. It won't be long before the cockroaches will be swarming at the school's doors. This school, this newspaper, this editor, they are all feeding you fake news pablum. Spit it out. Reclaim your space like we claim this one. We are everywhere. This place is ours. Wake up.

I am the herald of lightning.

It was *my* column. *My* byline. But crossed out and replaced by a racist manifesto? I felt like I'd been slapped. I looked up at Asma. "What's a herald of lightning?" I asked, a fireball whirring in my chest. Whoever the hell Ghost Skin was, I wasn't going to let them get away with this.

PART III

GHOST SKIN

JAWAD

Sometimes I like to visit old places. The ones I used to go to.
Like Juniper Park—my favorite playground when I was little. I was
so scared of the tall slide. The one that was shaped like a rocket at
the top and had a tunnel you slid through for the first half. You'd
only be in there for a second, but I hated the feeling of being
closed in, of not being able to see the sky. And that's how I was
left. Closed in, no sky.

Once Baba even went down the slide to show me that he could
make it through. He had to tilt his upper body back so he wouldn't
hit his head. I waited at the bottom for him, so scared the slide
would swallow him. I blinked and there he was, laughing. Raising
his hands in the air. Trying to get me to smile. I don't think my parents remember how to smile anymore. All their smiles were stolen
when I was taken.

Now when I go visit the dry cleaner shop my parents own, I watch them working through the big plate glass windows, and I feel how quiet it is inside. How the silence makes my mom's shoulders bend down over the sewing machine. The other day, she looked up for a second, rubbed her arms like she was cold, then pulled her blue sweater over her shoulders. I wanted her to see me. I wish she could see me. But I don't know how a ghost becomes real.

SAFIYA

JANUARY 3, 2022

Truth: When people show you who they are, believe them.

Truth: This statement is false.

Lie: This statement is false.

Asma was talking, but I didn't hear her. It was like my entire body was screaming but my brain was frozen. All I *could* hear was my heart beating in my ears. I kept staring at my phone, looking at the definition of "ghost skin": *a white supremacist who hides their beliefs to blend into a group or society and be undetectable.* What the hell? A neo-Nazi had hijacked my column? Our principal, Dr. Hardy, was probably going ballistic. Maybe if I was lucky, he'd been too busy with back-to-school stuff to check the site. Maybe I could take the whole thing down before he saw it. Why would anyone do this? How? I had to get to the newspaper room. I had so many questions and zero answers—the absolute worst-case scenario for a journalist.

"Hey. Hello? Safiya, are you listening?" Asma's hand on my shoulder jogged me out of my fog. "You're going to see Ms. Cary, right? I have to go ask Ms. Arch for an extension on my paper, but I'll meet you after. This is seriously effed up." She gave me a small smile as we stood and headed toward the building.

Ms. Cary was our journalism teacher, and we ran the *DuSable Spectator* out of her classroom. Asma was right: I had to get inside, take down Ghost Skin's article. But there was a pit in my stomach. Everyone had already seen the rant, or would see the screenshots that had probably been taken and were floating around in group chats. They'd all be staring, whispering about me. I was the editor. It was my responsibility. But right now, I didn't want it. Right now, I felt sick.

As soon as I walked in and turned down senior hall, I saw our principal in front of the journalism classroom, feet planted, arms crossed, face scowling. "Safiya Mirza," he hollered, unnecessarily loudly, down the hall. "I need to speak with you. Now." Hardy was big on public shaming. He would've made a great Puritan. He had the whole "Sinners in the Hands of an Angry God" vibe down cold. All he needed was a ruffled collar and shoes with wide buckles.

"Dr. Hardy, I understand and share your concern, but it's highly unlikely that anyone on the newspaper staff would have written that...that...statement. And certainly not Safiya. She is—"

"You think I wrote that?" I asked, my voice rising. I'd been silent, listening to him go off on editorial responsibility and slipshod management and inappropriate pranks and accountability. But now he was accusing me and the *Spectator* staff. Hell no.

Ms. Cary subtly gestured at me to take it down a notch. I took a deep breath. A wave of annoyance passed over Hardy's face as he narrowed his eyes at me, making the wrinkles on his forehead even more prominent. He didn't even try to hide how much he didn't like me. But being an admin butt kisser was never my goal.

In the fall, I'd written about how the administration was a dinosaur—out of touch with the times and the student body. He gave me a ton of grief for that column, a lot of side-eye, but right after Thanksgiving break, he made sure that either he or the assistant principal was in the lobby greeting students. A few of the very wealthy parents must've read my piece and called to question his administrative style—that was usually the only way anything got done around here. But he'd made it clear I was on his crap list for writing it. "Be careful, Ms. Mirza. You mess with the bull, you get the horns." That was one of his favorite phrases, which he repeated to me many times after my piece was published.

Also, he never let me forget that I was a scholarship kid who should be constantly grateful. I was at DuSable only by the grace of others. How could I possibly forget that, even for a moment, when he was always there to rub it in, like it was a wound.

"Ms. Mirza. If not you, then who was it?" Hardy asked.

"Obviously some racist who hacked the school website. Oh, and a happy New Year to you, Dr. Hardy." I added a wide fake smile to punctuate my sarcasm.

"Don't play coy with me, young lady. This is not how I hoped to start the winter quarter, but here we are. No surprise that you're involved with this mess."

"Involved? I had nothing—"

"Dr. Hardy," Ms. Cary interjected, somewhat softly. "As I said, I'm certain Safiya had nothing to do with this." I could tell she was nervous—she was twisting the ends of her strawberry-blond hair, and her face looked pale and more pinched than usual. She was a new teacher and didn't have tenure. And Hardy had the uncanny ability to make everyone around him uncomfortable, no matter how big or small the crowd. He was one of those administrators who seemed to dislike all kids except for…well, students like Richard. The shiny, beautiful ones, whose parents made big donations to the school.

"It's obviously not me. I mean, look at me." I didn't mean for him to glare at my scuffed Docs, ripped jeans, and blue-and-green-plaid flannel shirt, which he did, without amusement. I meant, *see me* for who I am. "I'm a brown-skinned Muslim girl with Indian immigrant parents. Why the hell would I hijack my own column to put up a bunch of poorly written racist crap?"

"Language, Ms. Mirza. Your intentions are beyond my comprehension. But perhaps this was a way to create drama. To stir some cancel culture fervor." He shook his head. I couldn't understand what he was saying. It made no sense. But he continued. "I expect you and the newspaper staff to get to the bottom of this. And beginning today, principal approval is required for every story you post to the *Spectator*. You get the paper in order ASAP, or I will shut you down. For good."

I opened my mouth to protest, to tell him that if anyone was creating cancel culture *drama* it was him, but Ms. Cary jumped in before I could speak. "Understood. I'll work with IT to see if we can figure out who hacked the site and how."

42

"And I'll address it in my column today—" I started to add.

"You will do no such thing," Hardy interrupted. "Were you not listening to a word I said? There is to be no reference to this so-called hack. If that is indeed what it was. If we don't talk about it, it will simply die out. Want to stop a fire from spreading? You cut off its oxygen."

"But I—"

"Don't press me. I will not hesitate to remove you as editor if necessary. This is a school-sponsored paper, and the buck stops at my desk." I had to hold myself back from laughing at Hardy mid-lecture. "The site doesn't go back up until it's been scrubbed and appropriate content is put up and approved by me. Have I made myself clear, Ms. Mirza? Now if you'll excuse me, I have to go deal with what I can only assume is a barrage of parent phone calls about this."

I nodded as Ms. Cary walked Hardy to the door. I quickly grabbed my phone from my back pocket, and when I refreshed the *Spectator* site, all I got was a 404 error. I wanted to throw my phone across the room. I wanted to throw it at Hardy. But that would only end badly for me. Besides, I had terrible aim. My stomach twisted in knots. Hardy was looking for an excuse to shut down the paper. To get rid of me as editor. After my column on the administration last semester, he'd called me a "thorn in his side." He was not big on being subtle. My head spun. If I didn't figure out who the hacker was, Hardy was going to get everything he wanted.

JAWAD

I may not be able to feel things anymore. But I get to see things now—things that people hid from me—from everyone—before. The thoughts they don't say out loud but admit to themselves when they think they're alone.

My English teacher? The one who reported me. I watch her sometimes. Not too often. Because it makes me sad and angry. I don't say her name. Can't bring myself to do it. Can't, period. Maybe because it would hurt too much. Like a wound that never heals. She doesn't work at my old school anymore. Her face scrunches sometimes when she looks at kids. Some kids, anyway. Like they are a walking bad word. Like they're a broken rule.

How did she mistake my costume jet pack for a bomb? Easy. She never really looked at it. She was only looking at me. Well, part of me, anyway. The Iraqi part. The Muslim part. The hard-to-pronounce-name part. She never ever got my name right.

I don't even know if she tried. Which is weird because sometimes she'd talk about this dead Russian writer she loved. He wrote a book about a guy who went crazy and killed an old lady. My teacher didn't seem to have any trouble pronouncing his name.

Sometimes I want to do mean things to her, to scare her. But I don't. When I was upset, Mama used to say, *Don't let them change who you are. Don't let them steal your goodness.* I haven't exactly figured out how to do all those scary-movie ghost things anyway. I whisper, though. Walk through leaves and crunchy, ice-hardened snow and across wooden floors that sometimes creak. Mostly people can ignore it, pretend it's nothing. But Safiya notices, I think. Maybe she's even starting to believe it's more than the wind, more than her mind playing tricks on her.

One thing I learned by being invisible: People see what they want to see and decide it's the truth. But it's not. Let me show you. Here are some things people thought were bombs:

A backpack.
A sack lunch.
A loaf of bread in a brown bag.
A camera.
An e-cigarette.
A science project about circuits.
A clock.

Police got called. Bomb squads. Bridges and stores were cleared out. None of those things were bombs. Guess what they all had in common.

SAFIYA

MAY 16, 2023

Alternative fact (presidential edition): The children of Muslim American parents are largely responsible for the growing number of terrorist attacks.

Truth: The director of the FBI testified before Congress that "a majority of the domestic terrorism cases we've investigated are motivated by some version of what you might call white supremacist violence."*

The police perp-walked a kid out of school over a Halloween costume. What a cruel joke. In eighth grade, a white student at my school dressed up as a "suicide bomber," which apparently some teachers found hilarious, too. He didn't even get suspended. All he had to do was take off the fake black beard and brown face paint he was wearing and put on a regular T-shirt. It was another reminder of who gets the benefit of the doubt. Of who America sees as innocent until proven guilty. Of who is always innocent, no matter what. Of who is always guilty, no matter what.

I didn't know Jawad then, not personally. He didn't go to my

---

* Testimony of FBI Director Christopher Wray, July 23, 2019.

school. I was at DuSable Prep. He was a first-year at Bethune High—a public school. Didn't matter, though. That picture of him, his mouth downturned, a panicky, confused look in his eyes, was splashed across every news site and on the television for days.

He was a minor, but it didn't keep the faux news sites from digging into his past—what kind of "past" can a fourteen-year-old kid have? They got a couple other students who'd gone to middle school with him on record saying he was "kind of a loner," that he'd "missed a lot of school in eighth grade," that he and his parents went on "a trip to Arabia or something." News stations edited and spliced the footage to make it seem suspicious. Showed pictures of Jawad fist-bumping another brown kid with the chyron TERRORIST FIST JAB?

They kept talking about how his family was Iraqi. *Eye-rack-ee.* Like that was a crime. Apparently, Jawad had taken a few pre-arranged absence days for a family wedding in Toronto. But it didn't matter when some media made corrections, because the first lie became the truth people heard. His family couldn't have gone back to Iraq even if they'd wanted to. His dad had been a translator for the American military; Jawad and both his parents were American citizens. But that didn't matter. They weren't *from* here. That was enough for haters, for xenophobes, for the alt-right. That was the not-so-hidden message they read between the lines.

Transcript of Phone Call with Patricia Jensen

May 17, 2023

Note: Regarding recording of phone calls, Illinois is a two-party consent state. Ms. Jensen now lives and works in Indiana. I drove across the Indiana border to make the call. Indiana is a one-party consent state. As long as you are one of the people talking on the phone, you can record the call.

PHONE RINGS.

Ms. Jensen: Hello?

Safiya: Ms. Jensen? Ms. Patricia Jensen?

Ms. Jensen: Yes? Who is this? I should be on the Do Not Call list for whatever you're selling.

Safiya: Oh, no. Sorry. I'm not a telemarketer. My name is Safiya Mirza. I'm a sophomore at Northwestern. Studying journalism.

Ms. Jensen: Okay, and...?

Safiya: I'd like to talk to you about Jawad Ali and the toy jet pack he made. You were the one who called it in to the police.

Ms. Jensen: Of course I did. He had a bomb! I was trying to save the lives of every child in that school. I was doing my job.

Safiya: According to the 911 tape, you said, "An Arab kid has a bomb. They want to kill us all. Why do they hate us?" But it wasn't a bomb. It was a costume—

Ms. Jensen: I know what it was. A threat. I know what you're trying to do—twist my words, take them out of context. One of the cops told me I'd done the right thing. That these people infiltrate our schools. They stay quiet, unsuspecting. Like ghosts, he said.

Safiya: And did you ask for Jawad to be removed from your class even when he was cleared by police? He was innocent.

Ms. Jensen: Why...I...I...Look. You should be ashamed of yourself, young lady. Harassing people on the phone. I know what you're insinuating. Like all the people who called me a racist. I'm not responsible for what happened to that boy—

Safiya: *That boy* had a name. It was—

LINE DISCONNECTS.

JAWAD

I've only been to one funeral. For an uncle at the mosque. He was Iraqi, too. He'd been in America a long time—he went to college here. Even though he was older, he was friends with my parents. "He helped us learn what it is to be American. And like us, he knew what it was to love and miss home," my dad said at his funeral.

I was in fourth grade and scared of seeing the body. I knew from movies that people visited dead bodies to say goodbye. But my mom told me that's not how Muslims usually did it. There wasn't an open casket. We bury our dead within twenty-four hours, she'd explained, after we cleanse the body and shroud it in clean cloths. "Then the Ummah, the community, offers the funeral prayer. The family has a three-day mourning period—that's when we can sit with them and cook for them and offer them our help.

Praying together, we ask God for forgiveness for the dead. We pray they will be at peace. For mercy and grace for the family. For all of us." She told me all of that so softly, while holding my hand.

My mom taught me what to say when we hear that a Muslim has passed away. Inna Lillahi wa inna ilayhi raji'un. *We belong to God, and to him we shall return.*

But now my parents don't even know I'm gone. *Really* gone. They only think I'm missing. I know they're praying I will come home. I don't know what they'll do when they find out what happened to me. I'm praying for my parents, too.

SAFIYA

JANUARY 3, 2022

Fact: For every action, there is an equal and opposite reaction.

Truth: The reaction is not always equal.

Ms. Cary shut the door behind Hardy and sighed. I saw her shoulders rise and fall a couple times before she turned back to me with a tight smile. "Safiya, do you have any idea who might have done this?"

"Why does everyone keep asking me that? Like I'm supposed to have a sixth sense for racists because I'm brown? That's not how it works."

"No…no one thinks that. It's—"

"What? They hacked my column, so somehow I'm responsible?"

"Is there anyone who might have something against you? Crossing your name out is personal. That was a choice they made rather than merely reconfiguring the home page."

Gut punch. I hadn't thought of it that way. Like crossing out my name meant Ghost Skin was going after me, wanted to x me out literally. The only person I could think of who had something against me and would want to cut me down like that was Hardy. I opened my mouth, but before I could say anything, Ms. Cary jumped in.

"Dr. Hardy is saying that only a few people had password access to the site."

"Wait. Wait. Hold up. What's he implying?"

"Has anyone on staff ever shown…you know, alt-right sympathies? Sometimes kids say things to each other they won't say in front of adults."

Alt-right. That word, *alt-right*, smacked me in the chest. It seemed too, I dunno, too unreal. Too not–high school. Too *I'm middle aged but live in my parents' basement, spewing conspiracy theories and pretending to be a teenager online.* It's white supremacist, oath-taking Proud Boys storming the Capitol. It's a Nazi rally with torches raised high in Charlottesville, Virginia. It's shooting the Emmett Till memorial sign. It's delusional trolls spinning conspiracy theories about pizza places and kidnappings and female presidential candidates. It's arguing at the school board meeting that the Civil War was about "states' rights" and that it's cool to teach *Huck Finn* and say the N-word out loud because of "historical context." The hacker was one-hundred-percent racist—but alt-right, here at our little school? Maybe it shouldn't surprise me that other kids at school can be as horrible as some adults. It's the adults who taught them.

"No way is it anyone on staff. Only five of us have admin powers on the site, and four of us are BIPOC and/or queer. And Rachel is Jewish. So, no." I shook my head. "Not a chance." I dug my heels into the uneven wooden floor, in the well-worn grooves from all the students before me. I imagined one hundred years of other kids biting their tongues, of not saying the things that should've been said, grinding their anger into the grainy surface, their frustration fossilized in the hallways we passed through now.

"It's most likely a dumb prank. But until we can prove it's not one of you, the *Spectator* staff will have to walk on eggshells or Dr. Hardy could pull the plug."

"But it's impossible to prove a negative. Besides, why would we sabotage our own paper? The only person who would be happy about the *Spectator* shutting down is Hardy. He and every adult in this school have network access that kids don't. And they're a lot whiter than everyone who works on the *Spectator*, which makes them more likely to be, uh, white supremacists?"

Ms. Cary's back straightened as she clenched her jaw. *Oops.* Did I say that out loud? "I would tread carefully, Safiya. Every teacher's first instinct is to help students, not hurt them. Accusing the principal or any other adult in this school is a dangerous path to take. You should know better."

Maybe I shouldn't have said that. But I doubted that every single teacher at our school felt the way Ms. Cary described. The admin definitely didn't. Ms. Cary had stood up for me for a minute, but her fighting for me clearly had limits. She had to protect herself and maybe the paper, too. I wasn't going to win the argument, and I didn't want to risk getting kicked off the *Spectator*, so I nodded and mouthed an okay.

Ms. Cary sighed. "I'll talk to IT. Maybe they can figure out where that screed was posted from. The passwords have been changed and—"

"Wait. We're all locked out? I mean, are you going to post everything? Some of the formatting needs admin privileges, too."

She knit her eyebrows together. "I'll get back to you on that. For now, let the other kids know there's a hold on new articles. The site will be down until I can convince Dr. Hardy to get it back up. It's been scrubbed, and as long as there isn't any more drama and you play by his rules, I'm sure he'll agree to it." Her heels clacked against the floor as she walked out.

Drama? White supremacist threats weren't "drama." They were serious. Possibly violent. Maybe Hardy wanted to sweep the hack under the rug, ignore it like he did that racist Facebook meme from last semester. More "drama," according to him. And when the Organization of BIPOC students wouldn't be quiet about it, the administration turned the table, blaming the group for being uncivil, for not following procedures. The admin was big on civility and accountability…for everyone else. But as far as Hardy was concerned, only students were supposed to face consequences.

I plunked into a computer chair. Swiveled on the squeaky wheels. Maybe the admin didn't care who was behind the hack, but I did. Hardy was looking for a scapegoat, and I refused to let it be me.

Issue XVI March 2021

FBI FINDS "GHOST SKIN" INFILTRATION AT HIGHEST LEVELS OF LAW ENFORCEMENT, GOVERNMENT

In a 2018 update of a declassified, still heavily redacted 2006 report, the FBI found an alarming increase in systematic attempts by the KKK and neo-Nazis to infiltrate law enforcement and attain elected office by "passing" for mainstream by hiding their racist ideology.

The FBI counterterrorism unit has been quietly investigating the ghost skin phenomenon for well over a decade now. "Infiltration or recruitment," the FBI notes, "can lead to investigative breaches and can jeopardize the safety of law enforcement sources and personnel."* Further, the FBI warns that local police departments must be on the lookout for ghost skins, who have been trained to avoid overt displays of their beliefs so that they can covertly advance a white supremacist agenda. It was only with the recent firings of officers in police departments in Los Angeles, Chicago, Cleveland, New York, and Houston that this once nearly buried report has come back to light.

---

* "White Supremacist Infiltration of Law Enforcement," October 17, 2006.

With the January 6 storming of the Capitol by a mob that included white supremacists, far-right militants, and Republican Party officials and donors, as well as other nationalist groups, there has been a renewed focus on rooting out extremist ghost skins in law enforcement, the military, and government agencies, as well as identifying the lone wolves who operate outside of organized groups but are perhaps even more dangerous and likely to act on violent impulse....

SAFIYA

JANUARY 6, 2022

Fact: There are no good white supremacists.

Truth: There are no good white supremacists.

Alternative fact: There are very fine people on both sides.

"So you think Hardy doesn't want to hear your theory about how the white supremacists' call was coming from inside the house?" Asma asked as we headed up the school steps. She was wearing a knee-length winter-white wool coat with a skinny braided black leather belt and deep-red riding boots. Every head turned to look at her, like always. And like always, she was unbothered and uninterested. It had been about seventy-two hours and Ghost Skin had gone radio silent. Maybe the hack was a one-and-done deal, but the story was getting buried. Plus, Hardy was getting exactly what he wanted: a fresh news cycle. But I still wanted to find the truth. Needed to.

"I can't even get an appointment to see Hardy to explain my theory. According to his assistant, he has been very busy with important meetings that all happen to coincide with every free period I have," I complained.

"Do you really think DuSable has been *infiltrated*, though? Doesn't that mean something organized? I mean, kids in this school can barely organize decorations for a dance." Asma was a good friend who always had my back. But that did not mean she didn't question me or push back.

"Well…when I Googled, it seemed like the phrase 'ghost skin' was mostly used for neo-Nazis or KKK who infiltrated law enforcement or military. Like sleepers. But the hackers' using the name Ghost Skin doesn't necessarily mean they're part of a larger, organized threat. More like they were announcing themselves: *We're here even if you can't see us.*"

"To completely change the subject, let's talk about people we—I mean, you—definitely notice." Asma nudged me and not so subtly tilted her head in the direction of the table by the big fireplace in the lobby where students were selling tickets for the Winter Ball. One of the students was Richard.

"Shut up." I raised my eyebrows at Asma. "We're barely friends. Besides, I think he's still into Dakota." I tilted my head toward the cute junior. She was at the table selling tickets, too.

"Yeah, right. Dakota. The Dakota who is one-hundred-percent not his girlfriend. The Dakota staring at him right now, desperately trying to get his attention while he can't take his eyes off you? *You*. Safiya Mirza. The girl he's been chatting up every day this week, despite not being in any classes together this semester?"

"We were lab partners. Basically shared a table. That's all," I said while turning my gaze to Richard and then quickly back to Asma when my eyes locked with his. "The entire extent of our relationship was—"

"About finding the *chemistry* in chemistry?"

I rolled my eyes. "Grow up. You're such a dork!"

"Ha! You love it. Catch up with you *laaaaater*," Asma sang as she peeled off, leaving me openmouthed and flat-footed within earshot of Richard.

He stepped toward me. "Wanna go?" Richard wasn't whispering, but his low voice made it sound like a secret question.

"Huh?"

"To Winter Ball? Gonna buy a ticket?"

"Oh, uh, no. Hard pass." I had not been to any of the school's formal dances. It wasn't because I didn't have a boyfriend. Which I didn't. Technically, every ticket was a single, and students usually went in groups. The admin did not "promote" dates at school functions. Mostly, I wasn't into dancing and didn't have the extra cash to splurge on a fancy dress. Kids at DuSable went all out for the formals. Slinky, sparkly dresses. Heels that pinch. Tuxes. Limos. For sure Asma would let me borrow something from her closet, but...

"Too bad." Richard made a fake pouty face. "It won't be as fun without you."

Record scratch. This seemed like flirting? My face flushed. He reached out and touched my elbow. It was barely a touch, more like his hand grazing my puffy coat. But I felt the warmth of his fingers through all my winter layers. I unzipped my jacket so I wouldn't overheat. I glanced past his broad shoulders and saw Dakota glaring at us, her arms crossed, jaw dropped. I guess it looked like flirting to her, too.

"Uh…you and I have never been at a single social event together. In, like, ever."

"What about when we volunteered at the Cradles to Crayons drive?"

I laughed. "You mean when we sorted toys at a giant warehouse with half the school? It was fun, but maybe not exactly a high-society event."

"It is for my mom and her friends. And I did bring you a water bottle."

"Oh! You're right. So chivalrous of you. How could I have forgotten that?" I grinned.

"Fine. Okay. But I stand by my claim: It won't be as fun without you. You're the only one I know who can make journalism sound hot," he said as he flashed me a toothy smile, the same one he rocked in his homecoming king photo. I'm no expert, but this probably, definitely counted as flirting. Maybe even more? Did I like the more? The Magic 8 Ball spinning in my brain was screaming ALL SIGNS POINT TO YES. Ugh. Who even am I? How am I this giddy over a boy? I tried to come up with some witty bon mot or scathingly sarcastic remark, but all I got was cotton mouthed.

Then the five-minute warning bell rang, so I shrugged with a small smirk. I didn't need to say *Saved by the bell*. It was now a flirty fact that floated between us. But the helium-filled moment I was having didn't last long. As I turned the corner to head to my locker,

I caught a glimpse of Hardy, who narrowed his eyes at me before he stepped into the boys' bathroom for his morning drug sweep.

"So, we're still totally clueless?" Usman was nothing if not direct. As he'd once told me, he saw zero reason to be coy around anything or anyone except, occasionally, boys he was crushing on. He readjusted his yellow kufi that he wore atop his almost-buzzed head. He'd dyed his hair three different colors so far this year, but currently it was in its natural state of chestnut brown. When I walked into the journalism room, I saw that he and Rachel had already written some bullet points on the whiteboard.

- Hacked either night before break ended or before 8:00 a.m. on first day back
- Ghost Skin = one or more people?
- "Free speech" diatribe
- Possible member of a white supremacist org? Or posers?
- Angry at social justice/multicultural curriculum
- Students? Adult? In school community?
- Nietzsche quote: Herald of lightning

The hack was on Monday, and it was now Thursday; it was already old news to everyone besides us—the few, the nerdy, the journalistically inclined. Winter Ball was coming up, and there was nothing like a dance to distract everyone from the anonymous neighborhood white supremacist running around our halls. Hardy agreed to let the *Spectator* site go back up, but only because he was censoring all our articles. The only things he and Ms. Cary didn't red-flag were sports and Asma's interview with major alumni donors about Winter Balls of the past, a story Hardy had suggested.

Hardy had vetoed every article on the hack, even the general piece I'd quickly written about ghost skins, which didn't even mention the hack but talked about the Chicago police officer who'd been arrested after he'd tortured over 120 Black men in police custody and was also found to be a legit KKK member. My story got returned with the words *NOT RELEVANT* scrawled across the front page in red Sharpie, like his words were bleeding into mine.

I guess I couldn't complain too much. I was the only one on the newspaper that Ms. Cary had given the new password to, after swearing me to secrecy. She also gave me a warning that as far as Hardy was concerned, I had a major strike against me. Two more strikes and I was out as editor, which is how I think that sportsball metaphor works. Part of me was surprised he'd okayed my having the password again, but another part of me thought he was hoping I'd mess up so he could ban me from the newspaper permanently.

I slumped into a seat next to Usman in the semicircle of chairs set in front of the whiteboard. "So, have we figured out if the Nietzsche quote connects to something else?"

"Besides our Ghost Skin maybe being a nihilist, I'm not sure," Usman said.

"Nihi-what?" Rachel asked the question I was thinking.

"Nihilist." Usman took in our blank faces. "A person who believes existence is useless and everything sucks, so destruction without any purpose is necessary. Did none of you take philosophy last year?"

I shrugged.

"Well, Nazis were pretty into Nietzsche, so maybe that's it? Doesn't prove much, though. Nietzsche quotes are everywhere. Like, 'That which does not kill you—' "

" 'Makes you stronger'?" I finished.

"Yup. That's him."

"I think it's the same assholes who put that meme on the school Facebook page. Another thing Hardy blew off," Usman said.

Rachel twisted her light-brown curls into a low bun and began doodling little blue flowers on the whiteboard. "Yeah, but that was different because it was added as a comment from a fake account. Ghost Skin had to steal the password to post their BS."

"Could be the same person escalating," Usman added. "That's usually how the delinquent life starts."

I elbowed him. "And you're basing this on?"

"A lecture my auntie gave me last weekend."

"Dude, you're in early admission to University of Chicago. You're the last person who needs a lecture on keeping your crap together," Rachel said.

Usman and I looked at each other. "Aunties!" we shouted at the same time before cracking up. His family was Shia Hazara from Afghanistan and mine was Hyderabadi Indian, but apparently aunties of every ethnicity had the tough-love gene.

While we were laughing, the fire alarm blared throughout the school, startling all of us.

"What the hell? Is this a drill? It's freezing out!" Rachel grabbed her hoodie and pulled it over her head.

The three of us headed out. It was weird because the school never held fire drills in winter. Then we heard the sirens.

JAWAD

When I went back to school after my arrest, I got switched into a different Honors English class. I was fine with it; at least I didn't have to see my old English teacher every day. The first time she saw me in the hall after I got back, she turned around and went the other way. I guess she didn't want to deal with me, either. My parents told the principal they thought the teacher should apologize to me for what she did. She didn't apologize, and she sure didn't seem sorry.

The first assignment in my new class was to read this poem called "The Hollow Men." Everyone was paired up except me. They'd gotten the assignment while I was suspended. Ms. Maley, my new English teacher, was nice and had these kinda sad eyes and a soft voice whenever she spoke to me. She offered to let me join another pair, but I didn't want to butt into a group. The poem was kind of hard to understand. It was about a bunch of dead guys who couldn't figure out what to do.

Now the last stanza is stuck in my brain like a bad song. One of the scary texts I got after I was arrested quoted those same lines.

> *This is the way the world ends*
> *This is the way the world ends*
> *This is the way the world ends*
> *Not with a bang but a whimper.*

Transcript of Phone Call with Rachel Kahn

May 20, 2023

Rachel is a first-year at Beloit College. DuSable Prep graduate, former *Spectator* staff, and Jewish Student Association member.

> **Safiya:** Do you remember that day? The fire in the boys' bathroom?

> **Rachel:** Oh yeah. We were in the journalism classroom. I think it might've been the only real fire alarm we ever had, right? Every other time was a drill.

> **Safiya:** The school admin hasn't been keen to talk to me, so I couldn't get them to verify. But I'm pretty sure, yeah.

> **Rachel:** [*laughs*] Even the new admin doesn't like you? Damn, you really made a mark.

> **Safiya:** Yeah, well, I guess the only alumni they have time for are the ones who will donate money and don't testify about the school's white supremacy problem. So...tell me what you remember. How did that day play out in your mind?

> **Rachel:** We were all across the street in the park at the school's designated meeting zone for fire drills. It was organized chaos. The teachers were trying to herd students together. Most of us had no idea what was happening. I could tell by the confused looks on everyone's faces,

including the teachers', that it was not planned. There was a good amount of smoke. Someone said there was an explosion in the boys' bathroom. A smoke bomb. Kids were coughing. I think you were coughing—

Safiya: Definitely. I think Usman had to use his inhaler. He also whacked me on the back a couple times to make sure nothing was stuck in my throat.

Rachel: He probably enjoyed that a little bit. Ha ha ha. I mean, you drove us pretty hard on newspaper.

Safiya: I was so grizzled, even in high school. [*laughs*]

Rachel: Anyway, yeah, it was a mess. I felt bad for the kids who had to come out in their gym uniforms. Shorts and T-shirts. They were probably minutes away from hypothermia; then some firefighters brought over blankets. I guess we were all so busy trying not to freeze our balls off that no one saw what was happening.

Safiya: And there was the singing. That was a big distraction.

Rachel: Oh my God! How could I forget. The fight song, a cappella, courtesy of the DuSable Clef Hangers.

Safiya: And then show tunes, with jazz hands and everything.

Rachel: [*laughs*] They really did a whole show out there in the butt cold, didn't they?

Safiya: It was surreal. And pretty impressive, considering the chattering teeth. [*chuckles*]

Rachel: [*pauses, sighs loudly*] It was so brazen. So stealthy.

Safiya: You mean painting the swastika?

Rachel: Yeah. Almost daring to be caught, like mocking the school's incompetence. I remember Hardy signaling the all clear and then the fire trucks pulling away. That's when we saw it. I couldn't move. My brain felt frozen. It was like a nightmare—the red paint dripping on the brick wall. Like blood. I think at first I thought it *was* blood. I felt like vomiting. I mean, I was terrified. I'd never seen anything like that...not happen before my eyes, I mean. Our synagogue had anti-Semitic graffiti painted on it, got threatening notes—more than once. But this, being at school, while I was there...It was...I don't know...When was the hack again?

Safiya: A few days earlier, on the Monday we got back from break. The swastika was Thursday.

Rachel: The timing...It made it feel even more threatening. More hateful. And Hardy getting the custodians to block everyone's view of it, making them scrub it off so fast. Before the police even came? I don't think he cared about how traumatizing it was; he didn't want anything marring his beautiful, perfect school. Or his reputation. He didn't want witnesses. But people got pictures.

Safiya: Oh yeah. Always get receipts. Sure learned that lesson.

Rachel: Then you posted your column, like a big FU to the admin.

Safiya: And got suspended for it.

BE THE CHANGE

BY SAFIYA MIRZA

The administration does not want us to address the ghost skin in the room. But all of you saw the swastika painted on our school at the same time I did. Just now, when we were outside freezing our butts off during the fire. We were all witnesses to a hate crime. Silence is not an option, okay?

We came back from winter break this week with the *Spectator* site being hacked by someone or someones calling themselves Ghost Skin, a reference to how white supremacists infiltrate a group like, say, the police, or maybe the unsuspecting student population at a fancy private school. Now, a few days later, there's a red swastika spray-painted on the facade of our school.

Sorry (not sorry), but I don't believe in coincidences.

Maybe I'm too cynical. Too hard. Maybe it's ridiculous for a seventeen-year-old to be so pessimistic and angry. Can you blame me?

The Amazon is on fire. The polar ice caps are shrinking. Black Americans are subjected to unchecked police brutality. Nazis are on the rise *again*. People have to put up GoFundMes for chemotherapy and their kid's liver transplant because God forbid we have free health care.

Hundreds of thousands of American lives were lost during a pandemic because of a president who didn't believe in science or simple masks that could have saved so many lives. There's money for tax breaks for billionaires, but there's no money for the city's public schools to have arts programs, nurses, and smaller class sizes. Meanwhile at DuSable Prep we have a state-of-the-art media center donated by a media mogul, and multiple nurses, and my biggest class this year has fifteen students in it.

Oh, and we apparently have at least one Nazi running around the school, blending in, acting like they're one of us. And instead of weeding out white supremacists, all the administration wants to do is erase the facts. That's why as I write this, Dr. Hardy is outside with custodians, scrubbing away evidence of hate before it can be reported on the local news. Before police are called. Before airing all the DuSable dirty laundry for parents to see at pickup.

So my question is, if you're alive and paying attention to this world, why aren't you angry? Angrier? And what are we going to do about it?

Maybe it all feels overwhelming. And you'd rather be drowning your sorrows in Medici's hot chocolate. I get that. I do. But the thing is, burying our heads and crossing our fingers and hoping the bad guys go away won't change anything. Action does.

If you don't want the administration to sweep our neo-Nazism problem under the rug, then please email the board of trustees and urge them to investigate. Have your parents call and email, too. And in case you didn't get any pics before the swastika was erased, here are some that I took. We were all there. We have to bear witness. We can't let the administration ignore it or whitewash what happened. Forgetting is not an option.

And that's one way you can be the change.

SAFIYA

JANUARY 6, 2022

Truth: She was warned. She was given an explanation.
Nevertheless, she persisted.

I posted that renegade column and walked right out of school.
I knew I was going to get suspended anyway, so why give Hardy the
pleasure of doing it to my face? I felt squeezed, like the walls were
closing in and I needed some air. It was chaos in the halls, everyone talking about that swastika, teachers trying to corral students
back into classrooms. Panic and confusion mixed with the lingering
smoke in the air. I figured no one was going to notice me walking
out, but they sure were going to figure out pretty fast that I was
gone.

Walking to my parents' store, I was feeling pretty good about
myself. Besides the clammy hands and wanting-to-throw-up part.
My parents were going to be mad. Furious. I'd never been suspended
before. I'd never even skipped school. And without a doubt, I was
going to get yelled at by a very red-faced principal. But I wanted to

be a journalist. I *was* a journalist. And the whole point of the press was to throw light in dark corners and crack open the doors that people like our school's administrators tried to close in your face, because hiding the truth let them control it.

I'd make my parents understand. It's not like they didn't know me. And when they saw the picture of the swastika, they'd get it. I mean, it's not like they haven't lived in this country. My mom always said that people think Islamophobia only started after 9/11, but she was an immigrant kid during the Iran hostage crisis, and that's the first time she ever heard a grown man—a stranger—call her racist names and yell at her to *Go home!* It was 1979 and she was a second grader. I can't get over that. An adult getting in the face of an eight-year-old kid because, what? Her tiny brown hands were a threat? My parents may be on the quiet side, but their eyes are wide open. They were the ones who taught me about complicity and finding the courage to speak up. I was sure they'd understand. I made myself think so, anyway.

I paused before I opened the door to our store to watch my parents for a moment.

My mom was busy helping a customer. She had a smile on her face, and her navy-blue chiffon scarf was gently drawn over her shoulders and around her salt-and-pepper bun. My dad was restocking teas. Our tea selection absolutely rocked. One of my favorite things to do when I was helping around the store was to refill the tea testers—the small round containers that held a couple teaspoons of loose leaf tea so customers could take a whiff. After a while they would lose some potency, and my parents always liked them strong. It was a source of pride, especially for my dad. If any customer was willing to listen, he'd wax on about, say, different types of Darjeeling teas. Or why he preferred the more floral first flush (spring) Darjeeling versus second flush (summer) and wouldn't even carry a monsoon tea (too oxidized). Why his recommended temperature for steeping a fresh first flush was lower (195 degrees) than a later first flush (205 degrees). *The oxidation! The bitterness!* And how steeping his beloved Darjeeling for over five minutes was a crime against tea tradition. Once a customer asked Dad if he took his tea the "British way," and, well, my dad *never* lost his patience with a customer, but the smile on his face was so strained in that moment, I thought he would burst.

You know how in holiday movies, they signal coziness with a roaring fire and a cute couple cuddled under a throw knit by someone's grandma? Well, that's what looking at my parents felt like. It had been a weird, scary week. It was winter outside, flurries falling, a bite in the air. But inside it was warm.

Maybe Mirza Emporium was only a store, but it was also home.

My mom spied me outside the door and scrunched her eyebrows at me as she finished bagging a customer's groceries. She wasn't expecting to see me, obviously. Then I saw her look down at her phone, and her jaw dropped. I watched as she yelled for my dad and gestured at her screen. My heart raced. Was it the school? They sometimes texted confirmations of absences, but this was unexcused, and I'm sure Hardy would be calling them to express his extreme disappointment in my behavior. God, I hope he wasn't going to threaten to take away my scholarship. No. He wouldn't send that in a text. That couldn't be it.

I slipped my mittened hand into my coat pocket. I hadn't heard my phone buzzing at first, muffled as it was by all my layers. I yanked out the phone, nearly dropping it as it slipped against my mitten. I checked the screen:

AMBER ALERT

Chicago, IL

Jawad Ali

14 years old

Brown hair

Brown eyes

5'6"

Dark blue or black four-door sedan

Last seen near 47th Street and Stagg Avenue

That's near here. That's this neighborhood. The name...it's familiar. Snowflakes fell on my face. The wind stirred, and I got cold all over. Oh my God. It's him. I swear it's him. The kid with the jet pack. Bomb Boy.

JAWAD

It's so cold. Someone took my coat.

I'm all alone here in the dark, in the falling snow. The only sounds I hear are the birds. I can't even feel my own heartbeat anymore, can't hear it. It's so quiet in my body.

I want to go home. Please. I need to go home. My parents must be so worried. And my shoes are wet. Mama told me to wear different shoes this morning. I should've listened to my mom. Why didn't I listen?

JAWAL

PART IV

WITHOUT A TRACE

State's Exhibit 3

Transcript of voice mail received by Suleyman Ali, via Burner app

> *Listen carefully. Your son has been kidnapped. Let me begin
> by assuring you that your son is safe, for now. So long as
> you follow the exact ransom directions that I will text to you
> shortly, no harm will come to him. However, if you alert the
> police or deviate from the instructions, the penalty will be
> your son's death. This is strictly a financial proposition, but I
> am fully prepared to carry out the punishment.*
>
> *I know who you are. I know where you live. Thirty thousand
> dollars. If you want to see Jawad alive, do exactly as I ask.*

SAFIYA

JANUARY 7, 2022

Lie: Cowards die many times before their death.

Truth: Haters who hide behind masks, internet trolls, the random guy who yells racists things out a speeding car window are all cowards. And they're thriving.

My suspension was basically for a day and a half—the rest of yesterday and today. I'm honestly surprised I didn't get a longer one, but Hardy was likely relishing the idea of making my life miserable, and I had to be present in school for him to do that. Ms. Cary was probably getting a lot of crap from Hardy about how she needed to control me. I sort of felt bad about it, but I'd done what I had to do.

I had today plus the weekend of working in the store to try to earn back my parents' trust; they weren't thrilled with my resistance journalism, even if they admitted I was in the right (sort of). "There are better ways of making the point than by defying your principal and breaking the rules," my mom argued. I didn't bother explaining that breaking unfair rules *was* the right thing to do. That administration is best that oppresses students the least. Isn't that what we were supposed to learn when they made us read "Civil Disobedience" by Thoreau in American Lit?

Technically, I was to get zero credit for any missed schoolwork while on suspension, but since I'd met all my graduation requirements and mostly had independent study, I wasn't worried about it. Ms. Simone had already emailed me the Senior Lit assignment and said as long as I answered the questions on the Gwendolyn Brooks poems we were reading, I'd be okay. I needed to get the book, which I was going to ask Asma to grab from my locker. Journalism, as my dad loved to say, was going to be a sticky wicket. I did not think Ms. Cary was going to give me any leeway.

It was still early, not even 9:00 a.m. The store wouldn't be open for another hour, so I meandered back to the pickle shelves and started sorting. I was reordering the extra-spicy mango pickles when my phone buzzed. I snagged it out of my back pocket to find a text from Asma.

> **Asma:** You're not here and you're still causing a riot
>
> **Me:** Oh no. Don't tell me
>
> **Asma:** There were flyers taped all over school when we got here
>
> **Me:** And...
>
> **Asma:** Don't freak out!
>
> **Me:** Asma!
>
> **Asma:** The flyer was your column about the swastika but there was a sentence like scribbled on top of it. Sending pic now

I stared at my screen. My fingers trembled, so I gripped my phone

85

tighter. It was my article printed out with the words *Swallow your poison, for you need it badly* scribbled over my column.

> **Me:** WTF?! Is that a metaphor?

> **Asma:** I dunno. I'm sorry. Hardy had them all taken down before the bell

> **Me:** Ugh. But it's gotta be the same people right?

> **Asma:** 😶 There wasn't even an announcement about the swastika or the leaflets

> **Me:** Of course ☹️

> **Me:** Any chance you can bring me my Gwendolyn Brooks book from my locker?

> **Asma:** Okay. I have debate so it might be on the late side. Gotta run 😬

> **Me:** 🖤 🖤

I stared at the photo of my column with that...I dunno... threat, I guess, scrawled over it in thick red marker, the same color as the swastika painted on the school. If the purpose was to terrify me, it was working. But why me? Ms. Cary asked me if someone had something against me. My heart thumped against my rib cage. I licked my dry lips. What was the poison they wanted me to drink?

I shook my head, glancing at my screen once more before shoving the phone into the back pocket of my favorite worn jeans. That Amber Alert was still on my lock screen. A chill slithered

86

through my veins, like ice crystals swirling in my blood. I swore I felt a gust of wind *inside* the store and heard a swirl of voices. No, a single voice. A whisper. But I figured I was tired. I rubbed my hands over my arms and went to grab a sweater. I hoped they'd find that kid.

JAWAD

It's cold. Everything. Everywhere.

Wet leaves stick to my forehead and cheek. I can almost smell the wet ground underneath my face. It's like a hard pillow. But I don't think it's real. I think smell and feel are only memories. I think maybe *I'm* only a memory now to everyone, including myself.

This isn't how my life was supposed to go. There were so many things I wanted to do. Things I wanted to build with my dad. Places I wanted to visit with my mom. And there were so many promises adults made me. Things that have no chance of coming true anymore:

The world is your oyster.
You have a bright future ahead of you.

Things will get better.

In America you can be anything you want to be.

It never got better, though. And there is no future. Not for me. Now everything is the past.

Everything but Safiya. She was in my past, too. But she's the only one who can hear me, and she may be the only chance at a *now* that I have left.

SAFIYA

JANUARY 7, 2022

Fact: Ninety-nine percent of the human body is made up of six elements—oxygen, carbon, hydrogen, nitrogen, calcium, and phosphorus.

Truth: We are more than the sum of our parts.

Truth: Some of the elements burn and consume all the others in their flame.

All morning and into the afternoon, I distractedly worked the register at my parents' store, thinking of those whispers I thought I heard earlier. I was sure it had been my imagination, but a Montage of Eerie Things™ ran through my mind: red letters, the flashing lights of the fire trucks at school, the name Ghost Skin, that swastika. Poison. *Swallow your poison.* I reorganized shelves, rang up customers, helped Dad unload boxes of whole spices: cardamom and fennel seeds and star anise. And that all had me craving chai, so Mom steeped a cup in the tiny half kitchen in the back storeroom. Two burners, a sink, and a small fridge. She didn't always add fresh ginger to the simmering pot of tea leaves and other spices, but this day she did, and with the constant shiver I was feeling, the warm, fragrant spices in the chai were perfect. How can a few simple ingredients stirred together be so magical?

I warmed my hand on the steaming cup as I lifted it to take a sip of the milky tea. We sat together in the late-afternoon light at the small Formica table with red vinyl chairs my parents kept near the big plate glass windows. Chicago winters could be bleak, gray skies for miles, but on the days when the sun did shine, it felt like a small gift. I watched as my parents sat side by side, in companionable silence, their chests rising and falling in sync with each other. There were many, many things going wrong. But for a moment, this was right.

"Do you think they'll find him?" I asked. "Jawad, I mean." My parents' faces looked drained.

"I pray they will, beta," my mom said. Between her sips of chai, my mom was running a tasbih through the fingers of her right hand—ninety-nine prayer beads looped together and strung with green silken threads that formed a tassel at one end. I knew that each prayer she whispered was for Jawad to be found. I was wearing a smaller tasbih bracelet around my right wrist, thirty-three beads of sandalwood. Thirty-three hopes for Jawad to be safe. I knew some of those prayers were for me, too.

"We met his mom once or twice, years ago when..." My mom got choked up and her voice trailed off as she looked out the store windows. My dad covered her hand with his. They didn't always show a lot of affection in front of me, so this small gesture surprised me. It worried me a little, too.

"The mosques in the city are joining to do a search—different groups going to different neighborhoods in waves, to see if we can help the police. I am going after we close the store," my dad said.

"I want to help. I'll join you."

"No...you can stay here with your mom. We don't know....I think it's for the best for now." My parents exchanged glances. My dad always scrunched his forehead when he worried. I had a feeling Mom and Dad weren't only concerned about the missing boy; they were scared of something happening to me. I didn't fight it. I understood it. Right then I decided not to tell them about my column being plastered everywhere with *Swallow your poison* scribbled across it. I didn't want to burden them even more. So I nodded at my parents, agreeing to stay back from the search.

My mom gave me a soft smile, her face relieved. "You know, beta, sometimes we forget to be thankful for small things. To be grateful for all that we have," she said.

My dad grinned and added, "Like your mom's chai."

I raised my half-full cup. "To Mom's chai." They both raised their mugs and clinked mine.

I knew my dad wanted to help with the search, so I suggested he go ahead while I helped Mom hold down the fort—it had been mostly quiet in the store. My dad headed upstairs to our apartment to get ready, and my mom went to make him a large thermos of tea.

I grabbed the window cleaner and sprayed the inside of the door. My dad wanted it spotless at all times. I bent down to put the bottle on the floor, and when I stood up, Richard was walking toward the store, a huge smile on his face. I grinned back at him as he jokingly mimed at me, pleading to be let in. I moved away from the door so he could enter. The cheerful brass bird bell rang as he stepped through the doorway. I tried not to read into his being here. It definitely did not mean anything. Anything like him liking me. Nope. I wasn't imagining us cozily sharing cocoa at Medici while watching snow slowly fall outside. Not at all.

"Hey," I said. "What are you doing here?" Gulp. It was one thing to play it cool. It was another thing to be an ice queen.

"Great to see you, too!" he said, chuckling while gently nudging me with his elbow. I nudged back, letting myself lean into him a tiny bit. Pretending to ignore the little spark of joy flashing in my chest. Pretending my face wasn't feeling all warm. And so, so happy that my dark-brown skin never revealed a full blush.

"Sorry…um…surprised to see you is all," I said, stepping to the counter to put down the cleaning rag. Wow. I'm not winning any awards for riveting conversation.

"Surprised in a good way?" Richard asked as he unbuttoned his dark-blue peacoat and walked over to the counter, across from me, and plunked down his backpack.

"Definitely," I whispered, and quickly looked away.

My mom chose that precise moment to pop back into the store. How do parents always know? An inquiring eyebrow shot up when she saw Richard.

Richard turned to look at her. "Oh, hi, Mrs. Mirza. Good to see you. Let me know if you need any help moving boxes again. Or taste testing your samosas. They're all I've been thinking about since Parent Night last month." He knew how to charm everyone.

My mom chuckled. "You should come for dinner sometime, Richard. We'd love to have you."

I was glad Richard's back was to me, because my jaw dropped nearly to the floor. But my mom could clearly see me shaking my head in a combination of embarrassment and horror at having a… guy…a guy who was maybe a crush…over for dinner.

"My mouth is watering already," Richard said, and my mom's face lit up. Complimenting her cooking—which is amazing—is a sure way to her heart.

"Wonderful! Now, if you two will excuse me, I forgot something in the storeroom," my mom said as she headed to the back. "Lovely to see you, Richard. Be careful when you're going home, okay?"

"I will be. Thanks, Mrs. Mirza. Good to see you, too," Richard called after her, then swiveled toward me.

"You are such a brownnoser." I grinned.

"What? I was being serious. I literally dreamed about those samosas….Does your house smell like this?" he asked.

"Like what?" I said, scrunching my eyebrows.

"Like this store. It smells so good in here," he said, glancing around. I braced myself for him to make some dumb comment about chai tea or naan bread. "Like cardamom and ginger. Maybe fennel, too?"

Whoa. Wait. I was used to people jumping to conclusions about me, not the other way around. "I'm impressed. You know your spices."

"I like to cook."

"You do?"

"Yes. I'm more than a muscly jock, you know. Like I said, I have layers." He laughed.

"So, cooking and tolerating journo movies I rec. What other secrets do you have?"

"I come bearing gifts."

I grinned. "Wait, let me guess: Your presence is my present?" Oh my God. I am a total, utter dork. Gah. There was this tiny fluttery feeling inside my stomach that I had to fight so I wouldn't blurt something even more ridiculously dorky and giddy.

"Of course. That goes without saying, right?"

I rolled my eyes.

"Actually," he continued, unzipping his backpack and pulling out my beat-up Gwendolyn Brooks anthology, "I brought you poetry." I'd bought the book secondhand at Powell's, and the worn cover showed it. I suddenly felt self-conscious about it.

"Oh. Thanks. I needed that." I quickly grabbed the book and put it under the counter and tried not to look disappointed that this was what he called a "gift."

"I may have one more thing." Richard reached back into his backpack and pulled out a small brown paper bag with some visible grease spots on it.

"Awww, you brought me trash. You shouldn't have!" I joked.

He handed me the bag. "One man's trash is another's—"

"Cookies!" I yelped as I unrolled the top and the delicious smell of chocolate wafted out. A Medici garbage cookie, to be exact. "These are my faves." I was absolutely addicted to these chocolate chip, M&M, and walnut cookies.

"I know," he said casually. "You brought them up once in chem, remember?"

I did not remember, but waxing on about my passion for this perfect cookie seemed like me. I loved the cookie, and I loved that Richard paid attention to details. Details about me.

"Thank you so much. It's super sweet of you. And I'm sure Asma appreciated you bringing the book by—one less errand for her."

"I wasn't doing it for Asma," he said softly, leaning slightly over the counter, closing the space between us. I took a deep breath as he leaned in a little closer, loosening the knot of his light-blue cashmere scarf.

"So, who were you doing it for?" Whoa. Did that suggestive sentence come out of my mouth? Maybe I was all stick-it-to-the-man when it came to authority, but I was not bold at flirting. Never needed to be. Never truly tried. Maybe I just needed the right nudge(r).

Richard rubbed his chin like he was feeling for stubble (there was none). "You know how sometimes something can be right in front of your face, but you never really see it?"

I gulped. Yes. I did. So very much. I looked down at my scuffed blue sparkly patent Docs, then back up at him. I placed my palms on the counter, and my body inclined slightly toward his, like he was a magnet gently pulling me in. We were close enough so that I could see flecks of gray in his eyes. I stopped breathing while electricity crackled between us.

My phone buzzed. Exactly my luck.

"Oh. Uh…hang on." My body jerked back like it had been released by that magnetic pull. "Probably Asma telling me you're going to be dropping off my book. I love her, but she totally has the desi lateness gene." I chuckled awkwardly.

But it wasn't Asma.

I gasped. "Oh my God."

SWALLOW YOUR POISON.

The number came up as private.

"What is it?" Richard asked, his brow furrowing.

"I...think it's...the person who put up the flyers. Ghost Skin." I showed Richard, who narrowed his eyes at the screen.

"That sucks. I'm so sorry." Richard placed his hand on mine. My heart raced. But I couldn't tell if it was out of fear from the text or because his hand lingered. It felt warm, comforting, on top of mine. His skin was so soft—he must've moisturized constantly. How else could his skin be smooth and uncracked in a Chicago winter? We locked eyes across the conveyor belt on the counter again. I bit my lower lip.

"How can your hands be so warm? You weren't even wearing gloves."

"I never wear gloves. I don't even have a pair. They're like prison for your hands. Besides, I run hot," he said, looking into my eyes.

Oh my God. I chewed the inside of my cheek. There was a chance I was going to combust. I gently pulled my hand away, and my eyes were drawn back to my phone screen. I was happy for the momentary distraction, but that scary message was still there.

"I wonder how this jerk got my number. What do you think it means?"

Richard rubbed his forehead. "I don't know. Definitely creepy, though. Is your number unlisted?"

"Nah. It's in the school directory they send home. I wonder if I should show the police the text?"

"The police?" Richard rolled his eyes. "They're as useless as Hardy, and they'd probably make you fill out a bunch of paperwork to pretend they were actually doing something. Can they trace it if it's from a burner?"

"It's not necessarily a burner. Could be someone *67'd their actual number?" I shifted my weight from one foot to the other, preoccupied.

"They'd be pretty stupid if they did that," Richard said, chuckling.

"Most criminals get caught for stupid stuff, though. Remember the Oklahoma City bombing? We studied it in history class last year? That dude was caught because he was driving without a license plate."

"What an asshole. Got what he deserved." Richard paused, looked down at his watch, and then cleared his throat. "Crap, I have to meet up with some guys from swim team. I'll see ya in school on Monday?"

"Definitely. Thanks again for my book and the garbage cookie."

"I aim to please." Richard smiled and began rebuttoning his coat. "Hey, give me your phone a sec."

"What for?" I asked.

"Trust me," he whispered, reaching across the counter. I handed him my phone, and he entered some numbers in it. Then his phone rang. "Let me know if you get any more creepy texts, okay? Or if you want to, you know, hang out or whatever." He grinned, dimples and all, as he handed me my phone.

"Cool. Thanks." I returned the smile and hoped that he couldn't hear my heart beating out of my chest.

I watched as he walked out of the store, his bag hung casually over his right shoulder. He looked back at me and winked. I shook my head and laughed.

I started cleaning again, but a few seconds later, my phone buzzed. I jumped. But it was Richard—a selfie with a goofy grin: So you'd get a funny text today too.

The smile on my face was so ridiculously huge, I was glad he wasn't there to see it. Even though we'd been lab partners, it was only when we'd spent that evening together as tour guides for Parent Night that his casual friendliness started leaning into slightly flirtatious and interested. And there was something about the way he'd helped my mom with all the food she'd volunteered to bring and how he'd stuck around and chatted with my parents that endeared him to me even more.

Of course, I hadn't shared that with him—I didn't want to give away all my secrets. There were so many things going wrong. So many things to be scared and worried about. And Richard was the most perfect, gorgeous, and sweet diversion.

I picked up my phone, hesitated. Then sent my own silly selfie back—head cocked, eyebrow raised, mouth open in mock surprise. He heart emojied it immediately.

I bit my lip, then scrolled through my phone, pulling up *that* text again: *Swallow your poison.* Richard was probably right about the cops doing nothing. There had been a rash of carjackings the last three months, and the police barely seemed interested in solving those crimes. So what were they going to do about an anonymous text? Tell me it was a prank or a wrong number? It would be way more trouble than it was worth to file a report. I tapped my thumbs against my screen. I pulled Richard's selfie up again and pinned it to the top of my text screen. The *Swallow your poison* text would get buried soon enough by new texts in my scroll. I smiled looking at Richard's goofy face. There were so many things I'd rather think about than some stupid troll.

January 7, 2022

SEARCH CONTINUES FOR JAWAD ALI, TEEN WHO DREW NOTORIETY FOR "BOMB BOY" ARREST

The Chicago PD issued an Amber Alert on January 6 for fourteen-year-old Jawad Ali. Ali was last seen leaving Bethune High School on Wednesday afternoon, near 47th Street and Stagg Avenue, possibly entering a black or blue sedan.

Jawad's parents, Dina and Suleyman Ali, were sent a ransom voice mail and text messages demanding $30,000 to assure his release. After securing the money, Suleyman Ali tried to wire the ransom to the account number indicated in the text messages, but no such bank account or routing number existed. There were no further texts or instructions sent to his phone.

There was nearly a full day's delay in initially issuing the Amber Alert, as police first suggested it was a hoax, citing a recent uptick in these crimes described as virtual kidnappings. Speaking under condition of anonymity, a source indicated that there was also some concern within the precinct that Jawad might have faked his own kidnapping to cover up running away or to gain sympathy, as he had been bullied at school after his arrest in October. Pressure from the local alderman's office as well as additional undisclosed clues moved the police to issue the Amber Alert, according to the source.

Jawad's parents, who came to this country as refugees, are offering the $30,000 ransom as a reward for information that will lead to the safe return of their son.

"We want our son back. That's all," Suleyman Ali said. "Please bring him back to us. He is the light of our lives."

Jawad first gained notice in the press in October of last year when a jet pack he'd made for his Halloween costume from recycled and salvaged materials was reported as a possible bomb by a teacher at his high school, resulting in his arrest. He was later cleared of all charges.

Jawad is described as 5'6" with wavy dark-brown hair and brown eyes. His family is of Iraqi descent. He was last seen wearing blue jeans, a gray hoodie, and a dark-blue puffer coat. Anyone with information is asked to call the police at 312-555-5555.

JAWAD

One time, in my Before, I asked Mama if she thought ghosts were real. We'd read *A Christmas Carol* in seventh-grade English class and then watched the movie. And all the chains on the first ghost that came to haunt Scrooge scared me.

"That's a very Western idea of ghosts." My mom grinned as she spoke to me. "We don't have those same beliefs. Of course, there are stories of jinn and other supernatural creatures, but I think the ghost in that story is more like a…uh…a symbol. An idea."

"An idea?"

"Yes. That your wrongs can haunt you. They can hurt you as much as they hurt others. No one expects you to be perfect. Just do your best to be a good person. The person we know you are," she said, and kissed me on the forehead.

My mom always smelled like the attar she had in a small glass bottle on her dresser—like a layer of something woodsy over a sweet flower. It was in her scarf and her hair. It was her. It was like the incense we burned. Sometimes on Fridays she and Baba would burn bakhoor in the small brass incense burner Mama had brought with us from Iraq. It had belonged to her grandmother and was one of the only things we had from back home. Sometimes she let me carefully light the charcoal disk the bakhoor wood chips sat on. I liked watching the smoke curl through the curvy slits in the burner and waft through our apartment.

Now I imagine myself like that smoke, slipping through cracks, filling a space, a whiff, then nothing. But a little bit of that incense stayed in everything—I could sniff it in the fabric of the sofa and the curtains in the living room, even my pillowcase sometimes. Maybe I'll be like that smoke. Maybe I can make a part of me linger everywhere, too.

USA Patriot Factor with Michael Kavanaugh

WCHN RADIO, SYNDICATED

January 10, 2022

Now, this so-called Bomb Boy and his parents are Eye-rack-ee refugees, supposedly. The dad claims to have been a translator for US forces when they were in the Middle East for Operation New Resolve, rooting out terrorists before they could strike here, on the soil of the good ol' US of A. *Supposedly.*

Don't get me wrong: I'm not saying all A-rabs are terrorists. Can you imagine the hand-waving hysterics from the political correctness police if I said that? They'd try to cancel me in a flash. Guilty even if you're innocent. Stupid anti-American cancel culture. But I'm a reasonable man. This show promises to show you all sides. And it is a fact that a few A-rabs, a few Moozlims, have sided with us. The good ones. The ones with modern beliefs.

But. But. But. This one? Su-lie-man Ali and his son, J-wad, the one *supposedly* missing? I don't buy it. Hear me out. This teen takes a jet pack to school, and his English teacher rightly calls the police because, did you see that thing? What with the dials and the needle gauge. The wires? That thing looked like a bomb. Now, supposedly he made it as part of a Halloween costume. But that damn thing looked real.

I don't know about you, but when I was a kid, I wasn't making things that looked like bombs to take to school. I mean, kids, what...They put things together with paper towel tubes, pipe cleaners, felt, that kind of thing. His jet pack was considerably more sophisticated. And if you research it—you can look it up, see for yourself. I guarantee you that it was made to look like one of those suicide bomber backpacks terrorists wear. Now, why would an innocent kid bring something that looked like that to school? Huh? I'll tell you why: his parents. They set up the whole thing—a planned hoax. They wanted to scare people. They wanted the attention. They wanted to cry "Islamophobia!" To get sympathy and money from the libs. And blame it on those of us who are trying to protect this country from Sharia law.

And what happened to this J-wad kid after? He gets suspended. A couple days of vacation from school. But huge, huge press coverage. All the liberals were fawning all over him. He got offers to go to summer camp for free. Bunch of these tech billionaires tweeted at him. He got some designer saying he would give the kid an internship in sustainable design, making costumes for the stage from recyclable items. What the hell is that? Outrageous! Why was this kid getting all this attention, all these offers? And I tell you what, I'm sure there was money involved. Some kind of deal with foreign entities, maybe. Look into it. I can sniff it from a mile away. That kid was a plant.

And now suddenly he goes missing, a few months later? Without a trace? And there's what...what? A supposed ransom note? A voice mail? Guarantee you some camel jockey was behind that. That kid is probably hiding out somewhere in some fancy hotel room paid for by some sheik or emir or what have you. Trying to play Americans for fools again.

I have a message to J-wad and his parents and the whole shadowy sleeper set behind this: This patriot is on to you.

SAFIYA

JANUARY 10, 2022

Truth: It is more important to outthink your enemy than outfight them.

Lie: Love your enemies because they bring out the best in you.

Asma practically body slam–hugged me when she saw me at my locker Monday morning after I got back from suspension.

"Jeez. I've only been gone since Thursday."

"During which time a threatening note about you was plastered all over school."

"I got a text saying the same thing, too."

"What!" Asma's yell was probably heard two floors above us. People turned to stare, but I shrugged. "Why didn't you tell me?" she asked.

"Because, one, I thought you might freak out. Not sure where I got that idea from. And, two, I knew you were knee-deep in prep for your cousin's wedding, so I didn't want to mess up the fun."

"So much shopping." Asma nodded with a small chuckle. "My mom is going overboard with the outfits, but my cousin wanted a full-on Pakistani wedding. So I need, like, a ton of new clothes."

"Plus, you have the added bonus of missing any Winter Ball drama since the nikah is the same weekend."

"Yes! I'll be scarfing biryani and rasmalai and hanging with my cousins. But hello! Of course, I'm freaking out that you got a text!" Asma gently punched me in the arm.

"Ow!"

"You wouldn't be interfering by calling me. Please don't make me burst into a musical number about what friends are for, okay?"

I nodded and laughed.

Asma continued. "What did your parents say? Did you call the police?"

"Uh...no. I didn't see the point." I twisted my lips and looked away, waiting for Asma to get incensed.

"What! Please tell me you did not delete it."

"No." I sighed. "I saved it, but seriously, you know the police wouldn't do anything about it, and it would be a huge waste of time. It's a prank from some troll. It's not a big deal."

"Uh...okay, except there was also a smoke bomb and Nazi graffiti at school."

"Fine. I hear you, but it came up from a private number, and Richard agreed that the police would be as useless as Hardy. I'm putting it out of my mind."

Asma grabbed my shoulders and shook them a little. "Oh, Richard agreed? The plot thickens. Or, should I say, hottens."

I shook my head. "That makes no sense."

"Uh, yeah, it does. I didn't realize Richard dropping off your book was going to be like a date. Were dimples bared?"

"Oh my God. It wasn't like that. I—"

"Please, tell me, what it was like *like*. Were there longing looks? His fingers grazing your hand? Something that made you see cartoon hearts instead of cold, hard logic?"

My cheeks warmed with embarrassment as I covered my eyes with my hands.

"Oh my God!" Asma continued before I could defend myself. "There was totally grazing!"

"Shhhh!" I bent my head down and leaned into my locker. "Okay, there might have been, a little, uh, flirting. And he maybe brought me a garbage cookie from Medici."

Asma's jaw dropped. "A garbage cookie?" She did a little twirl. "It must be love."

"Ha ha, I doubt it. I think half the girls in this school have crushes on him."

"So what? I am one-hundred-percent, absolutely in support of you having crushes, and you're more crushworthy than anyone I know. Don't tell Usman I said that." Asma jokingly glanced around.

I laughed. "I swear I'll take it to the grave."

Asma continued. "Look, Richard is over-the-top cute and charming, and a lot of girls do have crushes on him. And he's definitely…uh…*reciprocated* some of those crushes. There's probably been reciprocation all over this school. Make sure you don't feel pressured to do anything you don't want to do, okay?"

I paused. Yes, Richard had dated around. And I'd dated…no one. But I'd never seen him be anything but a solid good guy. "Are we using reciprocation as a euphemism now? If so, don't worry. I've never *reciprocated*. Reciprocation is not something I'm casual about.

My ability to say no is strong. Even in the face of dimples and hotness, I can make reasoned decisions about, uh, reciprocating."

"Good. Now go forth and have much flirty fun and maybe even get a little mushy. I'm totally on the side of you letting other people see past your hard candy coating to your soft gooey interior."

I grinned and nodded but cringed a little on the inside. Asma was right. People did see me as indifferent sometimes, or tough, but I had to be. When you're the odd one out, you don't want to let people know how easily you can break.

Asma smiled. "I'm guessing you didn't tell your parents about the flyer or the text, either?"

Busted. "I couldn't. They are so worried about Jawad's disappearance—I guess they met his mom at the store once or twice? I didn't want to make it worse. My mom has been praying nonstop for Jawad and also for me. They're so scared of something else happening. My dad's gone out a couple times to help scour the neighborhood for clues, but they didn't find anything, and there's no leads on that car, either."

"Ugh. It's only been a few days, and he's barely in the news. It's like they're forgetting him already," Asma said.

"Except for conspiracy theorists. Have you seen what some supposed news sites are saying? That maybe the whole thing is a hoax to try and place the blame for Islamophobia on the right wing? I mean, duh, we don't need hoaxes to blame the alt-right for hate crimes. We have actual facts."

"You know it'd be different if he were some rich white kid who'd gone missing," Asma said as the first bell rang.

I slammed my locker door shut. "That's the perfect story idea for my next column."

"If Hardy ever lets you write a next one."

"Heading his way now. Wish me luck."

"Ha, he'll be the one who needs it." Asma smiled as she turned down the hall, her bright-yellow sweater like a beacon making its way through the throng of students.

I paused. For a second, I swore I smelled incense in the hallway. Weird because I smelled it while walking to school this morning, too. It was musky and woodsy. I felt the faintest pressure on my eardrum, then a ringing for a second. Before it faded, I swore it sounded like a faraway voice—like the one I heard the other day in the store. The whisper when I was alone. Maybe I needed more sleep. I sighed as I dragged my heels to Hardy's office.

"You're aware, Ms. Mirza, that I can call the admissions office at Northwestern and relate to them your various escapades since your acceptance? You wouldn't be the first person to have a college offer rescinded." Hardy sat at his desk, his palms flat on the surface in front of him; he looked ready to spring up at any moment. His nostrils were wide, like he wished he could breathe out fire.

I thought he was bluffing. I assumed he was, but there was a small part of me that was scared I'd put my scholarship at risk. Both my DuSable scholarship and the financial aid I'd gotten for college. No way we could afford Northwestern without it. But honestly, it was bullshit that I was the only one getting any consequences for everything that had gone down since we got back from break. "I understand, Dr. Hardy. But I was reporting the news."

"You were trying to cause trouble."

"The trouble was caused by whoever that Ghost Skin person is."

Hardy talked right over me. "And you were insubordinate, posting that column without permission. You are on a very tight leash from now on. Nothing, and I mean nothing, from you is going to be up on the *Spectator* site without preapproval. And you've lost password posting privileges. You are one tiny misstep from being permanently banned from the paper."

Tight leash? What the hell. Like I'm a dog or something? He was fine with cancel culture as long as it suited him. I tried to hide my anger, my disgust, but I couldn't. This was *exactly* what Hardy wanted. He was like one of those guys who thought it was worse to be *called* a racist than to actually *be* a racist. "What about Ghost Skin? The swastika? The poison threat on my column that was plastered all around school? Any chance *that* person is going to get caught? It's like you'd rather shut down the newspaper than white supremacists!" Oops. I was such a blurter when I got angry. I knew I was pushing it.

Hardy narrowed his eyes at me. "It is being handled. The adults in the room do not need your pesky questions or interference." Hardy clenched his jaw, then scratched his neck, which was getting redder as he spoke, like his tie was tightening itself. "You have been volunteered by me to assist in the library during your morning study hall for the next three weeks. You start tomorrow. See if you can't help this school that has given you so much. Maybe learn to be grateful for all that you've received."

"But, I use that time for *Spectator*—"

"Very. Short. Leash. Ms. Mirza. You're dismissed."

I balled my hands into fists, my brain about to explode as I walked out of the principal's office.

Richard was waiting for me outside the door. "Hey, you okay?"

"I…you…hi," I said, my shoulders relaxing from my ears. "How are you here?"

"I saw you walk in when I was getting to school, figured you might need to see a friendly face after dealing with Hardy."

I grinned. "That's so sweet of you. And, yeah, he's the worst. He's making me work in the library during study hall as punishment or whatever."

"What? Can he do that? That's, like, indentured servitude or some bullshit."

"Apparently he can, by threatening my scholarship here and at Northwestern." I sighed. I was angry and scared, all my feelings jumbled up inside me. On top of all that, it was not escaping my notice that this was another thoughtful thing Richard had done. And I liked it.

"I'm sorry," he said, touching my elbow. "It's so unfair. I'm here if you ever want to—"

"Place a curse on Hardy?"

"Sure." He laughed. "I'll grab a cauldron and bring my eye of newt." The bell rang, sending us in different directions.

Richard was right; none of it was fair. None of it made sense. I refused to be sidelined reshelving books in the library when I could be using the time to figure out who Ghost Skin was and what they were after, since the school was clearly not going to do it. Hardy wanted to shut me up. I wasn't about to give him the satisfaction.

JAWAD

One day, not long after I came back from suspension, after "Bomb Boy" took the place of my real name, I found a note slipped into my locker. I held my breath, afraid of what it could be. My fingers shook as I pulled out the flat cream-colored card from the blank envelope. I was so angry at myself for being scared. I didn't want to cry, not at school. Not in front of everyone. That would have made it all so much worse.

But it wasn't what I thought. It was a quote from a poet named Hafez:

> I wish I could show you, when you are lonely
> or in darkness,
> the astonishing light of your own being.

Even before I saw the signature, I knew it was from Ms. Ellis. It was exactly the kind of nice thing she'd do. Like how she could smile at you and nod her head in a way that felt like a hug when you needed it. Like she was the only one who saw you.

I slipped the note into the pages of my Global Studies textbook. I bet it's still there. I wonder if someone found it—someone who needed those words, too. I wonder who's using that textbook now, if they see my name on that *This Book Is the Property of* sticker. It's right there, under *Issued to*. It's a reminder that I had an everyday, boring old life. Like every other kid who hated Global Studies. Maybe they won't recognize my name: Jawad Ali. But I bet they remember Bomb Boy.

More sticky residue that outlived me.

Zoom Interview with Ellen Ellis

May 4, 2023

Ms. Ellis is the physics teacher at Bethune High School and the sponsor of the makerspace club. She agreed to be recorded for this interview.

Safiya: Ms. Ellis, can you give your impressions about the day Jawad was arrested?

Ellen: I was furious. When I saw that the police had been called and that they'd cuffed Jawad? A perp walk? For a fourteen-year-old? And all because Ms...uh...his English teacher thought a costume jet pack was a bomb. [*shakes head*]

Jawad was telling the truth. All they had to do was believe him when he said he'd built it with makerspace materials for Halloween. I could have verified it all. He was so proud of his idea. It was so creative. The sketches he did. How he dug through all the recyclables to find the exact right pieces. He only took it home because he was eager to finish. I approved the whole thing.

Safiya: When did you learn about the police being called?

Ellen: I heard the sirens, like everyone else. By the time I walked down to the first floor of the school to see what was going on, it was total chaos. There were dozens of cops in the hall. Dozens for one boy! Students were gawking, recording on their phones. Lots of faculty and the admin standing around, doing nothing.

They'd already walked Jawad out the door. Even when I ran up to the police to tell them it was part of a costume. A jet pack. Not a bomb. That I vouched for him. They didn't believe me. Brushed me off. Said they'd sort it out at the station. No one believed a brown Muslim boy could be anything but a terrorist, I guess. No one believed the Black teacher, either.

Safiya: Could you tell us a little bit about what happened at school afterward?

Ellen: They suspended Jawad for three days. Even *after* the cops had cleared him. It made no sense. He'd done nothing wrong. And it wasn't over for him when he came back from suspension. No one would let him forget it. The dirty looks—sometimes from adults in the building! And the name-calling. Bomb Boy. [*shakes head*] Treating him like he was a criminal. It broke my heart. And the admin didn't lift a finger to help him. I absolutely had words for them. They were not happy about that.

Safiya: When did things get back to normal?

Ellen: Normal? Never. Not for Jawad. The press hounded him. Waited for him right off school grounds. There were conspiracy theories, too. That his parents had orchestrated it to entrap the school in a racist incident. The media kept running that picture of him in handcuffs, startled and frowning. Did they run the picture of him winning a ribbon for a district robotics competition? No. Or even his yearbook photo, for God's sake? No. The police treated him like a criminal, and that's how the press depicted him.

There was that one TV interview Jawad and his parents did…and the sadness in his voice…I'll never forget it. Do you know the one I'm talking about?

Safiya: The one after the arrest? Right when they were leaving the police station?

Ellen: Yes. Yes. That one. He was describing the scene at school, the chaos when he was getting arrested. And he said something like *I kept looking around at all the kids, all the teachers. They were staring at me. Holding their phones up. And I thought, why won't someone help me? Please, someone help me.*

Lots of people tell me I should keep my mouth shut now. But I don't care. I stayed quiet too long. Maybe if more of us had spoken the truth from the beginning, none of this would've happened. Maybe we could've protected Jawad. That brilliant, beautiful boy.

SAFIYA

JANUARY 10, 2022

Fact: The level playing field does not exist.

Alternative fact: "We hold these truths to be self-evident, that all men are created equal...."

I was still fuming about my conversation with Hardy as I grabbed my notebook for my current events class. The entire senior class did independent projects for the last semester, so our course load was light—mine especially, since I'd already met my graduation requirements. I'd planned on cruising through this semester without too much homework, academic drama, or lost sleep. Ha ha. Joke's on me.

I loved Mr. Terkel's current events class, though. The irony of him teaching this course was that he's approximately seven hundred years old. Still, that gave him an encyclopedic knowledge of history because he was always complaining that America looked at current events in a vacuum. "The past is prologue" was one of his favorite cryptic aphorisms, which he doled out like candy on Halloween.

I took my seat at the large, round oak table in the center of the room as Mr. Terkel stepped to the old chalkboard and pulled down the movie screen. His classroom was one of the originals. There was stained glass in the windows that filtered the midday light through prisms of blues and reds. The wood floors creaked from age and unevenness. The room even had some sort of historical society designation that alumni applied for. They would've flipped out if we tried to change anything. I got the importance of preserving history, but this school needed to change with the world around it, and some alumni gave the distinct impression that they wanted to make it back into what it was: *Make DuSable Great Again.* As if being a fossil were something to aspire to. Attempts at progress or inclusion can anger people when they've never had to compete on a level playing field. Maybe that was why they didn't want to fix our crooked floors.

Mr. Terkel was pretty spry for an old guy. His white wrinkly skin, messy silver hair, and tweed vests gave him a frazzled academic look. We all complained about his tough grading, but he was one of the most beloved teachers at DuSable. Our own absentminded, somewhat radical professor who always wore red socks. He was one thing about the past I wanted to keep. And judging by his speech patterns, he was around when the school was founded 120 years ago.

He cleared a week of phlegm from his throat. "Gentle people of Current Events. In my many years of teaching this class, it has been rare indeed to have a moment like this, where the topic I want to discuss is an event that has occurred right here at our school." He looked at me and nodded. "Welcome back, Ms. Mirza. Glad you could be with us."

Oh no. I'd spaced out for a second while he was talking, my mind drifting to Richard's visit, then to that heady incense smell that kept floating in and out of my presence, and the sounds like whispers on the wind, even when I was inside. I shook my head to snap myself out of it.

Mr. Terkel clicked the remote in his hand, and a slide of the hacked post flashed onto the screen. Then he clicked again to a slide of the *Swallow your poison* flyer. I sank lower into my seat, feeling the weight of every pair of eyeballs in the room on me. Finally, he clicked one last time and left my photo of the graffitied swastika on the screen.

Welp. I guess no one was going to let me lie low today.

Mr. Terkel continued. "Now, moments before class, the administration sent out *another* faculty email alert asking us to keep quiet and carry on as if our own *Spectator* hadn't been hacked by this so-called Ghost Skin. As if this heinous Nazi symbol hadn't been painted on our school. As if a smoke bomb hadn't gone off in the bathroom. Of course, it has also been decades since I listened to direct fiat of this or any other school administration. That, my young friends, is the benefit of old age and tenure. Perhaps we should've spoken about this on the day it occurred, but I'd hoped we'd have a culprit and an explanation by now. So…this incendiary post was merely nine lines long, and yet I find that we could talk about it for the entire week—unpacking its claims and debunking the myths therein. Let's begin there."

God. I'm not going to have a moment where I'm not being forced to think about this. Nine lines that set everything in motion. That got me even higher on the principal's shit list. That had our journalism teacher walking on eggshells. Had some students terrified that the next incident was going to be more than a smoke bomb, even more violent than a swastika. My question-riddled anxiety was running full steam ahead. DO NOT PASS GO. DO NOT COLLECT $200.

"For now, I'm particularly interested in this phrase: 'This school is where free speech goes to die.' Yes, it's hackneyed, and yet it is also this Ghost Skin's, um, dare we call it a thesis? What are your thoughts as to the veracity of this statement? Who'd like to begin?"

Mr. Terkel made eye contact with me but didn't call on me, which I was thankful for. There were only thirteen students in Current Events, so I wasn't going to be able to hide forever, but I wanted to hear what other people were thinking.

Rachel was in the class, too, and she piped up. "I think it's BS. I mean, whoever wrote that is obviously a racist. Snowflakes? Fawning multiculturalists? Please. And if it was the swastika guy—which we assume it is, right?—he's an anti-Semitic white nationalist, too."

"That's not what Mr. Terkel asked," Nate burst out. He sat directly across from me, but I don't think I'd ever genuinely looked at him. He had the lean body of a long-distance runner and perpetual dark circles under his eyes that were magnified beneath his fancy new green plastic glasses. Before this class, I don't think we'd ever spoken. "He asked if this school is where free speech goes to die. And the answer is yes." Joel, the school's single source for various stolen pharmaceuticals and Nate's best friend, high-fived him and laughed.

A bunch of kids started speaking at once, and I watched a sly smile spread across Mr. Terkel's face. He loved arguments but tried not to let them get out of control. He raised a hand to calm the class. "Explain, Nate."

"We don't have freedom of speech, and we should. Students don't leave our constitutional rights at the schoolhouse door." Nate straightened in his chair, like he was going to rise up out of it.

"And antifa sucks!" Joel shouted, completely out of context. This was the most animated I'd ever seen him or Nate. I didn't bother explaining how ignorant it was to say you were *anti*-antifa. That means you're pro-fascist. Congratulations, you've just told everyone you hate freedom.

"Are you trying to quote *Tinker v. Des Moines*?" Rachel pointed at Nate, ignoring Joel's outburst. "That case related to *public* schools. We're private. Constitutional law doesn't apply. Contract law does. As in, when your parents decided to fork over the cash to let you go here, they agreed to the school rules, and spewing hate is against the school rules. Which you should know, since your daddy was on the school board before he became an alderman," she scoffed.

"Buuuurrrrn," someone whispered a little too loudly under their breath.

Nate blushed a red so deep, it was almost purple. He opened his mouth to speak. Paused, took a breath, then said, "Believe me, I know what is hate speech and what isn't. I'm saying whoever wrote

124

that article might be right—some speech is protected at this school, and some isn't."

Joel fake coughed and muttered, "Political correctness." Maturity was not his strong point, apparently.

I raised my hand. I couldn't help myself. I was not in the mood for a fight. But I wasn't going to back down.

"Ahhh, our editor in chief would like a word. Go ahead, Safiya."

I nodded at Mr. Terkel. "Not all hate speech is protected, even in public spaces. Speech that incites violence, like from, say, neo-Nazis or even presidents, shouldn't be. Actions have consequences—that's one of Dr. Hardy's favorite phrases, right?"

"Oooh. Someone's triggered," Joel mocked.

"Seriously. By the way, censoring people is totally *un*-American," Nate spit out at me.

I felt the heat rise to my skin, like I was about to explode into a billion particles of rage. I hated how words like "un-American" were used as weapons against people of color. Like *But where are you really from?* And *You don't look American.* Or *Wow, your English is so good.* But before I could respond, Rachel jumped back in.

"You sound like a fascist crybaby," she said to Nate. "You're the one who's un-American. Racist!"

Everyone in the class started shouting at once. While Mr. Terkel tried to quiet us down, I saw Nate lean back in his chair, his arms crossed. "God is dead," he said to no one, to everyone, to me, an enigmatic smile crossing his face as he exchanged glances with Joel.

"Safiya, hold up." I turned to see Rachel jogging down the hall toward me. I'd rushed out after class. I was furious about Nate's un-American dig and had this churning, sick feeling in my stomach.

"Hey, thanks for calling out Nate. It was the best thing about this whole day," I said as Rachel caught up to me.

"It felt good. Not as good as punching him in the face might have felt, but less likely to get me kicked out of school."

"Always punch Nazis, sometimes metaphorically and, when needed, literally," I added.

"Seriously, what was up with him? Nate was like a rhetorical dumpster fire, but happening in real life. And Joel? Have you ever heard that dude speak in class? He's absent, like, half the time."

In terms of the school social ecosystem, Nate and Joel barely registered on any scale. Nate transferred two years ago when his family moved to the area because the alderman seat was open and his dad wanted to run for it. Nate and Joel mostly started hanging out early last semester. They were an odd pair. And mostly stuck to themselves.

This was the first class I had with both of them. Rachel was right; Joel was absent a lot. I guess truancy wasn't such a big deal when you had rich alumni parents. And Nate—well, even though we all sat at a round table, facing each other, he kinda always faded into the woodwork. I shrugged. "Doesn't Nate have, like, a YouTube channel? I think he mentioned that once."

"Yeah, about birds," Rachel explained.

"Birds? As in bird-watching?"

"He's in my Senior Seminar." Rachel rolled her eyes. "His senior project is a study on the birds of Jackson Park. I guess he's like a birding celebrity? He's been published in nature journals, and he's been profiled in the *Tribune* and other places."

"I bet colleges are going to love that. The weirder, more niche your hobbies are, the better."

"I don't think he has to worry about that. He doesn't only have the alderman dad going for him; his family is Harvard legacy— multiple generations. A fact that he actually goes around sharing." Rachel faked a gagging sound.

"Gross. But let me guess: They're vehemently against affirmative action—"

"Except when it applies to rich white families."

I felt a pinch in my chest when Rachel said that. There were so many ways everything was stacked in your favor if your family was white *and* had money. I wondered what it felt like to never have to worry about affording tuition. To not be constantly reminded of how lucky you were because you were the scholarship kid, thanks to the (strings-attached) generosity of rich families at the school. Or to always buy whatever clothes and shoes you wanted. To never be stressed about what your parents were going without so that you could go on the annual school trip to DC with all the other kids.

"Also, did you hear him muttering at the end of class?" Rachel asked. "I couldn't figure out if he was talking under his breath to Joel or trying to make some kind of statement."

I thought maybe I'd imagined it. But the goose bumps on my arms told me that it was too much of a coincidence to ignore. The police had never found out who mailed that threat to our mosque using the very same words that Nate mumbled at the end of class. Maybe I was being paranoid, but did it mean I was wrong?

Rachel continued. "'God is dead' is a hell of a way to end a conversation."

"Yeah," I said. "Or to start one."

January 2022

IT'S 2:00 A.M. DO YOU KNOW WHO'S RADICALIZING YOUR SON ONLINE?

BY RENA DAVIS

Picture it: a young man, thirteen or fourteen years old, a little lonely, maybe a little isolated, turning to the internet for people who get him. The blue light of his laptop or phone shining late into the night as he's slowly drawn into a trap, his busy parents unaware of what is happening in their own home.

Young people in search of connection often turn to popular online communities, such as YouTube, iFunny, MPGs, Reddit. The very same platforms that are being used as tools by extremists eager to recruit young people to their often violent causes. Extremists, in some cases, advocating violence against American institutions. No, these aren't the designated terrorist organizations from overseas, recruiting our young people to a so-called holy war. They're other Americans—usually white men—laying the foundation for potentially violent rebellion right here at home. The January 2021 siege at the Capitol was one example. Experts warn that the Capitol was merely an opening salvo to potentially larger acts of revolt.

"These groups have savvy social media platforms, and with little online regulation for hate speech, they've been able to run rampant while hiding behind the anonymity of the internet," said Nasiha Hussain, director of the American Anti-hate Network, an organization whose efforts include uncovering and labeling hate groups. "Recently, some of these white nationalist groups have rightly been labeled terrorist organizations by the State Department."

Over the last three years, white nationalist hate groups have more than doubled, and they've grown largely through the online recruitment of young white males. "It begins with funny memes," Sara Small, author and anti-racist educator said. "Subtle ones that are racist, anti-Semitic, Islamophobic, homophobic. These young men are encouraged to share and spread the memes, and when, inevitably, they are called out for doing so, by a teacher or perhaps a female fellow student, they feel ashamed and also angry." That anger, Ms. Small explained, is "a toxic seed" that leads them to lash out at girls, at people of color, at those in authority—that is, "snowflakes" who they believe are trying to censor them, impinge on their rights. From there, they become pawns in a much larger game.

Eighteen-year-old James Kyle is often cited as a case study in how white nationalists are recruiting and radicalizing young men to commit acts of violence. Kyle attended a peaceful interfaith vigil in Chapel Hill, North

Carolina, in memory of a young Muslim who had been murdered. According to a note found on Kyle's laptop, he had planned to go on a shooting rampage. Only the quick action of two college students who overpowered Kyle when they saw him reach for his gun prevented a potential mass shooting. Speaking from his jail cell, against advice of counsel, Kyle, who once aspired to be a police officer, was not repentant. "They're taking over this whole country. Trying to steal our guns. Change our way of life. Trying to bring Sharia law here. I was there to defend America."

Kyle's internet use showed a history of him logging on to alt-news websites and commenting as BlueLives4Eva. In one comment after the police shooting of Khadijah Omari, an unarmed Black woman, inside her own home, Kyle wrote, "The use of force was justified. Police were protecting the neighborhood that was infested." At a Protect Our Cultural Heritage event to protest a city council ordinance to replace a statue of a Confederate general with a monument honoring a Black poet, Kyle spoke to local news outlets. "They're tearing down our history and the legacy that made America great."

"We were lucky that James Kyle was caught," said Anna Cho, author of *Clarion Call: The Fight for America's Soul.* "Unfortunately, his arrest led to him being lionized by the very right-wing media that helped recruit and radicalize him online. His story should be a cautionary tale to all parents. What are some early red flags? Have your children started making racist or sexist jokes, or do they talk about 'triggering snowflakes'? Observe and, yes, even stalk their social media accounts. What are their online media habits? Search through their YouTube favorites. Sit down with them and review the Reddit explore page and discuss the hate in the memes that your child has accessed or shared. I often hear parents say they don't want their child to think they're impinging on their independence or their personal life. But you're their parent; if you don't pay attention and intervene when you see these red flags, who will?"

JAWAD

People see what they want to see. Hear what they want to hear.

But if you listen, there is a small voice inside you that talks. That says, "Don't trust him. Don't get in that car." There is so much noise, though, so many other loud voices, the ones that say:

Make friends.

Don't make waves; get along.

You're so paranoid.

In America you have to act like an American.

BE NORMAL.

Criminals are poor. Black. Brown. Thugs. Terrorists.

Cockroaches.

They're not the best people.

Why would rich white people need to commit crimes?

What the voices don't say: It's not need; it's want.
What the voices don't admit: They're wrong.
What the voices don't do: Save you when you cry out.

('Til human voices wake us and we drown.)

SAFIYA

JANUARY 11, 2022

Lie: "What you're seeing and what you're reading is not what's happening." —Donald J. Trump, July 24, 2018

Truth: "The party told you to reject the evidence of your eyes and ears. It was their final, most essential command." —George Orwell, *1984*

Fact: Truth is stranger than fiction.

"No way," Asma said in a voice that was too loud for the library. I immediately shushed her. It was the first morning of my forced volunteer work, and I wanted to keep my head down, even if I was the only one at the checkout desk while the librarian was in the back room sorting through new acquisitions.

Asma rolled her eyes at me but lowered her voice and continued. "You think Nate sent that threatening note to your mosque?" Despite all of us being Muslim, Asma, Usman, and I all went to different mosques for a combination of reasons linked to ethnicity, sect, and geography. It was pretty old-school. None of those differences mattered to us—we were all Muslim.

"Don't you think it's weird he blurted out 'God is dead'? The exact same line that was in the letter my mosque got?" I asked, pulling my hands into the sleeves of my cozy sweater.

"It's strange, but he's pretty strange, too, so…" Asma shrugged.

"That's not all, though.…I thought it was just some Islamophobic thing that someone wrote, but after Nate said it, I Googled it. It's a Nietzsche quote, too. And so is 'Swallow your poison.' "

"What. The. Hell. You have to tell the police. You think Nate sent the text, too?"

"Shhh," I whispered, looking around the library. "It could be a coincidence, but that's a bizarrely huge amount of Nietzsche. Like, I never even heard of the dude until Usman mentioned him, and now he's everywhere in my life."

Asma shuddered. "Something's rotten in the state of DuSable. It's creepy. Dangerous. And with that kid missing—"

"Jawad. His name is Jawad," I whispered. I hated how everyone seemed to forget his name. Especially the press, who constantly referred to him as an "Arab American teen" or the "son of Iraqi refugees." Taking away someone's name was how you made them an object instead of a living, breathing human being.

Asma nodded. "Jawad. With Jawad still missing and you getting that text and the hack and that swastika…"

I paused. Took a breath. A chill ran through me. It seemed impossible that it could *all* be Nate. "So you think it might all be connected, too?"

"I'm saying a lot of scary, violent stuff is going down all around us, so be careful. And tell the police. This is like a true crime story waiting to happen, and it's way above your editor-in-chief pay grade to figure it out."

"My pay is zero."

"Exactly!"

I rubbed my forehead. "I don't trust that the police are going to believe it, believe me. Besides, I don't want my name associated with this mess. My parents would find out and they'd freak."

"Safiya, seriously. Even if it's not Nate, at the very least there's some psycho white supremacist running around quoting a dead German philosopher. Your parents going ballistic should be the least of your worries."

Asma was right. I knew she was. So why was I hesitating? I know a part of me didn't think that the police would do anything. But a part of me wondered if I was paranoid and making connections where none existed. I mean, Nate? He's a friggin' bird-watcher. That doesn't exactly scream criminal mastermind.

"Look," Asma continued, "you can report it anonymously. You don't have to share your text, but your suspicions about Nate seem legit. Do it now. I remember we got a postcard from our alderman about a tip website. Hang on." Asma whipped out her phone, looked up the site, and then handed the phone to me. "Boom. TipSubmit. Hurry up and use the librarian's computer if you're worried about them tracing the ISP."

I smiled. "Fine. Hang on." I typed in the address, agreed to the terms, and wrote a few sentences about overhearing Nate utter the same words that were in the threatening note to our mosque. I named our school, but not the specific class. Of course, if the police wanted to figure out who sent it, it wouldn't be that hard. The Venn diagram of Muslim kids who go to my mosque *and* attend this school was a complete circle, and I was the only one in it. "There," I said, tilting the computer screen and hitting ENTER as Asma leaned way over the counter. "One more hot tip for the police to ignore."

"The note to your mosque was postmarked from London, right?" Asma asked. I nodded. "Well, where did Nate go during winter break? I was in Paris. I could've sent a letter from there."

"I can't exactly go up to Nate and ask him if he was in London in December. I've never spoken a single word to him outside of class. Barely in class, either."

Asma groaned. "Have you seriously not listened to any of the true crime podcasts I rec'd?"

"They give me nightmares." I seemed like the kind of person who would be a true crime, murderino type, but I couldn't deal with gruesome. "I listened to *Gone and Forgotten*, but I was tossing and turning all night, thinking about that girl in the trunk who has never been identified. Like, how can no one have claimed her? Plus, it's messed up that a lot of stories make the murderers famous while their victims are forgotten by everyone but their families, who have to relive their trauma over and over because we're all obsessed with true crime."

"I hear you. But what I meant was, you have to be stealthy and resourceful about your research. If only you knew a plucky journalist who enjoyed cross-referencing and other nerdy pursuits. Oh, wait." Asma folded her arms across her chest.

"Ha! I'll let you know if I meet one," I said as the bell rang, rushing Asma off to her next class. I gathered my things. I didn't know why I was dragging my heels. I had an actual possible lead—okay, maybe more like a tiny hunch—connecting Nate to the threatening letter the mosque had gotten. But it was an even bigger leap from

there to the stuff that had happened at school and my text—a leap with no net below. Still, it did all go down in this neighborhood....
There was a voice inside my head telling me that if I pulled on this thread, I was going to unravel a whole mess that would entangle my entire life.

I stepped out of the library into the busy hallway. There was a faint ringing in my ears again—the sound I'd been hearing on and off since my suspension. I thought maybe I'd been listening to music too loudly with my earbuds. But I swear to God, underneath that ringing, I heard a whisper: *Help me.* I looked over my shoulder, but no one in the hall was paying attention to me. I turned around and continued walking to class. Then that incense smell wafted over me again, like an echo. Like a moment that was about to become a memory.

JAWAD

Mama and Baba had a customer who would always say "Hindsight is 20/20." A rich lady with shiny blond hair, who smelled like a whole perfume aisle. She always made a point of talking to me if I was helping at my parents' dry cleaning place after school or on the weekends. But every time she asked me how I was, she never waited for me to answer.

"Oops, shouldn't have worn cashmere while making pasta sauce," she might say, showing my mom a red stain on a white sweater. "Brain freeze! Hindsight is 20/20!" Her voice was tinkly and high-pitched, and she always seemed a little embarrassed when she was in the store.

My mom would nod and smile and place a few stickers around the stain, which would need extra attention. When the lady left, my parents would exchange a glance I never understood, but I think they didn't quite get American small talk. I don't think I quite got it, either.

Hindsight is 20/20! That sentence got trapped in my brain. You know how sometimes there are phrases that can mean more than one thing? That's what those words seemed like. *That phrase* could mean:

> I'll know better next time.
> Live and learn!
> I made a mistake, and now I need you to fix it.
> I should've been looking closer.
> I guess that was important. Oops!

I tried to use that saying once in school, when I was back from suspension for the jet pack and the principal pulled me into his office.

Him: Young man, do you understand the ruckus you've caused? What do you have to say for yourself?

Me: [*looking down at the floor, whispering*] Hindsight is 20/20?

He angry-frowned when I said that, crossed his arms in front of his chest while looking down at me. I shrunk back, tried to make myself as small as possible. I was invisible most of the time, except when I really wanted to be. It was like everyone was finally paying attention to me when all I wanted to do was hide.

I shouldn't have gotten into that car. But it seemed safe. My backpack was so heavy, and my feet were cold. I wasn't wearing the right shoes. My mom had told me to wear different shoes. I guess I thought it would be nice to get a ride. To be warm.

Hindsight is 20/20.

SAFIYA

JANUARY 12, 2022

Fact: There is no such thing as ghosts.

Truth: There is no such thing as ghosts.

Lie: There is no such thing as ghosts.

I'd tossed and turned all night. The desi dark circles under my eyes were even more pronounced, and my head pounded. Staring at myself in the bathroom mirror, I couldn't shake the feeling that eyes were on me. In the middle of the night, I swore I heard some-*thing*. Another voice whispering inside my dreams that wasn't my own. My name ringing in my ears when I was alone. A creak on the wood floorboards when no one was around. Then a whiff of that incense that had attached itself to me. It lingered everywhere, wrapping itself around me.

"Are you okay, beta? You're not hungry?" my mom asked at breakfast. It was just the two of us. My mom had let my dad sleep in—he'd been out again with the search group the Chicago mosques had organized. Still no trace of Jawad.

I gave my mom a small smile and pushed my scrambled eggs

around on my plate. Even my mom's freshly made parathas were not enticing enough to get me to eat. Behind her head, the local news was on TV. This morning, there was a brief story on Jawad—nothing new, a clip of that same sad interview of him after he was arrested and released. His scared voice spilled out of the screen and echoed around our kitchen: *Why won't someone help me? Please, someone help me.* I stared at the image of Jawad on our TV, his wide, confused dark-brown eyes gazing back directly at me.

"Mom, do you believe in ghosts?" I blurted. I expected my mom to dismiss the question. She was too pragmatic to believe in supernatural things. I used to think I was, too.

She leaned back in her chair and pulled her light-brown wool shawl over her shoulders. In winter, she always put it on before morning prayers. "You know, in Hyderabad, sometimes jinn stories and ghost stories intermix. Nani's family in Hyderabad would sometimes tell stories of the Kacheguda railway station being haunted."

"Haunted how?"

"Some say that on new-moon nights when it is darkest, a woman in a white sari can be seen roaming by the side of the tracks, weeping."

I shuddered. "Do they know who she is?"

"It's only stories, beta."

I opened my eyes wide at my mother, imploring her for more details. Sometimes my parents still acted like I was a three-year-old afraid of the dark. "Okay, okay," she said. "Supposedly, the woman wanted to marry a man who her family disapproved of, and when her family refused his offer and sent him packing, he was so

144

brokenhearted, he decided to leave Hyderabad forever. When she heard the news, she chased after him to the new railway station that the Nizam had built in Kacheguda—"

"So this was, like, around World War I?"

My mom nodded. "When the girl arrived at the station, she caught a glimpse of her beloved in a window as the train started to leave. She hurried after it, but the pallu of her sari that was draped over her left shoulder caught in the wheels of the train, and she was pulled under the train car and died."

I gasped, then covered my mouth with my hand. "That's horrible!"

"They say the man she loved never realized that she died trying to get to him. He joined the Indian Army and was killed during World War I."

"Oh my God. That's so tragic. It's like Romeo and Juliet, but without the oblivious friar who could've easily cleared everything up."

My mom nodded and gave me a sad smile.

"Mom, do you believe that story? I mean, did you ever see her? The ghost?"

"No. I never saw her. But I don't believe my aunts and uncles were making it up. Sometimes there are things in this world that logic can't explain. Sometimes you have to look beyond what you can see. Sometimes a ghost is only a memory."

"Whoa. That's either really deep or a misattributed Rumi quote."

My mom laughed, opening her mouth and quickly shutting it like she was going to say something but stopped herself. Then she shook her head and spoke. "It's not exactly the same, but do you remember your Naqui chacha?"

I nodded. My great-uncle—I'd met him once, when we'd gone

to India. I was around six years old. I remembered him playing hide-and-seek with me in the gardens of Golconda Fort while I pretended I was a princess.

"He was the uncle I was closest to. Well, about ten years back, I bolted out of bed in the middle of the night because I swore I heard him saying my name. A few hours later, we got a call from Hyderabad that he'd passed away. He'd been writing letters before he died. They found him propped up in bed with a pen in his hand and a notepad on his lap. Apparently, the letter he was writing was addressed to me. He never finished it." My mom wiped a tear from her eye. "We belong to God, and to him we shall return," she whispered.

"Ameen." Goose bumps sprang up all over my skin. "How come you never told me that story about your Naqui chacha before?" I asked.

My mom ran the knuckle of her left index finger across my cheek. "I thought I would, at the right time. I guess that time is now."

"Do you ever wonder what he was going to say in that letter?"

"I think I know," she said, and smiled. "I'm not sure if I believe in ghosts, exactly. But maybe the dead are with us in a way we can't explain. Any reason you're asking?"

"Not really." I shrugged and bit into my cold paratha, not knowing how to answer her question. I couldn't bring myself to say *I think I'm being haunted*. So many times in the last couple days, I'd thought about Googling "Are ghosts real?" or "How can I tell if I'm being haunted?" But I stopped myself every time. Didn't matter, though. The constant incense smell swirling around me and the whispers in my ear, in my dreams, were telling me I had an answer, even if it was one I didn't want to believe. And it was Jawad's own voice from the TV pushing me forward: *Why won't someone help me? Please, someone help me.*

I slunk to school with my eyes glued to my phone, scanning for more news on Jawad. In journalism class we'd talked about the history of news cycles and how because of cable and social media, the news cycle was now twenty-four hours, so stories—even important ones—faded fast. That's why things like political scandals that used to dominate the news for days or even weeks now dropped off the radar so quickly—another breaking story always popped up. I can't imagine what that old, slower world must have been like, because this is the only world I've known: the blistering pace, the clickbait, the press outlets trying to outgun one another for viewer and reader attention. But too many important stories fell between the cracks, like the story of a missing boy that had gone from national news to conspiracy sites within a few days.

My face burned with rage as I doomscrolled through Twitter, looking for news on Jawad but instead finding hateful, anti-Muslim tweets, egged on by some racist right-wing radio host:

The only good Muslim is a dead one. #bombboy #JWad

That raghead got what he deserved. #bombboy #JWad
#NoShariaLaw

#Bombboy planned his own "kidnapping" so he could get the
reward money.

Ready Aim Fire #JWad? #bombboy [Photo of Jawad in a target]

If you want me to believe in your Redeemer, you're going to
have to look a lot more redeemed. #bombboy

Of course, none of the accounts tweeting that hate used their
real names. Most of them were a string of random letters and numbers or statement handles, like AmericanPatriot2002. That weird
redeemer quote was from some loser who called himself Zarathus-
tra1488, whatever that was.

"Whoa. Heads up."

I stopped in my tracks and looked up at Usman's grinning face.
He was wearing a dark-gray wool kufi on top of his head, and his
hands were stuffed into matching wool mittens.

"Sorry I missed your text last night," he said. "Some of the guys from
the tennis team booked indoor court time. Then we went out after."

"Cool. I didn't realize practice had started already."

"It hasn't. But I'm number one varsity doubles this year, love.
Not going to destroy everyone at sectionals if we don't practice off-
season. My drop shot needs some serious work."

"I only understood, like, twenty-five percent of that. But fully
understand you have a crush on your doubles partner. Isn't love a
way of keeping score in tennis?" I grinned.

"Awww. You've been paying attention to my sportsball talk?"

Usman formed a heart shape with his mittened hands. "Now, why are you in a snit?"

"A snit?"

"Yeah, why were you staring at your phone like you were trying to make laser beams shoot out of your eyeballs?"

I sighed and showed him some of the tweets I was looking at. "Everyone's forgotten Jawad's disappearance except for Islamophobes. And…his family, I guess. I mean, he got more press coverage for being wrongly arrested than for going missing."

Usman rubbed the patchy stubble on his chin. "Yup, they hate us. So brave of them to hide behind anonymous accounts," he scoffed, peering closer at my phone. "Is that an avatar of a Confederate statue wearing a red hat?" He shook his head.

"I know. Not even sure if there's a point reporting them. Nothing ever seems to get done about it."

"In the before times, when you had editorial control, I would have suggested writing a piece about the Islamophobia angle of Jawad's disappearance," Usman nudged.

"Maybe we should do it anyway—try, at least."

"I volunteer as tribute."

The gears in my brain started spinning. Hardy would veto it for sure, but maybe that didn't matter. Maybe trying was the important part. "We could do a spread. A story on the alleged kidnapping? Interview the people involved. See if we can unearth anything new. You could do the Islamophobia angle, and maybe Rachel could write a more general piece on kidnappers and, um, what did that cop call it? Virtual kidnappings."

"I'm totally in. But do you think Ms. Cary would even go for it, let alone Hardy? He barely let you stay on staff."

"If we prep something great, maybe Asma can use her charm to convince Ms. Cary to plead our case to Hardy. If she says no, we'll figure something else out. Self-publish if we have to." We were basically being censored, but this was an important story, and it was worth a shot. Ask for forgiveness, not permission—we'd seen so many examples in history class where that was the only way things got done. "This could be amazing. But first let's do a little digging and see what we can come up with and who we can get on record. We can't let Jawad be forgotten."

JAWAD

By the time I got into that car, it was already too late. I was already a ghost.

I was talking about school, about the Bulls game. The floor heater was on in the car, and I was glad my feet were warm.

Then something hit me in the head. Everything went blurry and slow. I raised my hand to my neck; it was sticky and warm. I yelled. I think I yelled. But then a cloth covered my face, pressing down so hard.

Help me. Help me. Help—

I thought of Baba. I'd told him I would go straight to the dry cleaner's after school. I thought of Mama and how she had burned some incense that morning. Normally, she would wait until later in the day, near dinnertime, but sometimes she liked to burn it on damp days. The smell reminded her of home, she said, where the damp cold didn't seep into your bones like it did here. I loved that our house smelled like that incense.

All my words got trapped. Crammed in my throat. Even now I want to scream. I want to scream who did this. But I can't. I'm stuck. It's like saying a name could almost kill me again.

Help me. Help me. Help—

It's the last thing I *could* say. I thought it was a scream, but I think it was only a whisper. A hope. A prayer. My last thought before the end, because suddenly everything got quiet.

Then it was dark, and there was a light in the distance. Shining.

SAFIYA

JANUARY 13, 2022

Fact: Hide-and-seek is a game for kids.

Truth: The older you get, the better you are at hiding.

The next day during lunch, we gathered at my thinking bench in the park across the street from school. It was sunny, and in winter even a cold sun feels good on your face. Asma and Rachel sat on the bench. I was too fidgety to join them, so I bounced on my toes in front of them with Usman almost statue-still next to me. He and I had shared our plan with Asma and Rachel for our secret (for now) spread on Jawad's disappearance. I hadn't totally figured out a plan B if Ms. Cary vetoed it, which she probably would, but I wasn't going to let this story die. I'd figure something out.

"So, what have we got?" I asked.

"I emailed Jawad's parents," Usman said. "They go to a different mosque, but our moms sort of know each other because they were on the Chicago Eid planning committee last year. His mom said I could go talk to them at their dry cleaner's. I'm free last period, so I'm heading out early to meet with them."

"Ugh. They still have to work?" Rachel asked in a quiet voice.

I shrugged. "They probably don't have a choice." If they were anything like my parents, Jawad's mom and dad probably were the owners *and* employees and couldn't afford to shut down their business for too long. My parents didn't talk to me about their money concerns, but if they had a bad month at the store, I could see the worry in their eyes.

"That sucks," Asma said. "I hope it at least gives them something to do. Can you imagine? My parents would absolutely be unhinged and terrified if it were me, but at least they wouldn't have to worry about losing their jobs, too, if they took time off."

"This country is total bullshit sometimes," I said.

"Sometimes?" Usman added.

We were all quiet for a moment. I dug the toe of my worn Doc Martens into a small pile of dirty snow and tucked my chin into my scarf. I was the only one of us on scholarship; the only one who lived the kind of life that we were talking about. It's why I understood. Maybe it's also why I couldn't let this story go.

"I went to the police station and asked some questions," Rachel said. Then, glancing at our three surprised-looking faces, she added, "What? I'm white. I told them I was doing a research project. Besides, my dad is the precinct sergeant's doctor."

Usman shook his head. I think we could all guess what he was thinking. Hard to imagine he'd ever be able to walk into a police station with his kufi on and ask questions without rousing some suspicion. I mean, Jawad had gotten arrested on suspicion of terrorism for making a costume jet pack out of plastic soda bottles.

"And…," Asma prodded.

"So, the sergeant gave me some basic background on virtual kidnappings and also real kidnappings and why time is of the essence. The first twenty-four hours are the most essential if it's a kidnapping. Most missing kids are found—I think he said only one in ten thousand or so is not. But of the ones who are murdered, like, over seventy percent are killed in the first three hours."

"Three hours?" I gasped. "It's been a *week* since the Amber Alert for Jawad, and everyone seems to have forgotten about him already."

Rachel nodded. "The sergeant said they are doing what they can. But there weren't any eyewitnesses except for the one who saw a car driving around, and even that was uncertain. Plus, Jawad's cell phone looks like it was turned off, because they can't locate it."

"People don't just disappear," Asma said.

"Sometimes, I think, they kinda do," Rachel added in a soft voice.

I felt an anger rising inside me, like a tiny flame starting in my belly, ready to turn into a bonfire and burn everything up. "We're not going to let that happen to Jawad," I said through gritted teeth. "No way."

Usman placed one of his mittened hands against the back of my coat. I took a deep breath. "No, we won't. Look, I found—"

Out of the corner of my eye, I saw Richard bounding toward us. "Hey, so what's the newspaper crew up to?" he asked as he slipped in between me and Usman. He leaned his arm into mine, and I leaned back, all while trying to be so cool, like this was no big deal even if my earlier flames of rage had started flickering into mushier *feelings*. I was surprised at how quickly my anger started to dissipate when Richard turned to me, dimples bared, his smile dazzling in the winter sunlight. Everything inside me felt like a whirly muddle almost all the time now. Even if it was sometimes good, it was dizzying.

"We were talking about how the *Spectator* desperately needs a full-page spread on the captain of the swim team," Asma deadpanned.

"Don't forget lacrosse." Richard smirked, then flexed his arm muscles. "I think Yo and Bro would look amazing in a pinup. Should I wear my Speedo?" he said, and pretended to kiss each of his biceps through the wool of his coat, his bare hands in fists as he curled his muscles.

"Oh my God, you're ridiculous," I said, gently elbowing Richard.

"It's the paper, not a thirst-trap challenge, dork," Rachel added.

"On the other hand, it might increase our hits." Usman laughed, and we all joined in.

"Why do I feel like you're not taking this seriously?" Richard asked, then turned to me with a wide grin. "Of course, it would need the right editorial touch."

I bit my lip and looked away, absolutely wordless, which was a rarity.

"As shocking as it may seem, there are more things in heaven and earth, Richard, than are dreamt of in your ego." Asma glanced at me and grinned. Richard burst into laughter.

Asma had been right. Richard was an expert-level flirt. He oozed charm. And he knew it. The thing is, I liked it. Maybe more than I was willing to admit out loud.

"We were talking about Jawad's case," Rachel said. "You know, the missing kid?"

I scrunched my eyebrows at her. She wasn't spilling state secrets, but I didn't want anyone to know what we were planning, not yet. Not that Richard would run and tell Hardy or anything. Ugh. I dunno, maybe I'm too paranoid. I do hold things close to the vest. A lot. Especially feelings. Maybe too much.

"Is there new info on the kidnapping?" Richard asked.

"No, but you think it was a kidnapping, too?" I asked.

"Isn't that what it usually is with kids who go missing this long?" Richard wondered. "I hope they find him. He seemed like a nice guy."

I think all our jaws dropped at the exact same time. "You know him?" Asma asked.

Richard shrugged. "Sort of? The entire varsity swim team kinda knew him. Cross country and soccer, too. All our coaches organized a volunteer program at Bethune, so a bunch of us did, like, ten hours of volunteer work there with ninth graders during first quarter. You know, like tutoring, painting lockers, helping out after school."

He turned to look at me with a sad half smile. I put my hand on his forearm for a second. "That has to be tough to know he's missing."

"He wasn't in my group, so I didn't really see him much. But I felt bad for all the crap he went through with that whole Bomb Boy thing."

157

"Did you ever see kids bully him? The police said he had problems with that at school," Rachel said.

Richard shook his head. "No. Nothing I can remember. But I was only in his school for those ten hours. It sucks what happened to him."

I gave Richard a small smile, and he squeezed my hand before he glanced back at the school doors. "I gotta grab some lunch before next class. Let me know if you need to take photos for the feature on me." He chuckled and then leaned over and whispered in my ear, "It's all happening." He smiled as he jogged off.

"Did you all see those looks those two were trading?" Usman said, fanning himself, as soon as Richard was out of earshot. "And so much suggestive nudging."

"Hello? I'm standing right here," I pled.

"That flirty banter?" Asma added, ignoring me. "Hot."

"And what does 'It's all happening' mean? What exactly is happening?" Rachel asked as my friends burst out laughing.

"Oh my God. Whatever. You're all drama queens. It's a line from a movie."

Usman raised an eyebrow at me.

"Nothing is happening, okay?" I said, then hid my face with my mittened hands. "Can we please get back to the point of meeting up?"

"Oh, was it not to discuss your bone-dry social life?" Usman grinned.

"Ouch. Besides, I have you three."

"A girl cannot live by newspaper friends alone. Especially when dimpled boys are, like, *happening* right in front of you," Rachel said.

"Exactly. Variety. Spice of life, et cetera," Usman added.

I shook my head at Usman. "Dude. I can't believe you referenced spices and a white guy in the same sentence." Rachel and Asma giggled. "Anywaaaaay," I continued, "let's check back in tomorrow after you've talked to the Alis, Usman. The rest of us will keep digging."

"And tell them all of us are doing dua for Jawad to be found safe," Asma added.

"Oh! I forgot," Rachel said as we started walking back to the building. "Why did you text me about wanting to know where Nate went for winter break?"

"You know how he whispered 'God is dead' at the end of Current Events?" Everyone nodded as we neared the red doors of the main entrance. "The threatening letter my mosque got during break quoted the same words. And it was postmarked from London. Usman said it was a famous quote and all, so it could be a coincidence, but—"

Rachel put her hand on my arm, stopping us all in our tracks. "On the first day back from break, some of us were talking in Senior Seminar about where we'd gone, and when Nate walked in, someone asked him. He said he was in London."

I sucked in my breath. Maybe there was no such thing as a coincidence.

Usman Haider Interview with Suleyman and Dina Ali for *DuSable Spectator*

Usman: Salaam and thank you for taking some time to talk to me. I know this must be so hard.

Dina: As-Salaamu-Alaikum. We just want to find our son. I...We...He is our everything.

Suleyman: We are worried people are already forgetting Jawad has been missing. We are praying and keeping our hopes up that he will come back to us, unharmed, Insha'Allah.

Dina: Did you see what some of these people are saying, that Jawad planned this? How can they say such things? He would never hurt us this way.

Usman: I'm so sorry. They're terrible people. Have the police given you any updates, or has there been any other news?

Dina: [*shakes head*] They say the same thing all the time, that they are following every lead, but they are not telling us what the leads are. I do not think they are following anything.

Suleyman: We have offered a reward. Can you put that in your article? And the number to report any information? People can report anonymously. Maybe some young person saw him around the neighborhood....

Usman: I'll make sure we do. I promise. Did the kidnappers send you anything else besides the ransom messages that first day?

Suleyman: I did get a strange text this morning, but it didn't say private number like the other texts. It wasn't a ransom and didn't say anything about Jawad.

Usman: Did you tell the police?

Suleyman: Yes, of course. I tried calling the number, too. But there was only a message saying "This number is no longer in service."

Dina: Such a strange message about dead gods. And Superman? The store has also been getting prank calls. Saying terrible things about Jawad, calling him Bomb Boy. And other worse things. Horrible, hateful things.

Suleyman: We don't want to change the number in case Jawad tries to call us. It's the only number we've had for our dry cleaner's.

Dina: Why are people so cruel? He's just a boy. Our sweet, loving boy. Yesterday, he was our baby. And now he's vanished, and no one seems to care.

SAFIYA

JANUARY 13, 2022

Truth: The simplest explanation is usually the right one.

Truth: Sometimes there is no simple explanation.

Alternative fact: You're wrong on both counts.

"Can I walk you home?" Richard was at my locker when I arrived after my last class. Not sure how he got there so fast since my classroom was a lot closer, but as Asma would say, he was eager. Eager was good.

"Are you going to hold my books, too? Let me wear your varsity letter jacket, maybe?"

"If you're cold, sure," he said, eyes sparkling.

"That was a joke." I spun my locker combination and grabbed my coat and hat, shoved my journalism and current events class binders into my backpack, and shrugged it over my shoulders. Did I mention that sarcasm was my fallback mode whenever I felt awkward? A disdainful worldview often made excellent armor.

Richard grinned and bent down to whisper in my ear. "I think sarcasm is hot."

My cheeks flushed. I turned to my locker and pulled my scarf from my coat pocket and wrapped it around my neck, tucking my chin into it. I felt like I'd been caught flat-footed, but I shut my locker, mustered up a little courage, and said, "I think you like saying things that get people all flustered."

"Not all people, just you." Richard's eyes twinkled as he spoke.

Ugh. The perfect lines rolled off his tongue. I shook my head as we started to head out. "You have my vote for Biggest Flirt, but you're probably a shoo-in anyway." The yearbook kids organized the senior awards ballots and named the winners of the goofy categories in a two-page spread with caricatures. Not sure which category they could invent for me.

"So my legacy is secure." He laughed as he pushed open the door.

"Legacy? What high school senior thinks about their legacy?"

"Ah, you haven't met my dad. Lucky you." Richard drew a knit navy-blue cap from his pocket and fitted it over his head. "He can't shut up about it."

"That's gotta suck, at least a little," I said, trying to sound sympathetic. My parents never used words like "legacy"; honestly, it seemed a term solely reserved for wealthy Americans, but maybe it wasn't that different from wanting to live up to your parents' expectations, which I definitely understood.

"More than a little. He drones on about all the things I *have* to do. About the things the family expects of me. That's basically why I'm captain of lacrosse and swim. One wasn't good enough for my dad. And it turns out that two wasn't good enough for Harvard." Richard looked away, his face twisted in a grimace.

"What do you mean? I thought you wanted to go to Yale."

"I do. But my dad leaned on me *hard* to apply to Harvard, and I didn't get in early action."

I was floored. Richard had never told me any of this before. And I'd never seen him look so bummed. He was generally the cheerful type, always smiling. "Sorry. I didn't know about that."

"Yeah. I didn't tell anyone. Not even the guys on the team. I wasn't going to apply, and I think I did a half-ass job on my essays. But, wow, my dad was pissed."

"Is that where he went?"

"That's the thing—he went to Michigan, but he's been obsessed with me getting into Harvard forever. There's pictures of me in a Harvard onesie as a baby." He shook his head.

"Gee. No pressure."

"Right? It's like he wants to live vicariously through me. He got even more pissed when I told him maybe Harvard didn't want another rich white kid who played lacrosse at their school."

I chuckled.

"Look," Richard said, "I'm not afraid to admit I'm a little vanilla."

"In fact, vanilla is a much more complex flavor than most people understand."

"Ha! Tell that to Harvard."

We continued walking quietly in the direction of my apartment. The midday sun had already started to fade. It would be dark in less than two hours. The gray of winter and the early sunsets always depressed me a little. The wind whipped up a few fallen leaves as we turned the corner onto a quiet street. I shivered and snuggled into my coat. Richard edged closer to me as we walked and then put his arm around my shoulder. I let him pull me closer to him. His arm was warm against my back. I could even feel the heat through the wool of his peacoat and the layers of my army-green parka—a hand-me-down from Asma, barely worn and so cozy. Her generosity never had strings attached, but it sometimes still pinched a little. I didn't talk much about privilege and money with my friends, not directly, but everyone knows when you're the scholarship kid.

Richard broke the silence. "You know, when I was in your store the other day and you were talking about working with your parents, I kind of envied it."

"Believe me, restocking shelves is not as glamorous as it seems." I nudged him a little.

"No. I mean, you seem to get along with your parents. Like you enjoy each other's company."

"I think that's called being a family," I said, but instantly regretted it when I saw the tight smile on Richard's face. "I mean…yeah, basically, we get along. And they're pretty cool about not pressuring me about school stuff, but I'm a kid of immigrants. I still feel the pressure to do well, to help them out."

Richard paused and turned to me as I stopped next to him. "God, I'm a jerk. Listen to me. Poor little rich kid with a bunch of first world problems."

"It's cool," I said. "You feel your problems how you feel your problems, you know? Like, I know it was hard to decide between a Benz and Beemer. I feel your pain."

Richard raised an eyebrow and then chuckled. "Touché."

I gazed up at him as we continued walking. My scholarship status and beat-up Docs didn't seem to matter to him, not like they did to so many of the other kids. And it felt good that he could confide in me, share a secret that was a little painful. More and more Richard surprised me, in a good way.

"So...um...I have a question." Richard paused, stretching out his syllables.

I pulled away so I could turn to look at him. "Go on." I bit my lower lip, unsure what to expect. I generally lived by an "expect the worst, hope for something not the worst" motto. But secretly I was hoping for more. Secretly I was optimistic.

"I know you were all hard pass on Winter Ball. But would you consider, uh, reconsider going?"

"Going?"

"With me, I mean. To the dance. Would you like to go with me?"

What my heart was saying: *YES!*

What my mind was saying: *Be cool. Don't be a dork.*

What my body was saying: *Don't worry, upper lip sweat in winter is totally normal.*

What my mouth said: "I don't really dance...."

Wait. What? No. My brain said be cool, not icy.

"Well... I would very much be into not dancing. *With you.*" A smile spread across Richard's face and made his eyes twinkle. "I'm sure we could find something better to keep us occupied," he added.

My jaw dropped. "Uh, *excuuuuse* me?" I said, pretending to be scandalized.

"I meant...um...I didn't mean it like that! We could, like, hang, talk, or take a stupid number of goofy selfies. You know, senior year, last hurrahs." I didn't know Richard that well, but I did know he rarely stumbled over his words. It was sort of cute.

"Sure, that could be fun." I rushed my words so I wouldn't chicken out, and quickened my pace. I tried to sneakily sponge away the sweat from my glistening face with the back of my mitten, but the truth was, I needed to take off my hat, my coat, my scarf.... My entire body felt overheated. Richard took a couple long strides to catch up to me and then followed in lockstep.

I was going to a dance. Winter Ball. *Me.* The girl who didn't like to dance and whose only fancy shoes were the khussa slippers I wore to Eid. Well, those and a pair of silver sparkly heels that I was forced to wear to a family wedding and that pinched and gave me blisters and were lost in the black hole of my closet. This was going to break my streak of never going to school formals. I had no dress to wear. Butterflies battered around my stomach and...was I possibly feeling giddy? Oh my God. I was giddy. I was embarrassed for myself. And yet...I finally understood why people broke out into song in musicals.

The wind continued to stir leaves and shake branches as we walked the last block to my place. "Our apartment is above my parents' grocery." I pointed to our building once it came into sight.

Richard nodded. "I think you mentioned that in chem."

"Well, that was forward of me," I joked. I liked that Richard paid attention to details, like with the garbage cookies. So many guys in our class only paid attention to their own BS.

My phone buzzed as we neared the store. It was Usman: Jawad's parents got another text. Maybe from the kidnappers.

"Holy crap," I blurted.

"Everything okay?" Richard asked.

"Yeah, hang on."

What did it say? I texted back after removing my mittens.

I stole a glance at Richard. His eyebrows were scrunched together. He looked worried.

"Everyone is fine," I said. Then hesitated. Rachel, Asma, Usman, and I had agreed that we'd keep our little fact-finding mission under wraps. But we were trying to keep it a secret from Hardy and Ms. Cary. Not Winter Ball dates. (I had a date?!) "Usman interviewed Jawad's parents."

"Whoa. That must've been intense."

I nodded, a bit distracted, looking from my phone back to Richard. "Apparently, they got another text. Not sure if it's from the kidnappers."

My phone buzzed again. Took Usman long enough. It was a photo of a text screen on a phone: **Dead are all gods: now we want the supermen to live.**

More gods and death? What the hell?

I texted back: **Call you in 5.**

"Sorry," I said to Richard. "I gotta call Usman."

He looked disappointed. "I was going to try and convince you to hang a little longer. Maybe do some homework at that table." He pointed to the Formica table in the store window. "But I get it. Maybe we can grab lunch tomorrow?"

"Oh, umm…I'm meeting up with my friends again." I winced. I didn't mean to make it sound like I wasn't friends with Richard. "Newspaper things," I explained. "Trying to keep some stuff from the prying eyes of Ms. Cary. I'm pretty sure she tells Hardy everything."

He gave me a half nod. Richard had asked me to Winter Ball,

and now I was kind of blowing him off? If there were rules or social cues for this moment, I didn't know them. And I was antsy to call Usman. Although I was torn because I wanted to hang with Richard. My Winter Ball date, who was very good at flirty banter and smiling and making me feel like some animated version of myself, a girl in a musical wearing a twirly skirt and singing alongside chirpy woodland creatures. But I had to focus on Jawad. This new text could be a bombshell.

My mind wandered, and an awkward silence filled the space between Richard and me. "More sleuthing?" he prompted.

"Something like that." I reached into my bag, fumbling for my keys. "I'll text you later?" I didn't want to be rude, but I *had* to call Usman. "I'm excited for the dance," I added as a consolation. Then, remembering what Asma had said about maybe letting my guard down a little, I let my impulse take over, stepped closer to Richard, and kissed him on the cheek.

He smiled. "Can't wait for it." He brushed the back of his index finger against my cheek. I had no idea how his hands could be so warm when he never wore gloves. It was nice, though, the perfect complement to my constantly cold hands. He winked at me and gave me a huge smile as we parted. Dimples appeared. Pretend fireworks went off in the air around us. Cartoon birds sang. There might have been heart palpitations. I waved at him as he crossed the street.

I stepped through the door into our apartment vestibule, those cartoon birds still singing. My phone buzzed, another text from Usman: That text is a Nietzsche quote.

Oh. My. God.

PART V

THE POISON OF SILENT TRUTHS

SAFIYA

JANUARY 14, 2022

Fact: Sticks and stones can break your bones…

Alternative fact: …but words will never hurt you.

Truth: Words can be terrifying. Sometimes words leave scars. Words can break you, too.

There were dots to connect, but I kept wondering if my overactive imagination was seeing links where there weren't any to see.

I sketched out what we knew so far after Usman and I spoke last night. And a common denominator kept popping up.

- Dec 16th: Letter postmarked from London to mosque: *You can pray all you want to your God. But God is Dead.*
- Nate in London during winter break, Dec 15–?
- Jan 3rd: Ghost Skin newspaper hack: "I am the herald of lightning."
- Jan 6th: Smoke bomb and swastika painted at school
- Jan 6th: Jawad's Amber Alert (missing day before?)
- Jan 7th: "Swallow your poison" flyer and text to me
- Jan 10th: Nate says "God is dead" in class

- Jan 13th: Usman interviews Jawad's parents and sees text: *Dead are all gods: now we want the supermen to live.*

"Wait. The text Jawad's parents got is from Nietzsche, too?" Asma asked, turning to look at me and then Usman as we flanked her on the bench across from school. Rachel had to meet with her Senior Seminar adviser during lunch and couldn't make it.

"But what does it mean?" I asked. "When I Googled, I read that white supremacists kinda glommed onto Nietzsche. He's all over their websites. Some of his stuff is even used…kinda like a code word or a secret handshake. There was an article about some bookstores seeing increased sales of his books recently."

Usman scoffed. "Wow. Rich racists like to read so they can be educated about their bigotry, huh?"

I nodded and continued. "So, Nate quoting that phrase could be a coincidence or not. And the text Jawad's parents got? That's gotta be an outlier, right?"

"Outlier?" Asma asked.

"It's already a bit of a stretch to link Nate to the mosque note, even if he was in London over break and blurted out the same words in class. I mean, there's no proof he actually sent it. I guess it would be circumstantial evidence, but barely, right?" I asked.

"Being in London gives him opportunity. And we can confirm he knows the Nietzsche quote. But motive?" Asma scratched her neck.

"So you're thinking Nate is the one who sent the threatening note, hacked the school newspaper, set off the smoke bomb, and he…" Usman's voice trailed off. "Look, I think the dude seems pretty messed up, and I checked out one of his birding videos from Jackson Park, which was creepy as hell. But maybe we need to step back for a second and consider that we're *looking* for him to be guilty because that's what we want."

"Confirmation bias." Asma nodded. "It comes up a lot in true crime podcasts when the police are convinced the murderer is one person and they totally miss the real killer because they're fixated on the wrong guy."

I took a deep breath. They were right. Nate was a weird loner except for being friends with Joel, a rich stoner, who was, also, admittedly strange. But it didn't mean they'd committed any crimes. Still, it didn't *feel* right. "I know it sounds ridiculous to even think about connecting Nate to Jawad going missing, but… this Nietzsche stuff keeps popping up. Seems like it has to mean *something*."

Asma nodded. "Same. But weird behavior and bizarre coincidences don't mean he's a kidnapper or even the hacker."

"What about the #bombboy tweets?" Usman asked. "Did you Google that odd one after you showed it to me?"

I scrunched my eyebrows together. "I didn't take screenshots right away and—"

"What! First rule of true crime club: Always get receipts," Asma yelled.

"I know. I was going to, but after I talked to Usman, I also kinda bumped into Richard. We were chatting, and then suddenly the bell rang, so I rushed off to class. By the time I remembered to grab screenshots, the tweets had been deleted."

"Wow. That must have been some bumping." Asma smirked.

Usman held an imaginary microphone to my mouth. "Could you please describe the bumping, ma'am."

"Shut *uuuuupppppp*," I said as my two friends burst into uncontrolled giggles. "Wow. So mature."

Usman coughed. "Fine. Okay. Was it only that tweet that was deleted or the whole account?" Usman asked.

I scrolled through my phone to get to the app and the hashtag. Then I showed Usman the deleted content message and shrugged.

"Give me your phone a sec," he said, his hand outstretched. I handed it to him. Staring intently at my screen, Usman furrowed his brow and started typing.

I turned to Asma. "So, um, there was a tiny bit of other news yesterday afternoon, which I was going to text you about, but I wanted to get your reaction in person....Richard asked me to the Winter Ball."

Asma's jaw dropped. "This is breaking news. I can't believe you buried the lede!"

"Going to a dance is not news." I tried to act all nonchalant, like my stomach wasn't doing summersaults every time I thought about it.

"*You* going to a dance is absolutely hot-off-the-presses clickbait. And with Richard. Oh my God. I cannot get over it."

"I can't get over it, either," Usman chimed in without looking up from my phone. "And I'm going to have plenty to say in a minute."

I tried to suppress my smile. But why did I feel like I needed to? Why did it feel so weird to be excited for a school dance? Maybe because dances were ridiculous, manufactured, forced-fun social events that I'd always looked down on. But I *was* excited. And my friends were, too.

"The account's deactivated," Usman said, still not looking up from my phone. "But I'm digging up their tweets on an internet archive. Hang on."

"Tell me everything," Asma said, ignoring Usman's much more important side note. "How'd he ask? What are you going to wear? I'm going to have extra new outfits for the wedding, so if you...Oh! My khala in Karachi sent me a gorgeous burnt-orange gagra choli that would look amazing on you. I still have to get it tailored to the right size, but it's yours if you want to wear it. My closet is your closet."

I grinned. "Thanks, but I think I'm going to wear that kurta pajama I wore last Eid."

"The dark-blue one with the silver-threaded embroidery?"

I nodded. "I think it'll work?"

"It's perfect. He's so lucky you even deigned to go with him. The mighty Safiya, slain by the captain of the swim team."

"Don't forget lacrosse!" Usman added, still busy with my phone.

We all laughed. But I shuddered a little. It felt wrong, surreal, to be talking about dances and outfits with Jawad still missing.

"Got you!" Usman yelled, holding the phone triumphantly. "This ass tweeted racist, Islamophobic, anti-Semitic shit. All. The. Time."

"Gross," Asma said.

"One more thing," Usman added, turning my phone so we could all see the screen. "That tweet you found, about the redeemer and being redeemed? It's a Nietzsche quote, too. And the account name, Zarathustra? It's one of his books."

I hopped up off the bench and started pacing. We all got quiet. Stared at each other. Like each of us was having the exact same thought at the exact same time.

Asma spoke first. "So…we're blowing way past coincidence here, right? There's gotta be a connection."

"The only common link is the Nietzsche thing, and the only connection to that is Nate. He's a bird-watching, conceited dweeb, and probably a racist who maybe sent that letter to my mosque. But hacker? Vandal? Kidnapper? We don't have enough evidence to accuse him of all that," I said.

Usman looked at the ground and reached down to pick up a dry twig near his feet and rolled it between his fingers. "We can't go around accusing rich white kids of anything. Period. Not of being Nazis or hacking the paper. And definitely not kidnapping. Not without super-obvious evidence. Like a video of them committing the crime. Sometimes that still isn't enough. That shit would blow back on us, though. Count on it." Usman looked up at me. "Hardy could pull your scholarship for making false accusations, which you know he's dying to do. And whose side do you think the police will be on? Yours or the rich alderman's kid?"

"Ugh. You're right," Asma said. "Plus, I can see the anti–cancel culture brigade screaming about it now."

I gulped. "Right. Okay. We can't name names," I said. "We don't have any real evidence besides Nate blurting out a phrase and being in London and having a BFF who sells Adderall and wears fatigues. Which all amounts to…basically nothing." Those were the facts.

Still, the whole truth felt out of reach. Maybe that's why my stomach was all twisted in knots. One thing I did know is that the longer Jawad was missing, the less likely he was to be found alive. And I was trying so hard not to think of what those whispers around me could be—the voice that no one but me seemed to be able to hear. Maybe my gut was trying to tell me something I wasn't ready to acknowledge.

Usman took a deep breath and rubbed the back of his head. "The kidnappers did ask for ransom. What…thirty thousand?" I nodded and he went on. "It's not like Nate needs money. That's practically pocket change for him."

"Look. This isn't a cold case, but the first rule of solving a mystery is reviewing all the existing evidence and making sure the police didn't miss anything," Asma said.

I scoffed. "The police can't miss something they never bothered searching for in the first place. We don't know if Hardy seriously looked into who hacked us. He's the only person who has something to gain from clamping down on the paper."

"Whoa. Now you're saying it's Hardy?" Asma's eyebrows shot up.

"You said look for motives. And he has motive. Shutting us down and shutting me up. It would be his dream to dump the troublesome scholarship kid."

"Sure, but no way he could've graffitied the school," Asma said. "He was around us the whole time."

"He wouldn't get his own hands dirty," Usman said. "He'd pay someone else to do it."

I chuckled. That tracked. Hardy was like a type A, hospital-corners neat freak.

I sighed and shook my head. A crack made me jump back, startled. I thought Usman had broken the twig he was holding. But he was still rolling it between his fingers. Neither he nor Asma seemed to have heard the sound. There was no one else around. I took a deep breath and let my eyes flutter closed for a second. I heard that voice again. So faint. But I knew what I heard. It wasn't a delusion. *Help. Safiya. Help me.* I opened my eyes. There was that incense smell hanging over us like a cloud. I was the only one who noticed that, too.

JAWAD

She heard me. This time I'm sure of it. She. Heard. Me. My words. *Help me.* I tried to whisper it so many times before. But my voice sounded like the wind and the rustling leaves. I don't know if sounds even come out of my mouth. I don't know how I say the words. My lips are blue.

I stepped on a twig. Imagined the feel of it under my foot. The sound of it if I pressed down hard with my toe. *Crack. Crack. Crack.* Maybe that's how it works with my voice, too.

Find me, I whispered.

I want my parents to know. I want to go home. I don't want to be alone anymore.

But I'm scared. For her.

Because when the truth bashes you on the head, it can make you bleed. It can destroy your world. The truth can be scary. And now the scary truth is so, so close to her.

Asma's Rules for Solving a Cold Case

Texted to Safiya

Jawad is missing, so it's not technically a cold case, but I think these still apply!

1. Know and name the crime(s) you are trying to solve.
2. Review all existing evidence. Pay close attention to any details that might have been missed.
3. Create a timeline.
4. Interview potential witnesses.
5. Follow every lead.
6. Treat everything as evidence.
7. Don't take no for an answer.
8. Don't go into a creepy house that white kids in slasher flicks would go into on a dare.
9. Trust your gut.
10. Document everything. And keep the receipts!

SAFIYA

JANUARY 14, 2022

Truth: Birds of a feather flock together.
Truth: Opposites attract.

I spent the afternoon parked in the school library watching Nate's YouTube channel, *Fowl Play*. I was technically "working" as part of my Hardy-mandated post-suspension punishment, but I'd set up my laptop behind the counter where I was sitting so I could research while checking out books.

I'd learned more about migratory birds passing through Jackson Park than I'd ever thought possible. According to Nate's narration, "Jackson Park is a world-class birding destination with fifteen million birds that fly through or live here on a yearly basis." He'd posted videos for the last two years and had over one hundred thousand subscribers. His Fowl Friends were also enthusiastic commentators on everything from his latest bird sightings to the special (and expensive!) binoculars he used, to his new "signature" green eyeglasses, which his fans fawned over. There were clearly people in the comments who had crushes on him. And birdtubers were apparently very passionate. *Very.* I shuddered. Who knew a hundred thousand people would want to subscribe to a birding channel run by a teenager? The internet is weird.

Nate documented everything—with video and still photographs—and did little voice-over narrations naming the bird type and Fun Facts! about the birds. He had clips of Caspian terns and cormorants soaring high above the park and patrolling the lagoons. There were eastern kingbirds, black-capped chickadees, warblers, woodpeckers, hummingbirds, great blue herons, green herons, cedar waxwings, and black-crowned night herons. And he went off on how the purposeful release of peregrine falcons into Chicago had decimated the bird population.

It was weird watching Nate on these videos. He was like a different person. At school he was usually quiet, awkward. Slightly weird. His only friend was Joel. I literally had no idea what the conversational intersection of birds and illegally obtained Oxy and Adderall was, but maybe they sat around being racist together. I don't know. Except for that outburst in Current Events, I'd barely even given Nate a second look or thought. But on these videos he was relaxed, engaging, and chatty; he even cracked bird jokes. Maybe he had only one IRL friend, but he had an army of people who loved him online.

"Caught you."

I looked up, startled, then burst into a toothy smile as I pulled out my earbuds. Richard leaned over the counter, a sly grin on his face, and whispered in my ear, "Don't worry, I won't tell Hardy if you're watching not-safe-for-school videos." His breath felt feather light against my skin, and goose bumps popped up all over my arms.

"Ha! You wish." I smiled and closed my laptop. He didn't need to see me obsessing over birding videos like the total dork I was.

"So," he said.

"So," I replied. Then murmured, "It's all happening." Crap! That was supposed to be internal monologue. Now I'd made that movie phrase a thing between us? Was it a thing?

Richard grinned.

I moved around some papers on the desk, scrambling for something to say. "Um...uh...oh, sorry I couldn't hang at lunch."

"No worries. Everything good with the newspaper crew?"

"Yeah. No. Still under Hardy's fascist rules." I sighed.

"No closer to solving the Case of the High School Hacker?"

"Oooh, that's so Nancy Drew of you to title the case."

"I used alliteration and everything." Richard grinned. "Hope you're impressed."

"Oh, I am. Very effective use of consonants."

"Good, I like impressing you."

"I like being impressed." My face warmed. I bit my lip and looked away for a second. We were having banter. Yes, it was nerdy and we were in the library and I referenced consonants, but I was engaged in flirty chatting with a cute guy. And I was good at it! Who had I become?

"So, the swim team wants to get fondue before Winter Ball. You game?"

I scrunched my nose. I was one-hundred-percent un-game to

spend a dinner avoiding hot cheese mishaps with the guys on varsity swim. "Maybe we could think of something else?"

Richard smirked. "Oh, I can definitely think of something else."

I was glad to be wearing a gray turtleneck. I rarely, if ever, blushed, but my neck sometimes burst out in tiny red hives when I got super embarrassed. Which I was. "Ha ha. Grow up." I tried to conceal my smile.

"Would you rather do dinner with your friends? Or I could cook for you at my house—show off my skillet and spice skills."

I would've liked to go to dinner with my friends, but Usman was going with his doubles partner and some guys from tennis. Asma had her cousin's wedding that weekend. Rachel and Adam always went to the dances alone. And that was the extent of the friends I could possibly consider doubling with. I was excited to go to the Winter Ball with Richard, but it was likely going to be my only high school dance, and a part of me wanted the Hollywood movie big-friend-group thing that would also end with me and Richard dancing in a gazebo under the stars. Not that I would ever confess that secret delusion to anyone.

I also liked the idea of him cooking dinner, but I felt self-conscious about it. Would that mean I'd meet his parents? That they'd have dinner with us? Would they even be there? Asma's voice singsonging *re-cip-rocaaaaaation* in my mind made me freeze up. I wasn't quite sure what I was ready for yet.

Since I didn't know what to say, I changed the subject. Besides, Richard's face was so close to mine, I thought I might combust—and I didn't want a *Fahrenheit 451* type of situation in the library. "So, umm…you know Nate, right?"

"That dude from cross-country? He lives a few blocks over from me, but I don't think I've ever talked to him. He and his pal Joel aren't exactly social. Why?"

"Oh, uh, nothing. He was being weird in Current Events."

"Weird how? Did he say something rude to you?" Richard straightened from the counter, tightening his jaw and squaring his shoulders, like he was going into protection mode.

"No. He was spewing some kind of alt-right crap, agreeing with that hacker who posted over my column."

Richard relaxed his shoulders a little, but his brow was still furrowed. "He what? What the hell is wrong with that guy? He's definitely a creep, but I don't think he has the balls or the brains to hack the site. He's probably trying to get under your skin. Don't let that bird-watching dork live rent-free in your brain."

I shrugged. "You're probably right."

"Do you guys have any clue who it might've been?"

"Not really," I said, leaning back in my chair at the library counter. "And I don't think Hardy is even trying to figure it out. He seems positively gleeful that the newspaper is getting screwed, and he's happy to take it out on me, like it's my fault."

"He has it in for you, huh? That's why he's working the hack to his favor, the asshole."

"Exactly! He's the worst."

"Whenever we lose a swim meet, I always tell the guys, what's done is done, you know? Learn from it and figure out a way to get back at Hardy the next time." Richard paused. I got what he was saying, but it was so hard for me to let things go. He smiled and showed a dimple in his right cheek. "Anyway. I came here to find you and ask if you wanted to meet up at Medici for cookies and cocoa. Maybe talk about the daring investigative techniques of Woodward and Bernstein. Seriously, who meets a source in an empty parking garage? That's got future true crime podcast written all over it."

I chuckled. "You know garbage cookies are my weakness. I have to check in with my parents, but I think they'd be cool with it."

"They keep close tabs on you, huh?"

"I don't mind," I said. "They've been super nervous about me walking around by myself since Jawad went missing. My dad's still been out searching for clues with a group from our mosque. They're not saying it out loud, but they're scared."

"I get it. At least they care. Tell them you're safe with me. I'll even walk you home, like a gentleman. And if your mom happens to have an extra samosa lying around, I wouldn't say no to it."

I laughed. "I'll let them know I'm in good hands."

"Oh, you totally are," he said, then winked at me as he headed toward the exit. I waved at him as he stepped out.

I flipped my laptop back open. I stared at the paused image of Nate on his video while I held my pen between my thumb and forefinger, wiggling it up and down until it looked all rubbery. *Are you a white supremacist? A Nazi?* It didn't feel plausible. The bell was about to ring, so I closed all the tabs I had opened and I deleted the history, only because Asma reminded me, like, a hundred times to be careful, even on my own devices.

On a whim, I decided to check to see if the library had any books on Nietzsche. Our philosophy section wasn't huge, but I grabbed a book called *Existentialism for Dummies* and a musty-smelling volume with a worn gray fabric cover that looked a hundred years old: *A Brief Introduction to Nietzsche*. Briefly is the only way I wanted to be introduced to philosophy. I went to check the books out, and another student librarian was already behind the desk. I told him I'd check it out myself, since he was stacking books onto the reshelf cart. As I scanned the books, the title and checkout history came up. No surprise they weren't the hottest volumes in the library. No one had even borrowed the Dummies book this year, and it looked like there was only one person who had checked out the brief intro book....I gasped when I saw the name: Nate Chase. He'd checked it out right before Thanksgiving and returned it this week. All those coincidences were starting to add up to facts.

Excerpt from *A Brief Introduction to Nietzsche*

Verily, I have often laughed at the weaklings who thought themselves good because they had not claws.

—Friedrich Nietzsche, from *Thus Spoke Zarathustra*

Perhaps more than any other philosopher's, the works of Friedrich Wilhelm Nietzsche (1844–1900) have been open to widely disparaged interpretations and debate. His writing on nihilism, morality, truth, the superman, eternal return, and the purpose of life had practical application. He did not believe philosophy to be a mere intellectual exercise but rather a guide for the individual to grow and overcome herd mentality, which he rejected as the path of fools. He believed that man's purpose was to overcome the herd compulsion, to better himself and become a higher man, a superman, who could look down upon the masses of sheep who blindly followed societal norms without question. Nietzsche believed that such supermen (his opinion of women was anti-feminist and even misogynistic) must constantly be questioning within a kind of solitude: *Why do I exist? Why do I suffer?*

While some of Nietzsche's work appears contradictory, his views are often interpreted as anti-democratic, anti-labor, and anti-socialist while espousing a proto-fascist ideal. He often made racist, classist, anti-Semitic remarks and was intrigued by a caste system where the upper class exhibited clear superiority over the lower classes. However, at times he denounced nationalism and widespread scapegoating. But he also strongly believed that mixed-race individuals were inferior, and he supported the ideals of racial purification.

There is some controversy as to how Nietzsche's ideas may have been manipulated by his sister, Elizabeth, who became his caretaker and sole editor after he suffered from physical and mental health issues that left him a recluse. Elizabeth was an outspoken anti-Semite and German nationalist and shaped her brother's works to suit those views. After Nietzsche's death in 1900, she published fragments of his *Will to Power* and became an important figure in the Nationalsozialistische Deutsche Arbeiterpartei, the Nazi Party. When Hitler rose to power in 1933, his Nazi government publicly supported the Nietzsche Archive. The Nazis sought German thinkers to espouse their philosophies. Nietzsche's works, edited by his sister, were used by German universities during the Nazi era, referencing soldiers as the ideal supermen. The will to power was adopted as a fundamental Nazi Party tenet, which Hitler expressed through military might, political power, and the extermination of those he deemed inferior.

In the later twentieth century, historians have tried to reclaim Nietzsche's philosophy from what some call his sister's "censorship" and "hijacking" of his work. However, even those who attempt to rectify supposed wrongs to his name concede that Nietzsche held reactionary views on women, egalitarianism, democracy, and racial equality. And Nietzsche's writing continues to serve as a foundation, a rallying call to fascists and white supremacists.

191

JAWAD

I follow her everywhere. Now that I know for sure Safiya can hear me. I can tell she sometimes tries to ignore me—wants to. But she knows. Now that I know that the truth is so close, so dangerous, I try to use the words I have, the ones that still come to me.

Help me, I whisper when she wakes up.

Jackson Park, I say as she brushes her teeth.

Find me, please, I cry as she walks to school. My voice makes her shiver, shrink into her coat. It makes her stuff her hands into her pockets even though she has mittens on. She pretends it isn't real. She pretends that it's maybe the wind and not my voice ringing in her ears. She looks around. Sees no one. Shakes her head. I don't blame her. I'm not sure if I'm real, either.

I keep whispering. My voice like dry leaves. Like a chill in the air. I try to make my voice not so scary. Even though I'm scared.

Even though scared was the last thing I felt. I don't want to scare her.

I'm so close.

I'm right here.

Please.

She knows more than she thinks. *Trust your gut*, I want to say. Isn't that what they tell you? I should've trusted my gut. But I was so cold. My feet were so cold. And I wanted to be warm.

Be careful.

Be careful. I should've been more careful.

SAFIYA

JANUARY 14, 2022

Truth: Reading helps you discover who you are. Reading makes you more empathetic.

Truth: In a war, books can be weapons.

On my way to meet Richard after school, I started flipping through the pages of the Nietzsche book. There was a whole section with his most famous quotes.

> *God is dead. God remains dead. And we have killed him. How shall we give comfort to ourselves, murderers of all murderers.*
>
> *Dead are all Gods: now we want Superman to live.*
>
> *Once you said "God" when you gazed upon the distant seas, but now I have taught you to say "Superman."*
>
> *I am the herald of lightning.*
>
> *You must have chaos within you to give birth to a rising star.*
>
> *All the truths that are kept silent become poisonous.*
>
> *And if you gaze into the abyss, the abyss gazes also into you.*

The next page was ripped out, leaving a jagged edge sticking out from the center. As I ran my finger along it, a sharp corner caught a piece of my skin where it met my nail. I pulled my hand away, nearly dropping the book on the slushy sidewalk. A tiny drop of blood popped out, and I watched as it spread, leaving a bright-red crescent under my fingernail. I squeezed my index finger and waited for the blood to clot.

My phone buzzed. I'd set up notifications for any news related to Jawad's kidnapping.

South Side Times Breaking News

Parents of missing student receive text from son's cell.
Police believe kidnapping may have been staged to cover
up running away. Chicago P.D. to hold press conference at
5:00 p.m. (CST).

What the hell?

I checked the time on my phone. I wasn't going to make that garbage cookie date with Richard.

Chicago Police Department Press Conference, Chief of Police Ken Burge

Good afternoon. I'm here to provide an update on the disappearance of fourteen-year-old Jawad Ali.

Shortly after 10:00 a.m., Suleyman and Dina Ali, parents of Jawad Ali, received a text message from their son's cell phone saying he had run away. The full text reads: "Sorry mom and dad. I'm okay. Couldn't take it anymore. Home soon."

Though it appears Jawad turned off his Find Me app, the last known location of his phone was the Chicago area. We are currently attempting to ascertain the exact location of his phone. The Alis have tried to call their son, but his voice mail appears to be full. Text messages have received no response.

At this point, we will pass along this case to our Runaway Interdiction Team, who will be investigating it under their auspices. Every effort will be made to locate this juvenile and reunite him with his parents.

January 14, 2022

BOMB BOY KIDNAPPING ANOTHER HOAX?

BY WILLIAM KEMP

The alleged kidnapping of fourteen-year-old Jawad Ali and the subsequent ransom demand that led to an Amber Alert and widespread search that turned up almost no clues has a new twist: It might not have been a kidnapping after all, but an attempt by a discontented teen to cover up running away from home due to "bullying." This, according to police who indicated that Ali's parents received a text earlier today from their son's phone.

Ali gained notoriety after being arrested and suspended for bringing a fake bomb to school, which he claimed was part of a Halloween costume. Among his fellow students at Bethune High he came to be known as Bomb Boy, a moniker he apparently disliked. "It was all a joke," a sophomore at his school told us, requesting anonymity for fear of being "canceled [by] the crazy libs at my school." Another student added, "It wasn't a big deal. Honestly, I don't think anyone even knew who he was before. At least it made him interesting."

The police investigation continues, according to sources inside the department. "It's cast a new light on him. On his whole family." Faking a kidnapping is a crime. Sources would not confirm whether Ali's parents were now also under investigation, possibly linked to a larger false-flag operation incorporating sympathizers at state and local governments who used the bomb hoax and kidnapping as a way to gain sympathy for Islamist causes.

SAFIYA

JANUARY 14, 2022

Fact: In the United States, citizens are promised equal protection under the law.

Truth: Some Americans are more equal than others.

"It's bullshit. No way his parents were in on it. No way. I saw them. They looked totally broken." Usman was pacing around Asma's foyer. Calling this space an entry hall was almost a misnomer; it was bigger than my living room. Asma's family lived in one of the massive brick mansions built in the early 1900s north of my neighborhood. It had three floors and five fireplaces, including one in Asma's room—she and her little brother essentially had their own wings in the house. Instead of meeting Richard, I'd headed straight to Asma's house, texting her and Usman for a 911 meeting ASAP.

Right before I was going to text Richard, he messaged me, saying he had to bail because his dad wanted to have a meeting with him. He'd accompanied that with an eye roll emoji. What parent uses the word "meeting" to talk to their kid? "I'll make it up to you," he'd promised. Even though it was necessary, I was still bummed I was going to miss garbage cookies and cocoa and studying next to him, inhaling the clean, soapy way he always smelled (but not in a creepy, obsessive, I-like-to-sniff-you way).

It was so weird how life could get all twisted up and confusing. I was angry about the hack and the vandalism at school. Terrified that a teen from my neighborhood was missing. But every time I thought about Richard, I got fluttery all over, like butterflies were flapping their wings over every part of my skin. How could any human hold all those contradictory feelings in one body without bursting?

I sat on a red satin settee (as Asma's mom called it), scrolling through my phone for more info about Jawad's kidnapping and the text his parents had gotten from him: *Sorry mom and dad. I'm okay. Couldn't take it anymore. Don't worry. Home soon.*

"Are the police even trying to find him?" Asma asked.

Usman scoffed. "Wouldn't count on it."

"I still think we should go to the police. Who else can we tell about our suspicions?" Asma said.

"What do we tell them about? A missing page of Nietzsche quotes, the newspaper being hacked, and a classroom outburst from a loner?" I asked.

"The note to your mosque, the text Jawad's parents got. And the swastika at school, too," Asma added.

"They already know about those things," I said. "And they're not in any rush to find who did them. My dad is still going out with the mosque group looking for clues, but they don't even have a police escort anymore. Besides, what are we supposed to tell them? A kid quoted Nietzsche in class; obviously, he's a white supremacist, a hacker, and maybe a kidnapper! Being a white supremacist isn't illegal, anyway," I said glumly.

Usman, who had come straight from tennis practice and was still sweaty (gross!), had been staring at a painting that hung in Asma's foyer. It was by this artist named Shazia Sikander, who put a modern twist on Mughal miniature painting. Asma's mom knew her from when they were kids growing up in Lahore. Sikander's art hung in museums now—and on the walls of Asma's house. Her work was so cool; you could study one painting forever and still not find all the tiny little details. But it was those little details that made up the big picture. I made a little game of trying to find new things every time I came over.

"What do we have to lose by talking to the cops?" Asma asked.

"Look, if you guys somehow think CPD are going to listen to you or even care about a missing Muslim kid, go ahead. But I'm sitting out a trip to the police station. I seriously don't think my mental health can take watching them actively ignore Jawad's disappearance." Usman shook his head.

"I think we have to try," Asma whispered.

Usman drew his shoulders in and stared at an invisible spot on the floor. "I wish I could be as hopeful as you. But they didn't care about the swastika painted on the school or the threatening note to Safiya's mosque. They don't care about us." He paused, then continued. "Look around. Like…in Wisconsin, cops literally ignored that white kid holding a giant gun after he murdered people, because the police were focused on arresting Black and brown protestors. They'd rather protect a Target than protect our democracy. Hell, if we went in there, they could arrest us and say we were filing a false police report. Hard pass."

I walked over to Usman and reached up to put an arm around his shoulder. We'd talked before about the discrimination and fear his Hazara Shia family in Afghanistan lived with. How scared he was for them; how much it weighed on him. They're an ethnic and religious minority. Not that long ago, the Taliban bombed a school in a Hazara neighborhood, killing eighty-five people, mostly kids; and the police and government didn't seem to be doing anything to protect them. Then Usman was almost arrested last year at a rally against America's refugee policy and the internment camps at our border. The police started kettling people, and Usman had an asthma attack as the cops corralled the protestors. Luckily, a nurse in the crowd helped him. Until right now, I hadn't stopped to consider how painful and triggering all this probably was for him.

"You're right," I said. "It sucks how much this country loves white supremacy. But I...I...think maybe we should still try telling the police. We'll need them eventually. We don't have other options." Saying that, I still wasn't sure, but maybe Asma had a point. It's not like I could make an arrest.

Usman nodded. "I'll see what else I can find online about that Zarathustra dude."

"I'll drop you off at home," Asma said to Usman, then turned to me. "And then drive us to the station."

"So let me see if I understand this…" The desk sergeant leaned back in his chair after we told him our story. He honestly didn't look much older than we were. He had short red hair and the kind of fair skin that probably needed 100 SPF not to get burned. "You think there's a connection between the mailed threat to the mosque, the DuSable Prep vandal, and Jawad Ali running away, and that it's tied to a kid in your school?" He gave us a half smirk, like he was annoyed but also slightly amused at our pluck. We'd decided not to use Nate's name. Not yet. Usman was right: It was too risky to name an alderman's kid.

"Kidnapping," I said. "We think…it's, uh, a kidnapping. Maybe. Possibly." Looking at Sergeant O'Keefe's face made me lose my resolve. His smile had turned to a grimace.

"That's a serious claim," he said. "You are aware it's a crime to file a false report. Especially in light of the text message that kid's parents received from him. Is there something you know that law enforcement doesn't? Some detail *you're* hiding?"

Asma nudged me aside and stepped closer to the glass divider between him and us. She smiled. "Oh no, Officer. Nothing like that. We were hoping to get some help is all. We work on the newspaper and are doing a story on…everything. We thought it was suspicious that N—that a kid quoted words from the mosque threat and that it seems linked to the hack and the text Jawad's parents got. And also to the words scribbled across Safiya's op-ed."

The sergeant's grin returned when Asma spoke, but he narrowed his eyes as he looked past her at me. "And you were suspended for violating school rules and posting an article to the newspaper, correct?"

"Yes, but actually, I disagreed with that rule, freedom of the press and all." I tapped my rubber Doc soles on the linoleum. "Civil disobedience is very American."

Asma turned her head and scrunched her eyebrows at me. Like, why did I think bringing up civil disobedience to a cop was a good idea? Then she turned back to the sergeant. She had this innocent, I-respect-authority voice down. "Sir, we felt it was our civic duty to report our concerns. We think that there is enough circumstantial evidence to connect the crimes."

The sergeant leaned forward, and his chair snapped back in place. "I bet you two are true crime buffs. Listen to a lot of podcasts? Am I right? Well, thank you for reporting your concerns. As journalists, you're aware, I'm sure, that I can't give any comment to the press about ongoing investigations. But you've certainly given me a lot to think about, ladies."

Asma and I walked out of the station in silence, our heads down until we got into her car. I thought about the creepy text I'd never reported. That cop wasn't even interested in a missing kid; no chance he'd care about me getting anonymous threats.

"Wow. Could he have been any more condescending?" I asked. "He wasn't even taking notes. It's like Usman predicted—that cop was trying to turn it around on us."

"Even my charm didn't work. Frankly, I'm kind of offended. But, yeah, he seemed more irritated at our presence than anything." Asma started the car and put it into reverse.

It was smart not to use Nate's name. We'd come so close to accusing an alderman's kid of vandalism, of being a Nazi, of kidnapping.

The cop seemed convinced that Jawad was a runaway—I guess that was the story they were sticking with.

A chill crept up the back of my neck and that voice floated in the air around me, ringing in my ears. Rachel had said that most missing kids are found okay. That only one in ten thousand is found dead. But 70 percent of the kids who wind up dead are murdered in the first three hours of their disappearance. The Amber Alert was issued eight days ago. Jawad was nine days gone.

January 16, 2022

Breaking: Text from missing student known as "Bomb Boy" casts doubt on kidnapping. Parents of Jawad Ali released statement today claiming text is fake, as their son never called them "Mom" and "Dad." Investigation continues. We'll be joined by the director of the National Center for Missing and Exploited Children at 10:00 p.m. (EST).

JAWAD

Mama and Baba. That's what I called them. Always. That's how I texted them. Even how I left voice mail messages, because my parents are very old-fashioned and wanted me to call them on the actual phone if I was going to be late coming home from the makerspace. I didn't always like calling them Mama and Baba, because when I started school, no one else called their parents that. For everyone else it was pretty much Mom and Dad.

It made my cheeks burn when a boy named David made fun of my lunch in second grade. I always brought lunch from home, and for Eid my mom made dolma mahshi—one of my favorites. He turned up his nose at the smell of the onions and meat that was coming from the small thermos my mom had given me. I tried to turn away, but he wouldn't leave me alone. *Why doesn't your ma-ma give you normal food for lunch so you don't smell up the whole classroom?* he'd asked, saying *mama* in a baby voice. Other kids around us giggled and pointed fingers. The teacher told him to stop, but from then on, I mostly stopped talking about Mama and Baba in class or with the other kids, or I found ways to avoid saying those words.

It made me a little sad. I didn't want to let the other kids wash all my own words out of my mouth, but I didn't know what else to do.

SAFIYA

JANUARY 17, 2022

Truth: The end justifies the means.
Lie: The end justifies the means.

"Can you get me Nate's locker combination?" I'd asked Rachel to meet me Monday morning before school at my bench. I rushed out the words, hoping I wouldn't lose my nerve.

"Oh, sure. No problem. I'll ask him in Senior Seminar: 'Hey, Nate, can you give me your locker combination so Safiya can check to see if you are the school hacker and maybe a Nazi? Pretty please?'" she said with an eye roll.

Rachel had been there for a lot of conversations about Nate, but I hadn't filled her in on every single one of my suspicions. She didn't know that I thought maybe Nate had done a lot more than send threats. It didn't seem smart to say it all out loud. My two closest friends were already involved—maybe too involved—and after the way that cop had looked at me and Asma at the precinct on Friday, like we were the ones breaking the law, it felt wrong to drag them even further down this rabbit hole.

If Nate was involved in taking Jawad, that meant he could be violent. Painting that swastika was a kind of violence, too. But kidnapping? That meant he was okay with up close physical violence against a person. That was even more bloodcurdlingly scary. Nate's dad was one of the most powerful aldermen in the city. And I guessed he would protect Nate no matter what he'd done. That's always how it went. We get cops coming to our mosque, asking us to rat out nonexistent terrorist sympathizers, but were white Christian congregations being surveilled and asked the same thing about white supremacists?

The police might not care about keeping my friends safe, but I did. And all my thoughts were simply that—feelings, suspicions. What if I'd led everyone down a dead end? It felt like everything pointed to Nate, *except* for his personality, motive, and limited opportunity. *Ugh.* I thought back to that whole confirmation-bias discussion I'd had with my friends. Was I looking for him to be guilty? That's what corrupt cops did—forced the evidence to fit the crime. That's how innocent people went to jail. I wasn't going to do that.

I needed a smoking gun. A single, clear, no-doubt-about-it piece of evidence for something—the hack, the swastika, the kidnapping. Ugh. Even linking those three things as, like, a crime spree felt absurd. But if I could find a real clue to prove even one of my suspicions, maybe others would fall into place. I had to search where Nate might hide something. I couldn't break into his house. But his locker, that was reachable.

"I wouldn't ask you if I didn't think it was important," I pled with Rachel. "Hardy refuses to listen to anything I have to say, but I'm sure that Nate was involved in the hack and maybe the graffiti, too. And...well, you work in the office first period, right?"

"You want me to steal his combination?" Rachel's voice was flat, her face expressionless.

In my sophomore year, the school had switched from allowing us to bring our own locks to using built-in-locks because of a stolen-test scandal. Hardy made sure to always inform us that the school had a right to search our lockers because they were school property, but I guess he got sick of using bolt cutters, and switching to built-in locks was another way he could control the students. "Isn't there, like, a master file of all the assigned lockers and their combinations?"

"It's on the server, password protected."

"But you have the password, right? Or a way to get it? I mean, isn't that how you managed to get a locker next to Adam all four years, or was it a coincidence?"

Rachel smiled. "Will not confirm or deny. But will say the front-office staff makes a beeline to the break room when freshly baked goods arrive, leaving their desks and computers wide open for the length of a coffee break."

"And you are an excellent baker." I grinned. "I'll owe you, okay?"

"Nah, don't worry about it. I'm in. If Nate is the asshole who put up that swastika, I'm happy to do a little crime for the greater good. When are you going sneak into his locker?"

"Fourth period. While everyone is at the assembly."

"Maybe I'll join you. I don't think I can deal with another

drinking and drugs are bad lecture from Hardy and whatever cop he's bringing in to show us a forty-year-old slideshow that refers to weed as Mary Jane." Rachel rolled her eyes.

I smirked, and we both headed toward the front entrance. "Oh, one more thing." I lowered my voice since we were getting closer to other students. "Don't text. Give me, like, a note or something I can get rid of easily."

"Oooh, that's very cloak-and-dagger, old-timey spy movie. I accept the mission. And be careful, okay?"

I walked into the auditorium in fourth period with everyone else. Once Ivy, the student body president, started talking, I told Mr. Byron I had a "female emergency," and he let me go out the side door. Normally we're not allowed to leave all-school assemblies, but from the face Mr. Byron made as he waved me off, I knew he wasn't going to stop me. Rachel had passed me a note, palm to palm, during the previous period: *Swallow this after reading. 237: 5-40-37 xo.*

During the all-school assemblies, pretty much everyone was in the auditorium except for two security guards and the custodians. One of the guards sat at the front desk and signed people in, and the other roamed the halls. After the second morning bell rang, all the doors to the school locked from the outside except the front doors. Senior hall was out of the sight line of the check-in desk, and I hoped the wandering security guard wouldn't wander toward me.

I hurried through the cafeteria and snuck into senior hall, which was completely clear. Nate's locker was across the hall and about a dozen lockers away from mine. My fingers shook and my heart pounded out of my chest as I spun the numbers on the lock. I'd never even stolen a piece of candy from my parents' own store. I passed the second number and then had to restart. *Hurry*, I whispered to myself as I glanced again and again down the hall, trying to silence the thoughts screaming in my mind that I was delusional, so I could listen for the footfalls of the school security guard or the jangle of the keys on a custodian's belt loop.

Calm down. I turned to the last number; the lock clicked, and I lifted up on the metal handle. I sucked in my breath. I hadn't been sure what I would find, but I didn't think it was this: a perfectly organized space. Nate's black coat hung on a hook, gloves stuck out of the pockets, and a gray scarf was folded and placed on the top shelf. His books and binders were neatly shelved on the bottom. There was no backpack. Like a lot of kids, he probably carried it with him during the day. God, this was ridiculous. *I* was ridiculous. What did I think he was going to have in here? A notebook with the word *CRIMES* scrawled in red Sharpie on the cover?

I shook my head and started closing the locker door, remembering I shouldn't slam it shut. But I paused, stole another quick glance down the hall, and then rifled through the binders to see if there was anything unusual. There wasn't. Then I stuck my hand into his coat pockets, moving the gloves aside. The left pocket was empty, but there was a folded-up piece of paper in the right one. I snagged it and unfolded it: the missing quote page from the Nietzsche book. My chest tightened. There was a quotation circled multiple times: *Swallow your poison, for you need it badly.* It was the same one scribbled across my column. It was the same one texted to me. I gently shut Nate's locker, shoving the page into my back pocket as I walked toward the auditorium, my palms clammy and my heart thumping out of my chest.

I paused.

If he realized the page was gone, he would likely know that someone took it. That someone had been in his locker. Did I put the binders back in the right order? And how the hell could I even prove it was in his locker in the first place! *Crap.* I was terrible at this. I couldn't present the missing page as evidence to the police. How could I explain how I'd gotten it? Rachel had stolen the combination for me. Nate could say that I'd stolen from him or that I'd ripped the page out myself, planted it. And my fingerprints were on Nate's locker. Would they take fingerprints? Could it come to that? I sighed. I needed to put that paper back.

The bell rang, and reality hit me in the head like a hammer.

My breath caught in my chest. It was too late. I was screwed. Students would be flooding the hallway any second.

I hurried to my locker, spun through the combination, and flung open the door. I crouched on the ground and jammed the page I'd stolen from Nate into my backpack, shoving the whole thing into the bottom of the locker.

"What are you, the Flash?" Richard's voice startled me out of my catastrophizing.

"Huh?" I jerked up, knocking a binder off the top shelf of my locker. It promptly smacked into the side of my face. Ow. That was going to hurt for a while.

Richard bent down to grab my binder. "Are you okay?" he asked, handing it back to me.

"Fine. I'm fine," I said as students started to fill the hall and I scanned for Nate. "Sorry, what were you saying?" I turned my eyes to Richard.

"That you must've raced out of that boring assembly even faster than I did." He grinned.

"Yup. I fled the first second I could." It wasn't a lie. Not exactly. I didn't like lying to him, but it wasn't like I could tell him the truth: *Oh, hey, I'm your Winter Ball date. Also a klutz and a thief.* Yeah. That would go over real well.

"Your cheek is getting all red," Richard said, gently touching the side of my face with his fingertips.

We locked eyes. And stood there, next to my locker, heat filling the space between us, everything else falling away. Seconds slipped by. Maybe it was hours. Maybe it was days. Maybe time ceased to exist in that tiny moment of life's perfection.

Asma called my name, and I shot her a glance over my shoulder. When I turned back to Richard, he pecked me on the cheek. "A kiss to make it better?" he whispered as he pulled his lips away.

I was certain I was about to spontaneously combust. God. I was a giddy teen rom-com cliché, but with more panic and terror churning in the mix. As Richard walked away, fading into the crowd, I saw Nate standing in front of his locker glaring at me, his shoulders squared, his face twisted in anger.

SAFIYA

JANUARY 17, 2022

Fact: I'm a trespasser and a thief.

Lie: Two wrongs don't make a right.

Alternative fact: Two wrongs could make a right.

What I wanted to do: Skip fifth period and head straight to Hardy's office and tell him that Nate was the one who'd plastered copies of my column with that *Swallow your poison* quote on it and texted the quote to me, too.

What I wanted to do: Go to the police and tell them that not only was Nate the hacker and the one who'd spray-painted the swastika on the school, but he was also the one who'd sent the threatening note to my mosque. And me. Show them the page he'd ripped out of the Nietzsche book. Make them believe me.

What I did do: *Nothing.* Well, not exactly nothing. I brooded. A lot. And yelled at myself for being TSTL, *too stupid to live*, my biggest complaint about fictional characters doing ridiculous, illogical things. In a way, I got it now, though. Sometimes it felt like there weren't any smart choices. I couldn't go to Hardy. It was too easy to imagine how quickly the entire conversation could go sideways:

Me: *Nate is the one who did it. All of it.*

Hardy: *And you are basing this on...?*

Me: *The fact that he quoted Nietzsche in class and that he had the ripped page from the Nietzsche book in his locker.*

Hardy: *And how did you happen to come across that page?*

Me: ...

Hardy: *Isn't that page from a book that you also checked out from the library?*

The real version would probably be worse than my imagination. I'd end up implicating Rachel, too, which I obviously would never want to do. And risk getting expelled.

So instead of reporting a possible crime, I was in the journalism room pretending to work on my next column, which had been assigned to me like a punishment. At least the newspaper was up and running, even if we were still under Hardy's petty oppressive rules: no school politics, no columns about racism or white supremacy. "Think positive. Think school spirit," he'd lectured. A swastika got painted on the school, but *We've got spirit, yes, we do!* Make it make sense. My next Be the Change column had to be about the highly "controversial" topic of recycling.

Usman scooted his chair over to my computer. One of the best things about the journalism classroom was the wheelie office chairs. Sometimes when we were here late putting a special issue to bed, we'd have chair races down senior hall. Hardy would've murdered us if he'd seen that. These days Ms. Cary might have helped him.

"What are you doing?" Usman asked, glancing at my blank screen. He was wearing a rainbow-colored kufi today.

Asma and I had given Usman the CliffsNotes version of our visit to the police department, but I hadn't shared every single one of my sinking feelings and suspicions with him. I was starting to feel guilty about pulling everyone into this mess. I was risking my own expulsion, but what if they got suspended for helping me? "Oh, uh, deep in thought about how to write a riveting column about the need for more blue recycling bins in common areas in the school."

"Sounds Pulitzer worthy."

I looked up at Usman's smile. "There might even be a documentary."

"Thank me when you win an Oscar."

I laughed. "Count on it."

I tilted my head toward the computer so Usman inched closer to me. Ms. Cary was across the room, but I didn't want her listening in. For all we knew, she was reporting everything to Hardy. Even if she wasn't, I didn't need to be advertising my recent locker breaking and entering escapade. The page from the Nietzsche book wasn't exactly incriminating evidence except of defacing a book, which *is* terrible but not like hacking, texting threats, Nazi graffiti evil. Nate was in London when the threat to my mosque was sent, but that wasn't real evidence. I needed to put him closer to the scene of one of the crimes; it was a place to start, anyway.

"Did you upload all the photos we got during the fire? Like, of the crowd when the Clef Hangers were singing?" I asked Usman.

"Yeah, I even got pictures from some of the yearbook kids and organized all of them while you were suspended, in case hell froze over and Hardy let us write about it."

"Perfect."

"They're all boring crowd shots."

"Boring crowd shots are exactly what I want." I gestured toward my computer and then scooted out of the way so Usman could open the folder. About thirty thumbnails of the photos popped up.

"What are you looking for?"

"I'm trying to follow Asma's cold case rules. Treat everything like evidence."

Usman knit his eyebrows together, confused for a second, then smiled and nodded. "You're looking for who had an alibi when the swastika was painted."

I pulled up the first photo and magnified each section, zooming in as much as possible. Usman turned to the computer next to me and started looking through different photos. The school was small enough—only about three hundred students—that it wasn't a giant crowd we had to look through. And the park across the street, within very specific boundaries, was the designated meeting spot for the entire school in case of fire.

Usman and I spent the rest of the period poring over every inch of the shots we had. I didn't have the attendance data for the day, but

I knew that both Nate and Joel were at school, since I'd spied them making snide remarks as some ninth-grade girls passed through senior hall. They'd seen me watching and sneered at me.

Neither of them was in the group shots.

I didn't finish my recycling column during journalism class because I was too busy scanning through all the photos from the day of the fire, so I was working after school. There wasn't conclusive evidence, but every new possible clue pointed toward Nate. *Trust your gut* was another of Asma's solving-a-crime rules. I couldn't get the connections out of my head. But I also couldn't run to the police again or to Hardy without something definite.

We weren't allowed to be in the journalism room by ourselves anymore, and even the tiniest of stories had to be approved by Ms. Cary, unless they were things that Hardy had directed us to put in, like sports scores or any of the three stories he'd "asked" us to write about Winter Ball. Basically, Hardy's draconian rules had destroyed the concept of breaking news for the *Spectator*. It's not breaking if it's stale as a two-day-old open bag of chips. Which, I would probably eat anyway.

"And done. My Be the Change column is in your inbox," I said to Ms. Cary as I handed her the pages. "And here's a hard copy."

She looked up at me, her face drawn. "I'm sure it's a winner," she said, her voice kind of far-off.

"It's boring and stale, so I'm sure Hardy will approve."

Ms. Cary gave me a tight smile and opened her mouth to speak but then snapped it shut. She turned to look out the window. Journalism class was on the first floor, and the windows along the western wall looked out onto the park and my favorite bench across the street. It was getting dark already, and the park was mostly empty now save for a few joggers. Lit by the harsh white light of the new LED streetlamps, we watched as a plastic grocery bag caught on the wind and floated like a balloon through the air until it was snagged by the slender end of a tree branch. With the tree swaying in the wind, its limbs curved in a single direction, it looked like the entire tree was grasping for the bag, stretching to keep it captive.

"That would be a great image to go with your recycling piece," Ms. Cary said.

"Where's a photographer when you need one?"

Ms. Cary reached for the DSLR camera that she kept locked in her bottom desk drawer. She adjusted some settings and then held it out toward me. "Today, the photographer is you."

"I'm okay with my camera phone, but I usually—"

"You'll be fine. I switched it to manual and set the aperture and shutter speed. Hold it as still as you can. You're editor in chief; sometimes you need to wear more than one hat." Ms. Cary smiled. She looked relieved to be talking about newspaper-y things that had nothing to do with getting censored or suspended.

I dragged myself out of my chair and took the camera. "I'll be right back," I said.

"I'm going to step out to the faculty lounge while you get the shot. I'll meet you back in the classroom. Don't forget to take your ID with you to get back into the building."

I wrapped my scarf around my neck and pulled my black beanie over my ears. I was only going to be a minute, so I didn't bother to put on my coat; besides, I was wearing my dark-blue wool turtleneck. Growing up in Chicago winters built up your cold stamina.

But when I stepped out, a gust of wind swept through the wide weave of my sweater, and I instantly regretted not taking my jacket. So much for being tough. I shivered and hurried across the street to grab the shot. There was a stark beauty to Chicago winters, emphasis on the stark. It was quiet, and some leaves scuttled by on the street as if they had tiny legs of their own; some were plastered against dirty mounds of snow. In the distance, a jogger bobbed in and out of the spotlights cast by the streetlamps. The caught bag made a rustling sound as it fought against the tree. Plastic grocery bags had pretty much been eliminated in Chicago, so whoever had let this one go was old-school.

Ms. Cary was right. The shots were great. Poetic, in an ironic, we're-destroying-the-earth kind of way. I snapped at least five decent ones. Maybe I'd add another line or two in my column about how many plastic bags you save a year by using a canvas tote. I also grabbed some shots of the school entrance—it looked so moody and gothic, and it wouldn't hurt to have a few images for future footage in case we needed stock photos for something.

Obviously, I couldn't leave the plastic bag in the tree, but it was too high for me to reach, even if I jumped. Figured a school custodian could help me lift the bag off the tree or lend me a broom so I could snag it. I crossed the street, my head down and shoulders hunched, scrolling again through the photos I'd taken.

"I know what you did."

I stopped short of the sidewalk.

It was Nate, standing on the top of the curb, partially in shadow, his shoulders squared and his hands in fists at his sides. Joel was next to him in his trademark fatigues, looking vaguely bored, as always.

Nate wore the black coat and leather gloves that I'd seen in his locker earlier. Goose bumps popped up all over my skin, and I suddenly felt a little dizzy. I had to force my feet to stay firmly planted as I stared up at the two guys cutting off my path. How did Nate know? Had one of them seen me? Was this all a bluff to scare me? A million thoughts tangled in my mind.

"What I did? You mean take photos for my next column? Wow. Excellent sleuthing," I said, holding up my camera, trying to make my voice sound firm.

Joel turned to Nate, rolled his eyes, and faked a snore. "Text me when you're done with...this," he said, tilting his head toward me. Then they exchanged one of those weird silent dude head nods and Joel walked off into the darkness. I wasn't sure if Joel's leaving made things better or worse. All I felt was a chill down my entire spine.

Nate turned back to me, narrowing his eyes. "Where were we? Oh, right. Be. The. Change." He spoke slowly, stretching out the pauses between words.

"Yeah, *okaaaay*," I said. "Ms. Cary is waiting for me to bring back the camera. So if you'll excuse me, I don't have time to stand here while you slowly enunciate the name of each column in the paper."

He stepped off the curb toward me, the scowl on his face much clearer in the beam of the streetlamp that spilled onto the pavement.

I inched backward, away from him and out of the light. "You're very funny for a scholarship rat who's about to get kicked out of school for being a thief."

My stomach clenched and my knees shook. My eyes darted past Nate to the school doors, but no one was on the steps and no one was coming out. The sidewalk was empty. We were alone. "Are you having paranoid delusions? What are you even talking about?" I muttered.

"Shut up!" Nate yelled. I don't think I'd ever seen him so worked up before, so loud, not even that one time in Current Events when he was defending the hacker. The hacker I thought was him. He took another step toward me.

"What do you think I stole?"

"You know what it was." He gritted his teeth.

"Was it your sense of humor? Because that totally wasn't me." I pretended to laugh, but maybe mocking him wasn't the best idea. Words were all I had, though.

He wasn't going to admit what he'd done. And I wasn't going to admit what I'd taken. But we both knew the truth. How did he know I'd been in his locker? A guess? If I was making huge leaps of logic, maybe he was, too? My brain was screaming at me to get inside the school, and I was suddenly very aware that I'd left my phone in the journalism classroom.

I steeled my voice, hoping it wouldn't betray the fear that was pulsing through me as he edged nearer and nearer. "I don't have time for…whatever this is." I gestured at him and tried to harden the muscles in my face so I looked tough, or at least not utterly terrified. A gust of wind blew some stray hairs into my eyes. I moved to brush away the strands. As I readjusted my cap, Nate closed the distance between us.

"You broke into my locker and took something from my pocket, and now you need to give it back." He was so close to me, I could smell stale cigarettes on his breath. I'd never seen him smoke, but I'd also never been this close to him. I moved left to try to sidestep him, but he blocked me.

The wind kicked up, and that woodsy incense smell that had been following me mixed with the smell of Nate's cigarettes. And I felt a whisper in my ear: *Run. He's so close.*

I sucked in my breath. "Back off," I said, but I don't think my voice sounded as strong in real life as it sounded in my head. I took a step to the right, and he mirrored my movement. He shoved his face even closer, 'til it was only inches from mine, my breath fogging up his glasses. For the first time I noticed tiny scratch marks and maybe a bruise near his left temple, partially obscured by his frames.

While my brain whirred and I scrambled to figure my way out of the situation, he started laughing. *Laughing.* Like he'd heard a joke. Like I was the joke. Like my fear was funny.

"Move!" I screamed, and shoved my hands against his chest to get him out of my way. The camera, which I'd strung across my body, bounced and came back hard against my hip. I winced. Nate stumbled back a step or two, clamped down his jaw, and balled his right hand into a fist. I swore he was going to hit me, but instead someone pulled the collar of his coat and jerked him away. Nate's glasses flew off his face as he tripped, stumbling back, then forward, before he fell to the ground.

Richard was standing behind him.

"What the hell do you think you're doing, asshole?" Richard moved to stand between me and Nate, blocking my view for a moment.

"Taking what belongs to me," Nate said as he stood up, brushing himself off. Without his glasses, his face looked boyish except for the dark circles under his eyes. He stepped toward us, but Richard put his hand on Nate's chest, blocking him. "Get your hand off me," Nate spit. I followed his eyes to his glasses, which were lying a couple feet away from me. I picked up the black plastic frames and handed them to Richard. My hands were shaking. My entire body was shaking. Adrenaline pulsed through me so hard I could feel it in my teeth.

Richard took the glasses and motioned for me to head back into the school. I wasn't going to argue. Hurrying up the steps, I turned to see Richard handing Nate his glasses and saying something to him with this look of rage on his face. Their words were lost in the wind. But Nate's head hung low, like a kid getting yelled at by their parent because they got caught in a lie. Richard gestured for Nate to leave, and Nate swatted his arm away but took off, walking down the street and getting into a parked white Mercedes.

Richard jogged up to join me on the steps and put his hand on the small of my back as we walked into the school together. His hand felt warm and steady against me. My brain spun. The moment felt like a flash. It felt like forever. It felt like…WHAT THE HELL JUST HAPPENED. We walked into the warmth of the school—it was the most relieved I'd ever felt walking *into* school. I stepped into Richard's arms, and he wrapped them around me. I released the breath I'd been holding since the moment I looked into Nate's angry eyes.

"Are you okay?" Richard whispered in my ear, and kissed the top of my head.

"Yeah. No. Sort of." We moved apart, holding up our IDs for the disinterested guard, who waved us through.

"What was that all about? Why did he think you had something of his?"

I stopped and looked into Richard's eyes. Under the yellow tinge of the annoying fluorescent school lighting, his pale-blue eyes had almost a liquid-crystal quality to them. Like water about to freeze. A part of me wanted to tell him the truth, but I couldn't. There were too many loose ends, too many other people who could be implicated. And honestly, I didn't want him to think I was ridiculous. I shrugged. "I dunno. Like I told you, he was going off in Current Events one day. Maybe he's mad about my column? Or, like, my existence."

Richard nodded and gave me a soft, apologetic smile as we turned to walk down senior hall. I needed to drop off the camera. My brain was still trying to make sense of what had happened. How had Nate figured it out? Had he been stalking me, waiting outside the whole time, waiting to confront me? I shuddered. If Richard hadn't been there, I'm not sure what I would've done. "I'm so glad you showed up, but how did you know?" I asked.

"Luck. Swim team meeting ran late, and I was leaving school when I heard him yelling." Richard tugged at his blue swim team hoodie that had *Captain* embroidered across the left side of the chest. "I'm helping out next year's cocaptains."

227

I smiled, almost automatically, because the energy for a real smile felt a million miles away. "That's nice of you."

"I try to make myself useful."

"You definitely did tonight. Did I thank you yet? Sorry if I didn't. I honestly don't know what I would've done if you hadn't shown up."

Richard pulled me into a tight hug. I took a couple deep breaths. It felt good to breathe in the clean-laundry smell of his hoodie. His arms felt safe, and my tightened muscles finally started to unwind.

"Nate is such a loser. I'm pretty sure he's all bark and no bite," Richard said.

"His bark was scary."

"Don't worry. He won't bother you again," he said as we pulled out of the hug and stepped toward my classroom. "I'll make sure of that."

The door to journalism was shut, but I could see Ms. Cary inside, gathering up her things. I turned the knob to head in but paused. "Do you think I should say something? Like, to Ms. Cary?"

Richard scratched his head. "Are you going to tell her Nate accused you of stealing something? Oh…wait. Did he touch you? If he did, I swear I'll—"

"No. No. But I shoved him when he got in my space." I sighed.

Richard rubbed his forehead. "Be careful. You wouldn't want him to turn it around on you. I'll tell Hardy what I witnessed, but he keeps blaming you for everything, and I'm worried he'd take it out on you again."

I gulped. It *was* self-defense. But it was also Nate's word against mine. I knew whose side Hardy would take, which one of us would get the benefit of the doubt and which one of us already had two strikes against them and was the scholarship kid. Dammit. It felt so scary in the moment. Like I wasn't in control. Like anything could have happened if Richard hadn't shown up. Nate was in my face and in my space. He was totally in the wrong. But I'd broken school rules, too, more than once. None of this was fair. I wanted to scream and grind my heels into the floor. "No, I guess you're probably right. We weren't even technically on school property."

"I'm sorry. It sucks. Forget about that loser. Can I walk you home? He's going to steer clear of you, but—"

"Okay." I grinned. My parents wanted me to call them when I was done so they could come get me, even though we lived so close. I could tell they were trying to keep their fears sort of hidden, but I knew they were scared. But they knew Richard, and his company would be nice. "I need to upload the pics and grab my stuff. You're welcome to hang in the journalism room."

"I forgot something in my locker. I'll meet you back here in a few."

He stepped away, and I walked in to show Ms. Cary the photos I'd taken. She seemed pleased. I made a comment about how it was strange that plastic bags floating in the air always felt so beautiful when they were basically litter, and it made Ms. Cary laugh. I let my parents know I was walking home with a friend and didn't need a ride. I also dashed off a quick group text to Asma and Usman, telling them I wanted to talk, but I didn't give them all the details of what had gone down with Nate. How could I put all that in a text? My shoulders, my entire body, suddenly felt stiff, achy, like I'd been hit by a wall of tired.

When I glanced up, I saw that Richard had returned and was concentrating on his phone, dashing off a text. I hadn't thought about how that whole scene outside with Nate could've been weird for him, too. When he glanced up and saw me, his brow relaxed and a huge smile swept across his face.

I walked out of the classroom and straight into Richard's arms. We ambled toward my home, him holding me close, holding me up. It felt good. Solid. He smelled like the outdoors, like woods and dry leaves on a crisp day, but with a stale whiff of Nate's cigarette smoke on him. I tried to focus on the comfort of being next to Richard, but my mind was back in front of the school, the scene on repeat in my head. Nate's twisted, angry face. His clenched fists. Richard stepping in. Nate stumbling. My heart pounding, one question screaming in my brain: How did Nate know I took the page?

JAWAD

I'm holding on to the woodsy, sweet smell of the incense Mama used to burn. Of the scent of attar on her clothes. I don't want my last memory to be the smell of car air freshener layered over cigarette smoke. I figured out I could carry the incense smell with me, almost like an object, a memento I could fit in my hand.

In science once, our teacher told us that smell is memory. That some people considered it our most important sense. I'm trying to hold on to it. I want to hold on to it. I close my eyes and try to imagine the smoke in curlicues wafting up from the incense and remember how warm and safe my home always felt. But it feels like everything is fading. Vanishing. Like all the lines around me are beginning to blur.

SAFIYA

JANUARY 18, 2022

Fact: Every memory is a code, layered into our brains.

Truth: Memory is a ghost in the machine.

Truth: Sometimes the body remembers what the mind cannot.

I woke with a start in the middle of the night. There was a noise. Rustling. A whisper. A creak in the wood floor. A faint voice: *Help me, find me, Safiya.* When I sat up, everything was quiet. Everything was still. There was no one else in the room. But a small, quiet part of me knew I wasn't alone, even when the rest of me was screaming *liar* at the part of me that knew the truth.

Listen. Listen.

It's soft. A twist of the air that entered my ear. Waves of light and sound, but bent. My own inner voice, the feeling in my gut, mingling with the other voice I was hearing.

My voice: *You know what it was. Scholarship rat. Swallow your poison. God is dead.* The scratched face. The bruised temple.

A whiff of incense swirled through my bedroom.

The other voice became louder, and so clear: *Jackson Park. Please. Help me. It's cold. I'm so alone. I don't want to be alone.*

I closed my eyes. Listened to the voices puncturing the silence. I didn't know what to make of it all. What I did know: There was a singular voice that kept telling me to go to Jackson Park. An echo. *Help me. Find me. Be careful.* And I needed to listen. I had to go to Jackson Park.

State's Exhibit 9

Fowl Play, Episode 77, transcript
Nate Chase's YouTube channel

[*Shot of birds flying over a lagoon.*]

[*Nate enters scene wearing jeans, dark-brown leather hiking boots, dark-navy fleece, green glasses, binoculars strung around neck.*]

"Hey, Fowl Friends, hope you liked my reports from across the pond! England's got some gorgeous birds. The kinds with feathers and also the kind with legs! Ha! I landed last night and headed out to Jackson Park super early—thanks, jet lag—because I saw some chatter about a bald eagle sighting here."

[*Begins walking through wooded area, down narrow path.*]

"Now, I know you're thinking *Bald eagles in Chicago?* And, yes, it's extremely rare, but we usually get one confirmed sighting in Chicago every winter. Sometimes two if we're lucky. The ponds and lagoons in Jackson Park are stocked with bluegills and black bass, which are eagle favorites. Sushi on the hoof! Yum!" [*Laughs to self.*]

[*Sounds of birds in background. Nate looks up.*]

"Sounds like winter finches. But we're not here for them today."

[*Turns phone camera so it's no longer on selfie mode, and films group of birders entering wooded area.*]

"Looks like we have some company, but we're going to steer clear of groups. Too noisy. Instead, I'm going to take you to a part of Jackson Park no one ever goes to. I've never seen a single person there. Shhh. It's my *secret*. A place only I know. I'm turning off my camera now because I don't want to share how to get there. I don't want my secret spot overrun. Sorry." [*Turns camera off.*]

[*Camera comes back on. Nate's face fills screen. Speaking in almost a whisper.*]

"Okay, gang. Here we are." [*Pans camera around to reveal pond surrounded by trees.*]

"And do you see that spot over there?" [*Turns camera to the left; finger appears in shot, pointing to embankment near crumbling bridge.*]

"Not sure if you can see it clearly, but that's an old stone culvert there that's falling apart, by that embankment. They say that spot is haunted. Some say there was a Mothman sighting around here years ago. I don't believe in ghosts. But the stories sure do keep the people away. Still, wouldn't come here at night. You never know what you're going to come across on the South Side of Chicago!" [*Laughs.*]

[*Turns camera back on himself.*]

"No one comes here because there is absolutely nothing to see. Or they're too scared of the things they think might appear. But I'm not afraid of ghosts. As my dad always says, fortune favors the brave."

SAFIYA

JANUARY 18, 2022

Fact: According to the FBI, 421,394 "juveniles" were reported missing in the United States in 2019.

Fact: The vast majority of kids are found. Only 1 percent are marked as missing under circumstances that suggest "disappearance may not have been voluntary."

Fact: That's still 4,828 kids who go missing under mysterious circumstances.

I woke up painfully early. Bleary eyed and exhausted from bad sleep, I tiptoed to the bathroom so I wouldn't wake my parents. They usually woke a bit after dawn for their morning prayer, but with the late sunrise in the winter, they slept in a little. I checked my phone. I had two missed texts. One from Asma: Sorry I didn't call! Wedding prep madness! Catch up later?

And from Richard: Sleep tight 🖤

Half of me was still screaming that I should crawl back in bed, stay home, not go to Jackson Park alone. I didn't have a choice, though. People would call me crazy if I ever said it out loud, but I swear the voice was drawing me to the park. Deep down, I knew it was Jawad's voice. Maybe I'd always known. Maybe that's what I was afraid of. The rational part of me wanted to say there was no such thing as ghosts. My heart wanted to have hope. But it had been thirteen days since Jawad was reported missing, and hope was dwindling. The police seemed to buy the excuse that he'd run away, which still meant they should've been looking for him, but it sure didn't seem like a missing Muslim kid was a priority.

Using a fake name, Usman had called the Chicago PD press office from a school landline and asked if the police had been able to track the location of Jawad's phone since his parents got that text message they were certain wasn't from him. The press office wouldn't give any specific details, since it was an active case. And when Usman asked a hypothetical about tracking where the phone was when a text was sent, the press people responded that the location could be detected, but if the phone was then turned off, it would be much more complicated to find where it was now, *hypothetically*.

I left a note for my parents saying I'd gone on a run. It was a weak but somewhat plausible excuse. I only ran once in a while, mostly when it was warmer, but I couldn't exactly tell them I was going to Jackson Park because of a voice, a threat, and a compulsion to look for clues about a missing boy. I felt sick thinking about all the things that could have happened...could be happening to Jawad. Maybe I'd find something hopeful in Jackson Park. A real clue to give the police. Can you make something true by wishing hard enough? I was too old to believe that now, but lately I'd started to believe in a lot of things that maybe I hadn't before. Like the voice of a ghost calling out to me.

I padded down the stairs, holding my boots in my hand, and laced them up on the last step before I walked out, making sure the door didn't slam.

But I only got as far as our storefront.

Red paint stained the windows my parents always worked hard to keep clean:

GO HOME FUCKING TERRORISTS 14/88

I went cold. My stomach lurched, and bile rose to my throat. I ran to the curb and dry-heaved into the gutter, my entire body convulsing.

PART VI

GAZING INTO
THE ABYSS

January 18, 2022

Police are investigating graffiti in a South Side neighborhood as a hate crime.

Between the hours of midnight and 5:00 a.m., a vandal struck the Mirza Emporium, a locally owned business. Painted in red letters on the store's window were the words "Go Home F*cking Terrorists 14/88." The 14/88 numbers are believed to be a nod to white supremacy, 14 being a reference to the fourteen words of a slogan used by a white terrorist organization and the 88 symbolizing "heil Hitler," *H* being the eighth letter of the alphabet.

"Since 2016, there has been a disturbing uptick in hate crimes in America, in general. In Illinois alone, we've seen an alarming increase in anti-Semitism and anti-immigrant and anti-Muslim hate crimes," said Noor Jackson, director of the city's Hate Crime Task Force. "In Chicago, diversity is our strength. We will not tolerate intolerance."

Police arrived at the scene early this morning and began canvassing the neighborhood for eyewitnesses. No arrests have been made. If you have information about this incident, the Chicago police ask that you call the tip line: 312-555-5555.

SAFIYA

JANUARY 18, 2022

Truth: "Go Home" is a xenophobic favorite.
Truth: Racists are really bad at geography.

The scene spun around me. Flashing police lights. My mom bringing me an extra shawl to drape around my shoulders. The cameras. The pedestrians stopping to gape. The neighbors coming by to offer kind words and to help clean up. All as the sun rose on a brisk, bright January morning. My mind felt jittery, images popping in and out, some bumping into other ones, like a muddled flashback in a movie, where the character is trying to remember something, reach for something they can't grasp. Except this wasn't a movie. It was real life.

And I knew who did it.

I didn't have proof. But I knew in my bones it was Nate.

A fireball whirled in my chest. My stomach clenched. How deep did Nate's anger run? Hacking the newspaper, vandalizing the school and my parents' store, threatening me. How far had he escalated?

Was he capable of assault? Kidnapping? With each new question, I felt my breaths grow shakier.

"Beta, are you okay?" my mom asked. "Why don't you go inside and sit down." She put her arm around me and led me to the door. "I made some tea when the police went in to look at the video from the security camera. Drink some. It will warm you up." My mother smiled at me. I'm not sure how she and my dad were holding it together. Those hateful words painted on the store were glaring at me and screaming in my ears. I couldn't think straight.

"Mom," I said right before stepping into the store, "how can you be so calm? Aren't you upset?"

"Of course I am, beta. I'm furious. It's a horrifying violation, and I hope they find who did this. What a sad, cowardly person to have so much hate in their heart and then to spew it under the cover of darkness."

"But you and Dad both seem so...unbothered."

My mom cupped my chin in her hand. "This isn't the first Islamophobe who has crossed our path. We might never be able to stop them all, but one thing I do know is that racists *want* to take our power and sap our energy. They want us to live in constant fear; we are not about to let them. Our existence is not controversial, and this is our home. Full stop. We don't have to prove anything to anyone." My mom kissed my cheek. I was too choked up to respond, so I nodded and headed inside, my heart squeezed like it was held in a vise.

There were still a few cops reviewing the security footage in the back room, so I tiptoed in to pour myself a cup of tea. They were at the other end, their backs to me, and their loud voices and the crackle coming from their radios were likely covering up the sounds of my shoes shuffling against the floor.

"Perp made a damn good effort to hide his face," one of the police said.

"Wore a mask, got that hoodie pulled up. Gloves on. Can't even tell what race he is," the other cop replied.

I dropped the spoon I was about to use to stir milk into my tea; the spoon clattered against the counter before hitting the floor. Both cops swiftly turned their heads. The shorter one put his hand to his holster. That made me jump back, sent my heart racing. Seeing me, he lifted his hands up in, like, a calming gesture. Like I was the one who needed to take it down a notch. But, hello, I wasn't the one whose first instinct was to reach for a gun.

"Didn't mean to scare you, miss," he said. "But best not to sneak up on armed officers."

"I didn't realize I was sneaking," I whispered, then cleared my throat. "I...I only came in here to get some tea. I didn't mean to—"

"No worries. I'm Officer Hill, and this is Officer Anthony," he said, pointing to the cop who was seated in front of the TV my parents kept in back to monitor the store. Officer Hill was standing next to the chair, and now both had turned to face me.

"So you're the one who found the graffiti," Officer Anthony said. "I know how scary that can be."

He and Officer Hill were both white, so I supposed they weren't speaking about personal experiences with racist graffiti. I nodded.

"Guess you're an early riser, huh?" he added.

"Going for a run," I said.

"You do that often?" he asked.

I shrugged. "Once in a while. I guess."

Officer Anthony's questions seemed basic, and he had this light conversational tone, so why did it feel so tense?

"You have any idea who might want to do this to your parents' store? Anyone who has a grudge against them?" Officer Hill took a few steps toward me.

I tilted my head up to look at him. "A grudge? Against my parents? Can't imagine any customer would be disgruntled over their tea selection."

Officer Anthony chuckled. "Oh, you'd be surprised."

I picked up my mug and wrapped my fingers around it to warm them. Should I tell them my theory? About Nate? My last experience with the police hadn't exactly filled me with confidence or trust. But everything felt like it was getting out of hand, and this was maybe my best chance to get them to pay attention. "Well, I... uh...it's a guess and..."

Officer Hill's wrinkly forehead softened a bit, and he took another step toward me. "It's okay. You know, if you see something, you should say something. You never know how it might help."

I wanted to laugh out loud. Asma and I had already tried, but we'd been blown off when we went to the precinct. The desk sergeant hadn't even written anything down when we were there. So much for "See something, say something." I bit back my words because a sarcastic remark could get me in trouble. If there was any chance that Nate was dangerous, then I needed the police to be on our side. I needed them to make sure my friends would be safe. I didn't know who else to ask for help. It's not like there were a lot of alternatives.

"Well," I started again, "we've had some incidences at our school."

"Right, right, there was the smoke bomb and the vandalism," Officer Anthony said. He scooted forward in the wheeled office chair.

"There was also a newspaper hack. And…and a column I wrote got copied and plastered all over the school with a Nietzsche quote scribbled on it that said *Swallow your poison*. The hack also had a Nietzsche reference."

"Who?" Officer Hill asked.

"Nietzsche. He's a German philosopher who was loved by Nazis, and white nationalists stan him now, too."

Officer Anthony adjusted his collar. "You think it's all connected…how?"

I took a sip of my tea with shaky hands. They both were giving me slightly different variations of the skeptical raised-eyebrow look, like they'd seen one too many obsessive true crime fans trying to crack cold cases. I put my mug down on the counter because I was afraid it would slip from my clammy palms. *Do it, Safiya. Say the words.* "I think I know who did it, because he confronted me yesterday after school. And he's also a big fan of Nietzsche, like quoting him in class and stuff."

"Confronted?" Officer Anthony stood up from his chair.

"Were you hurt? Did you call 911?" Officer Hill furrowed his brow while he rushed out his questions.

"No. It was more like a verbal confrontation. It's this guy, Nate, he cornered me about some stuff at school. He was yelling."

"What was he yelling at you about?"

My stomach fell. I couldn't tell them I'd stolen the combination and broken into Nate's locker, because then I would be the one who'd committed a crime, even though he'd done worse. And I couldn't tell them I was the one who shoved Nate, even though he was the one in my face, because they could twist it into some kind of assault. With me being the assaulter. I didn't trust that they'd believe me. "He was going on about me supposedly taking something that belonged to him. I dunno. He wasn't making much sense."

"And did you?" Officer Anthony arched an eyebrow. "Take something of his."

"No. I didn't take anything that belonged to him." Technically, the book and the page he ripped out belonged to the school library, so I wasn't exactly lying. "He seemed...irrational." I shrugged.

"And how did you leave it?" Officer Hill asked.

"Oh, my friend Richard stepped in, and then, uh, Nate backed off. That's all. I didn't think it was that big a deal, so I didn't—"

"You didn't tell your parents?"

"Nope," I whispered, shaking my head.

Officer Hill continued. "Are you involved with this kid Richard romantically? Could Nate have been jealous? Did you not tell your parents because you're not allowed to talk to boys? Or maybe they don't want you hanging with boys who aren't your culture?"

"I'm sorry?"

"Like, because they want you to have an arranged marriage, like, back home? Maybe you're promised to someone?"

My jaw dropped. I could not believe what I was hearing. This country was our home. "No. No. That's not it at all." My voice got louder. How did this get to arranged marriage when the actual conversation was supposed to be about racist graffiti?

My mind slipped back to the time when my US history teacher basically made me and Usman explain our feelings about 9/11 in front of the whole class. We weren't alive when it happened! And he asked us stupid questions about whether we condemned the act. *Duh.* But he never ever asked white kids if they condemned slavery, or the Trail of Tears, or the assault on the Capitol, or took responsibility for the culinary crime that is chocolate hummus. I took a deep breath and tried hard not to get a tone. Getting a tone with the police was the most dangerous thing I could do.

"My parents didn't have an arranged marriage. Besides, that's not even—" *Deep breaths, Safiya.* "All I'm saying is that Nate seemed mad and then our store got vandalized and there's been a lot of weird stuff happening at school and…Oh! There was also a Nietzsche quote on the threatening letter our mosque got. You know, the one mailed from London right around Christmas? Well, Nate was in London over winter break. He's the common denominator."

"What's this kid's last name again?" Officer Hill asked, completely glossing over his earlier stereotyping and assumptions.

"Nate Chase."

"Nate Chase? You don't mean the alderman's kid?"

"Yeah," I said. My heart sank because I knew what was about to happen. "Him."

The officers exchanged looks. Officer Anthony took a breath and began, "Listen, that kid was probably born with a silver foot stuck in his mouth. Hundred-percent. But you know how boys are….Sometimes when they like you, they're mean to you."

My blood boiled. I was getting the *Boys will be boys* BS? The *If a boy hits you, he probably likes you* excuse. The *If he calls you a bitch, maybe it's because you rejected him* line. Because it's always, always the girl's fault, right? What. The. Hell.

Officer Hill continued for his partner. "Look, we're not saying he wasn't outta line. But kids like *that*.…This kind of vandalism isn't a rich-kid crime. They don't like to get their hands dirty with this kind of thing. But, of course, we'll, uh, check into it." Officer Hill turned to Officer Anthony, who nodded as if he were taking me seriously.

I felt like I'd been sucker punched. I was glad I'd put down my mug, because I wanted to smash it on the ground, and they'd probably arrest me for assaulting an officer or something. So I did the smartest thing I could do. I lied. I nodded. Picked up my tea and took a sip. I turned on a huge smile. "Yeah. I get it. Boys will boys, I guess."

Officer Anthony smiled. "Exactly," he said. "Better to move on."

"Now if you see anything suspicious, you let us know, okay? We want to do whatever we can to find the person who vandalized your parents' store." Officer Hill reached into his pocket and then handed me his business card.

"Sure thing, Officer. Will do." I turned and walked out of the back room, every cell in my body raging like a bonfire.

SAFIYA

JANUARY 18, 2022

Lie: To make someone go away, ignore them.
Truth: The more you ignore me, the closer I'll get.

I walked into school late. I'd texted Asma and Usman updates, but it was second period already, and if a teacher even glimpsed a student's phone during class, they'd confiscate it and hand it over to Hardy. My head was still spinning, my heart still broken at the sight of my parents outside in the cold with buckets and rags cleaning up those racist words on the window. A few neighbors had offered to help. I wanted to stay and help, too, but my dad had nudged me to go to school, as if I could concentrate on anything. *It's okay, go be with your friends*, he'd said.

Everyone at school was going to know—the news cameras had shown up. Not sure who'd tipped them off. I'd already gotten a flurry of texts from friends. Richard had checked in, too. I was going to be the center of attention *again*. This year felt like it was already six months long, when we were only two and a half weeks into January. There were a million things I didn't want to face or deal with, but I had to. Jackson Park was looming above them all.

My phone buzzed and I reached into my back pocket to grab it—a photo of my parents and some friends smiling in front of the squeaky-clean store window. Tears stung at the corners of my eyes as I turned to head to my locker.

"Uh, hello? Maybe pay attention to where you're walking." I looked up to see Dakota, tall, thin, two tight blond French braids draped over her shoulders, staring at me, a hand on the hip of her short gray skirt. She wore navy thigh-high stockings trimmed with gray velvet bows, and a blue scarf was tied around her neck.

"Excuse me? The entire hallway's clear. What's your problem, umm, uh…"

"Dakota. Don't act like you don't know who I am."

"And why would I?" Of course I knew her. Maybe I was being petty, but Dakota had been giving me side-eye ever since she saw Richard talking to me when they were selling tickets for Winter Ball.

Her face scrunched up like she'd shoved a lemon into her mouth. "I went to homecoming with Richard. And Sadie Hawkins."

"Well, aren't you special?" I saw where this was going, but it was literally the last thing I wanted to deal with. "I gotta get to class." I stepped around her.

"Are you going to Winter Ball with him?"

I sighed and glanced at her over my shoulder. We both knew she knew the answer. "Yeah. So?"

"So, I guess he's slumming it. Can you even afford a dress? Aren't you one of the scholarship kids?"

I dropped my backpack and turned to face her. She took a tiny step back, like she was worried I was going to hit her. "As opposed to having my daddy get me in with a big, um…what's that fancy word for bribery? Oh, right, a *donation* to the school."

"Shut up. I don't get what Richard sees in you. It won't last long." She flipped the end of her scarf over her shoulder, and my eyes trailed the movement. "Do you like my scarf?" she asked. "It was a gift. From Richard. He brought it back from London."

"L-l-ondon?" I stammered.

"Yeah, he went there over winter break. Oh, did you not know? I wonder what else he's not telling you," she scoffed, and turned on her heel and walked away.

Richard had been in London over winter break. What?

I scratched my head, confused. Nothing made sense. How come Richard hadn't told me he'd been in London? We'd talked about winter break—I was sure of it. He'd said the most exciting thing he did was watch the movies I'd rec'd. Was he so blasé that London didn't qualify as interesting? Had he known that Nate was there, too?

I clutched my stomach. Richard and Nate weren't friends. I'd never seen them speak to each other, not even when they passed in the hall. Except for last night, when Nate was in my face. And the way Richard had shoved him away from me…I could tell how furious he was at Nate. No. No way. This had to be a coincidence. It wasn't like London was a remote part of the world. Half our class was always off to Paris or London or Madrid every school break.

It wasn't even lunchtime, but this whole day had already been too much. I couldn't deal with school or the idea of seeing Hardy or Nate.

251

I walked to the nurse's and told her I felt sick. She stepped into her office to call my mom, and I heard her suggesting that I talk to the counselor, saying that it was natural that I could have a delayed stress reaction to seeing the violent words on our window. That was the word she used: "violent." Words could be weapons—any writer, any journalist, knew that. But I hadn't fully considered that word, "violent," before. But of course she was right. The whole point of a weapon is to cut you and make you bleed. Words are the weapons we carry with us all the time.

JAWAD

The devil fooled us.

His greatest trick was making it seem like he was a demon, a monster. But demons are everyday people. The most terrifying monsters are the ones you know. The ones who smile. The ones who say *please* and *thank you*. The ones who hold the door open for elders. The ones who always look clean, who dress nice, who smell like money. Sometimes they even help you when others are calling you names. Then you trust them. Then you owe them one.

They're invisible in a way, too. They blend in. Like ghosts. I think that's what my English teachers would call irony.

Now, from where I am, I see who they are, the ones who wear faces like Halloween masks. I see their calculated kindness. I hear their hollow laughs when their victims turn in shock to see who they really are, unmasked. It's an extra cruelty before the end. The cruelty is the point.

SAFIYA

JANUARY 18, 2022

Fact: It's important to know your enemies.

Truth: You need to know your friends, too.

When I got back from school, my mom suggested I take a nap. Ha. Right. I was too jittery to sleep or even lie down. My backpack was tossed in the corner of my room, my homework calling to me, but that wasn't the call I needed to answer. Instead, I paced across the floor of my bedroom, a thousand times because it's small. Images and conversations jumped around in my brain until they were all jammed and mixed up together. I imagined Asma telling me to write everything down on note cards, tape them to my wall, and connect them all with red string in true crime fashion. But I knew where all those red threads were going to lead: Nate.

I flopped onto my bed and closed my eyes to think.

My phone buzzed. *Crap.* I'd fallen asleep. My mom had willed my nap into the universe. I lunged for my phone, which I'd left on my night-stand next to my journal. It was already afternoon.

> **Asma:** Are you okay? I stg I'm going to kick Nate's ass. I can't believe he tried to attack you. Now this?? WTF

Before I fell asleep, I'd texted Asma and Usman again, this time with photos of the window and my suspicion that Nate was the vandal.

> **Usman:** I heard Nate yelling at someone

> **Asma:** What? Nate wasn't in school today. Who was he with?

> **Usman:** 👤 It was by the loading dock. I was at the Botany Pond with science class, only glimpsed Nate. But heard angry voices

> **Me:** What were they saying?

> **Usman:** Nate said something like "You're having second thoughts now cuz of her? She doesn't scare me."

I bolted up in bed. My stomach somersaulted.

> **Me:** WTF Are they're talking about me?

> **Asma:** Who's they?

> **Me:** Joel. 100% He was with Nate for a second last night but took off

I almost typed out Richard's name as a suggestion, too. Because of the scarf. Because of him being in London at the same time as

Nate. But I didn't. I couldn't wrap my head around even the remote possibility of that. No. NO. WAY. It wasn't him. I mean, Joel had actually been there. He had to have known what Nate was going to do to me, but he was too much of a coward to stop him.

Usman: WTF WTF WTF Richard should've kicked Nate's ass

Asma: And find Joel and kick his ass too for fun

Me: I'll make that suggestion

Usman: Gotta run. Be careful okay?

Asma: I'll call after my ortho appt 💚💜

Me: 💜 💜

I got out of bed and rubbed my eyes. It was chilly in the room, so I grabbed a hoodie and pulled it over my head. My phone buzzed again. This time it was Richard. My hands got clammy and my pulse quickened, but the reasons weren't clear.

Richard: Hey you okay? I heard you got in a fight with Dakota. Is that why you left school?

Me: Wasn't a fight, needed a mental health day

Richard: Feel better 💜 Ignore Dakota. She's A LOT

Me: She *really* wanted to rub my face in the scarf you got her from London

Richard: WTF She can be a real bitch sometimes

I recoiled seeing *that* word. Maybe Dakota was stuck up and jealous. But calling her that wasn't okay. And I couldn't believe he'd said that.

Me: Dude not cool

Richard: Sorry. She's been stalking me since break 😳

Me: You didn't tell me you went to London

Richard: I did. At the bench remember? I've been so many times NBD

I paused. My hands got all clammy. I forced myself to take a few breaths. I was sure he hadn't mentioned London to me before. Pretty sure, anyway?

Me: Did you know Nate was in London then too?

Richard:...

Richard: Not like we're friends. Especially not after the shit he pulled with you

Me: I think he spray-painted the store

Richard: No way. I friggin warned him to leave you alone! Wanna hang after school?

Me: Can't. My mom banished me to my room

Richard: Text me if you can sneak out. I'm an excellent distraction 😂 😘

My mind whirred. Richard had helped me last night. I didn't know what I would've done if he hadn't shown up. So why was I so annoyed at him right now? He was trying to protect me, but it felt, I dunno, dismissive? I stared at that kissy emoji on my screen and tightened my grip on my phone. Everything felt upside down.

I couldn't see straight. Think straight. And that voice—what the raised hairs on my arms were telling me was Jawad's voice…It was whispering everywhere, in my dreams, in the swirls of incense-scented air around me. I didn't know what to think. I was trying to pretend that so many things weren't there, weren't real, ignoring what my gut was telling me, ignoring what I was seeing and hearing. Suddenly it felt like my entire world was a tangle of lies, and I had to stop lying to myself and find the truth. And everything was telling me I'd find the truth in Jackson Park.

SAFIYA

JANUARY 18, 2022

Truth: Sometimes the thing that scares you most is the only thing you can do.

I remembered Asma's cold case rules, so I texted her that I was walking to Jackson Park to clear my head. I didn't tell her why, because she'd probably try to talk me out of it. Besides, I was having a hard time fully understanding the reasons myself. I tucked my phone into my pocket and walked straight to the park, heading for the "secret" birding spot Nate went to in one of his YouTube episodes. The place he said was haunted.

My footsteps started confident, thundering against the pavement, but by the time I'd reached the edge of the prairie grass, they barely made a sound. Like I was only a shadow. I shivered even though it was a little above freezing, pretty warm, for a January in Chicago, anyway. The late-afternoon sun was getting low, and soon it would be dark and the temperature would drop.

I ground the toe of my boot into the damp gravel path. Testing if it was solid ground. Testing if it could hold me up, because as I was standing there, on the edge of the park, the weight of the last few days hit me square in the chest and took my breath away.

I hesitated. Waiting for a whisper on the wind. Scared of what I might find. Scared I might find nothing. Scared, period. Everything paused. The sounds. The breeze rustling dead leaves. Bare branches bent, reaching over to claw at me.

Headlights of a stray car on the street behind me rounded a curve and briefly lit up the area. The sound of the car's engine startled a few birds who cawed and lifted from the trees, the swoosh of their wings flapping as the winter darkness crept into the afternoon. I watched until they were dots in the sky.

I took a half step forward, gravel shifting and crunching under my foot.

JAWAD

I can hear you.

I'm here.

Help me. Please. Hurry. You're so close.

Find me before the dark.

The dark is the scariest part.

It's when all the ghosts come out. And the monsters come back to visit you.

SAFIYA

JANUARY 18, 2022

Lie: That which does not kill you makes you stronger.

Truth: Strong is overrated.

Truth: Sometimes the school of hard knocks knocks you down and makes it impossible to get up.

The breeze picked up and stung my cheeks. The gray sky hung so low you could almost touch it. And the farther I walked into the park, the denser the trees, the more the chill clung to my skin and settled into my body.

Wet leaves stuck to the gravel path; some lay scattered, damp and lifeless, across the footbridge that connected the main part of the park to Wooded Isle, the small island set off by lagoons. I put my head down and kept going, beyond the Garden of the Phoenix, beyond the birding trails that Nate highlighted in his videos. Beyond all that was the quiet place. The part of the park that was still not redeveloped. The dried stalks of wildflowers that bloomed purple and yellow in the spring, the limp prairie grass, the gnarled roots of fallen trees—it was like all their colors had been drained.

The only signs of life were the pops of bright-green moss that thrived in dark, damp places and clung to rotting trees.

I pulled my scarf over my mouth and nose so that it warmed the air I breathed. I had no idea what I was doing. Or thinking. But my body knew where to go. This was the place where the ghosts were, according to local urban legends. In the past few years, there'd been Mothman sightings all over town, and the mostly abandoned area beyond the Garden of the Phoenix was one of those spots. I shoved those images out of my mind. My heart already had enough reasons to pound in my chest, and I didn't need rumors of a red-eyed har-binger of death to add to it. But it didn't matter, because I couldn't push the heaviness out of the air.

The sickly sweet stink of decaying leaves swirled in the air around me, making my nose twitch. And then a hint of that incense underneath all that rot. My pace slowed. I'd searched on Google Earth to find the area that Nate had called his "secret" in one of his *Fowl Play* episodes, and made my way there through the park. It was a place, Nate had said, where no one went but him. A short walk in front of me was the culvert he'd pointed to, almost completely hid-den by the grasses of the embankment, slightly beyond the crum-bling old bridge that went over a nearly dry stream. I hopped over, but my boot slipped on the muddy bank and I fell into a pile of leaves and twigs. I pushed myself up, then wiped away the dirt and bits of leaves that stuck to my knees, my jeans dampened with cold. I straightened up and sighed. Took a look around. What the hell was I doing? I shook my head, upset at my runaway imagination, at my belief that I would find answers here.

That's when I saw the shoe.

A charcoal-gray sneaker ringed with salt stains, sticking out of the culvert, toe pointed down in the semi-frozen earth. Wet leaves piled up against it.

My breath froze in my chest.

Every part of my brain screamed *STOP!* But I still took a step forward. Then another. And another. My pulse throbbed in my ears until that was all I could hear. The entire world slowed around me. I shined a light from my phone into the metal culvert.

That's when I saw the body.

JAWAD

I'm scared, too. I didn't want to scare her. I'm sorry she was scared.

You're here, I whisper to her.

She seems to hear me because she moves a step closer, her hand over her mouth.

She doesn't want to look. But she does. She has to.

She has courage.

This is the second kindness she's shown me. I carried the first one with me, like a secret, all the time. Like a souvenir. Like a promise. We were both little. I think it's a moment maybe only I remember.

Will I be warm now? Surrounded by that soft light growing in the distance? Can my parents say the funeral prayers now? Will there be peace?

Can I rest?

SAFIYA

JANUARY 18, 2022

Truth: The simplest explanation is usually the right one.

Truth: Sometimes the truth is a lot more complicated than the facts lead you to believe.

I don't know how long I waited. Just me and him. I stood there so he wouldn't be alone anymore. There was no way for me to identify him. I didn't touch the body; I couldn't see his face. But every part of me knew it was Jawad.

I should've called the police right away. The second I saw that shoe. But I needed a minute. A moment of quiet. To tell Jawad that I'd heard him. That he wasn't alone, not anymore. To say a prayer for him: *We belong to God and to him we shall return.*

I finally dialed 911, my voice barely a scratch, hardly believing any of this was real.

Jawad had been alone that whole time. Missing. Gone. It wasn't fair. How did a person get so lost? Forgotten by everyone but their parents? How could one human being do that to another?

I'm so sorry, Jawad. You deserved so much more than this. You deserved a whole life.

I paced but didn't get too close to the culvert—still, probably closer than I should have. I wasn't thinking. Not really. Not about the crime scene or evidence. Or what I was going to do or what I was going to tell my parents. All I kept imagining, as the light faded and as the sirens screamed out in the distance, drawing closer, was that he must've been so cold. He didn't even have a coat on. Did the killer take his coat? And Jawad wasn't wearing the right shoes for winter. Why didn't he have the right shoes? He looked so small there in that pipe, by himself. So alone.

I turned away from his body, sadness and anger twisting my insides. I kicked through small piles of soggy clumped leaves. Brown and wet and rotten. My toe connected with something, and a pair of glasses arced through the air.

A pair of green plastic glasses.

My mind raced back to the night when Nate confronted me outside the school. When Richard pushed him and he stumbled and his glasses fell off into a pool of light. They weren't the new green glasses he'd been parading around on his YouTube channel. They were his old black ones. Where were his green glasses?

I thought my heart had frozen in my chest, but it jumped back to life with a jolt. Bile rose to my throat. I doubled over. When I lifted back up, I felt dizzy, unable to stand straight. I stumbled a couple steps to where the glasses had landed. I had an impulse to reach down and pocket them. The police had already made it clear they wanted to protect Nate. They'd ignored Jawad's parents. They'd ignored everything I'd told them. What if they ignored the glasses, too? I couldn't let them do that. Jawad had died all alone. Someone had to be on his side now.

But what would happen if they found out I'd taken evidence from a murder scene? I mean, this *was* evidence, right? A real clue? I could get arrested for taking the glasses, for interfering with a criminal investigation. My insides twisted at the thought of explaining to my parents. I still had the ripped page from the Nietzsche book I'd taken from Nate's locker. How was I going to explain that? Instead of reaching down to pick up the glasses, I pulled my phone from my pocket and took a bunch of shots at different angles and zoomed in to get a snap of the words and numbers inside the frame. If these were Nate's, I was going to find out.

The sirens were in the park now. But I couldn't quite tell where they were coming from. I left the glasses in the damp grass and turned back to face the culvert. Stared at his shoes. The muddied exposed part of his sock. The slightly frayed cuff of his jeans. Then I walked away, up the sloped embankment to wait. My breath caught in my chest. My lungs seized. Jawad was dead. This was real.

The police cars and ambulances drove up behind me from a dirt access road that I thought was closed off, their tires kicking up mud. The narrow road ran behind the golf course that was to the south of the park and then along the east side. I honestly had no idea how to get to it, but I also didn't spend time at the golf course. First one police car, then others, skidded to a stop not far from me, sirens blaring. A voice on a loudspeaker told me to stop and put my hands up. I didn't react at first. I couldn't move. My mind was stuck. My body, frozen. The voice from the car yelled at me again. First, I was confused: Why was I getting screamed at? Then I slowly raised my hands; they felt like lead. I took a small step back, stumbled a little before righting myself. Police surged out of their cars, and an officer started yelling at me. I lifted my head to face them, but tears blurred my vision. All the sounds muffled in my ears. I couldn't hear what the man was yelling; all I saw was a white man with a gun. My brain froze. I was terrified, my eyes fixating on the words *Serve & Protect* on the cop cars; I knew right then that they didn't apply to me. Another cop, a Black woman, her hair pulled back in a low, tight bun, turned to look at me. Then said something to the man with the gun. He nodded and started to lower it, but he still looked angry. All the cops did. Even though he lowered the gun, it didn't make me feel any less terrified. Last year, Chicago cops had killed a thirteen-year-old brown boy who had his empty hands up, just like me.

They sat me on the back edge of an ambulance, a blanket wrapped around my shoulders. I heard one of the EMTs saying something about shock, but it was kind of a blur, and it took me a second to understand they were talking about me. One detective and then another came to interview me. I explained what I could. The same explanation I would have to give to my parents: I was on a walk. Clearing my head after what had happened to our store. That was the truth. Part of it, anyway. The whole truth was much more complicated than that.

I stood and inched closer to the embankment as they gently removed the body. My limbs were numb. My mind blank, erased.

I moved closer, as close as the yellow crime-scene tape would let me. I'd already trampled on the murder scene, a cop complained. I wanted to scream, *The only reason I stepped anywhere near the crime scene is because the police ignored the crime.* A missing Muslim boy, a refugee, an Iraqi, wasn't worth too many news cycles. Wasn't worth the full investigation. And now Jawad was dead. They didn't say it was him, of course; not to me, anyway. Something about notifying the parents to identify him. They talked around me like I wasn't there. A part of me felt like I wasn't.

They placed his body on the stretcher, their gloved hands gentle like his cold skin could bruise. My veins filled with ice. Every part of me felt locked, dazed. I shivered, even with the blanket around me. I didn't want to look, but I couldn't turn away. His face looked so soft. So young. Sometimes my mom says that when she looks at me, she can see my face as a baby in my face now. I wondered if that's what Jawad's parents would see. Like he'd never had a chance to grow up, like he would always be a baby. Their baby. I wiped my dripping nose with the back of my coat sleeve.

That's when I caught a glint of blue and silver as the EMTs lofted a gray blanket, air buffeting it before it came to settle on his body. A flash from his belt loop. A key chain. A small silver hand of Fatima, a blue-and-white stone in its center. An amulet to ward off evil. To protect him. My mind paused, trying to grasp at a moment vaguely reminiscent of this one. Not about the body or the murder. But him, Jawad. Goose bumps popped up all over my skin—my body remembered, even if my mind didn't have the words yet. That key chain had once belonged to me.

My mother screamed my name from across the field as my

parents hurried up the path. She looked frantic, her normally perfect high bun now low and loose at the back of her neck, wisps of hair flying around her face. My dad's face was a stone. I put my hand up in a half wave, then turned back to the culvert when I heard one of the detectives say something about the glasses. I'd pointed them out to the woman officer right away. It seemed like hours ago. It seemed like a minute ago.

"The kid wear glasses?" a tan-skinned detective in a dark-blue suit asked the Black officer, the one I'd told.

She shrugged. "Let me check his school ID again. She"—the officer tilted her head in my direction—"inadvertently kicked them."

"Fantastic." The detective sighed.

My parents appeared at my side, out of breath and gray faced. My mother threw her arms around me, and my dad rubbed my back.

"Beta. Beta. Are you okay?" my mom whispered.

I straightened up, my breath hitching. "Those glasses…," I muttered under my breath.

"Sorry?" my dad said.

I couldn't stop my hands from shaking, but I pointed to the detective with the glasses in his gloved hand. I raised my voice. "I know who those belong to."

Anatomy of an American Murder transcript

PBS DOCUMENTARY SERIES

April 2023

Part I: When the World Breaks

Suleyman Ali, *48, Iraqi American, former translator for Coalition Forces 2003–2007. Owner Greener Day Dry Cleaner. Father of Jawad Ali.*

Dina Ali, *46, Iraqi American, Owner Greener Day Dry Cleaner. Nurse by training. Mother of Jawad Ali. Founder, Jawad Ali Foundation for Refugee Youth.*

> **Dina:** The world is broken. Our world is broken. It was ever
> since that voice mail. A voice mail was the end of everything.
> The end of life. The end of hope. That...that...[*voice breaks,
> trails off*] Over a year later...I still don't know what to say when
> people ask me about our Jawad. Do I tell them about the grief
> that never goes away? Do I tell them about the love that never
> fades? Do I tell them how those twinned emotions live in me
> symbiotically? That their coexistence is both necessary and
> impossible? Grief kills you and love keeps you alive. Then you
> wake up, if you can sleep at all, and the cycle begins again.
>
> **Suleyman:** Even after all this time, all these months. I still
> look down at my phone thinking he will call. Thinking this is a

nightmare that I will wake up from. That the phone will ring and it will be him. No. That's wrong. He never called. Even my delusions are wrong. He texted. That's it. Jawad always said only old people called on the phone. [*chuckles*] I guess he was right.

We kept his number. The police gave us back his phone finally, after they'd recovered it from that house, after the trial. We still pay the bill. When I got him the new phone he wanted for his birthday, I told him he had to record an outgoing voice message. In case someone called. Someone important. You know what he did? Let me show you.

[*Suleyman gets up, walks to the shelf, and returns with Jawad's old iPhone X. He hits PLAY.*]

"Hey, this is Jawad. Your son. I know it's you, Baba. Or maybe it's you, Mama. No one else calls me. Go ahead and leave a voice mail. I know it makes you happy. And if I'm about to get in trouble, remember that I'm such a good kid, I left this outgoing message just for you. Like you asked. See? I listen sometimes! Love you guys."

Dina: [*sucks in breath, reaches for her husband's hand*]

Suleyman: [*clears throat*] He was such a good boy. A good son. May God shower him with blessings.

Dina: [*voice barely a whisper*] I used to tell him he was my bright, bright star. And now in our life there is only darkness. A black hole where joy once lived.

273

January 18, 2022

This is Karen McManus, reporting from a gruesome scene. A few hours ago, the body of fourteen-year-old Jawad Ali, missing for nearly two weeks, was found near a rarely frequented area of Jackson Park.

An area resident walking through the park came across Jawad's body in a culvert and notified police.

Police are canvassing the neighborhood to determine if anyone might have seen something suspicious. An early search for Jawad included the woods in Jackson Park but apparently stopped at the lagoons. Neighbors are wondering why police did not bother to push farther into the park.

Lizzie Chao, local resident, had joined in the initial search. "I don't understand why they didn't comb through every inch of Jackson Park. The police established the search perimeters and we stopped at the Garden of the Phoenix. My God. To think that he was here the entire time." [*shakes head*] "I wish we could've done more. For him. For his poor parents. No one should have to face that."

When asked, the police commissioner responded, "The department followed protocol. There was inclement weather, and we had to take necessary precautions to protect both our officers and citizens who were aiding in the search. Let me assure the community, we will find the perpetrator of this crime."

Local residents worry for their children. "If there's a kidnapper and murderer on the loose, why aren't the police doing more?" Ellie Ngyuen, a local social worker, asked. "We haven't gotten any other information besides the alerts. What are we supposed to do? Our kids walk home from school all the time."

Police initially believed Jawad's disappearance was a kidnapping when a ransom attempt was made. But then they classified Jawad as a possible runaway when his parents received a text allegedly from their son.

The police have been hampered in their efforts by little apparent evidence and seemingly no eyewitnesses. Police ask anyone who might have seen Jawad since January 9 or seen anything suspicious at all to please contact the tip line. You can report anonymously. There is a reward for information leading to the capture of Jawad's killer or killers.

JAWAD

The police won't let my parents bury me. Not until the case is solved, they said. I traded the cold metal of a pipe for the cold metal of a drawer in the morgue. It's dark in here, too.

At least my parents know now. At least they know where I am. Thanks to Safiya. I called to her and she came. She saw me when no one else did, even when I was alive.

I thought it would make it better for my parents if they found me. But my mom still cries all the time. I could almost feel her when she touched my hand and my cheek when they showed her my body.

Now I see Baba watching her as she tries to sleep. How he puts his hand on her head. How he puts his hand to his heart.

Safiya feels it, too, the dark, the scary shadows coming to life. I'm sorry for that. I didn't know that would happen. I didn't know what else to do. She's the only one who heard me, who listened. The only one who believed.

Be careful, I whisper when Safiya is at her breakfast table, shivering, her hands wrapped around a cup of tea her mom made. *Be careful. You're so close to everything.*

In sixth grade we did a unit on how courts and laws work in America. In our book there was a sketch, a line drawing of a figure that kind of looked like the Statue of Liberty, but wearing a blindfold and holding scales that weigh things, like at our little corner grocery. She was called Lady Justice. Because "everyone is equal under the law," my teacher said. I didn't get it because if you can't see, how can you make sure everyone is treated equally?

A lot of the things we read in the textbook didn't match up with the things I saw outside of school. And on the news. One time, a protest march passed my parents' dry cleaners. A lot of people of different ages and races. Even kids in strollers and toddlers on their parents' shoulders. They were holding signs that said BLACK LIVES MATTER. There were signs with a picture of a smiling Black woman. She looked happy and young. Not young like me, but like someone in college. She'd been killed by a cop. In her own house. All she was doing was sleeping. And there was a picture of a Black boy in a hoodie. He was maybe my age. He was killed, too. For walking around. For being Black. The news kept talking about him like he was an adult, but he was a kid, like me.

There were people chanting "No justice, no peace." It made me think of that Lady Justice drawing. About how some things they taught us in school were a lie. About how sometimes adults betray you. About how sometimes it feels like you can never win, no matter what you do, even when you didn't do anything wrong. But *some* people get to get away with murder.

I saw Safiya sitting still for a long time, staring into her cup of tea. She's scared. I know what that feels like. She was scared, but she came to find me anyway. *Shukran*, I breathed next to her. She turned her head, and her eyes landed on a slant of light streaming in through the window.

Thank you. Thank you. Thank you. You saw me when no one else did.

SAFIYA

JANUARY 18, 2022

Lie: Forewarned is forearmed.

Truth: Nothing can prepare you for your world shattering.

It was dark by the time we got home. The police had questioned me, and one of them—Detective Diaz—gave me his card in case I remembered anything else. My parents and I were mostly silent on the way home. They'd left the car at the edge of the park. I guess my parents didn't know about that access road, either. My mom escorted me to the car, our arms around each other's waists like she needed to hold me up. Maybe she did. Maybe we held each other up a little. My dad walked a half step ahead, blocking the wind, blocking everything. Like he was my shield.

Inside, our apartment felt warm but also somehow wrong. My entire world felt jagged, like I was looking through a cracked lens. I wondered if I would still hear Jawad's voice. I wondered if he felt at peace. I excused myself to take a shower while my parents got dinner together. My steps were heavy, and every muscle in my body ached. I felt so, so tired. My stomach lurched, and I barely made it to the bathroom, flipping up the lid of the toilet to puke my guts out; dry heaves followed. I turned the shower on, left my clothes in a pile on the floor, and dragged myself into the stream of hot water. I shivered, even in the steam. I don't know how much time passed, but my dad knocked on the door to tell me dinner was ready.

I barely touched my daal and rice. It was always what my mom made for me when I wasn't feeling well, making sure the rice was extra soft and the lentils not too spicy. My parents watched me eat, like I was a baby bird learning to feed itself. Too scared to take their eyes off me.

Of course, I hadn't told them the whole truth. The parts I did have to share with the police and my parents made my mom's face pale. Some things they'd known about: the newspaper hack, the swastika, the graffiti on our store. Others they didn't: the threatening *Swallow your poison* text and Nate confronting me after school. I'd kept the rest simple. I didn't lie. I *was* walking and thinking in Jackson Park. A lot of the weird things at school *had* pointed to Nate. Nate seemed to have white supremacist sympathies. And he'd worn those green glasses at school, in his birding videos, and he'd even pointed out the area around the culvert as a place where there were ghosts. His "secret spot," he'd said. It had to be him. Occam's razor, right?

What I didn't tell my parents, or anyone else, was that maybe the ghosts were real. Maybe one of the ghosts talked to me. And that ghost was Jawad.

"I'm tired," I said, pushing back my chair.

My parents both leaped up, startling me.

"Beta, you have been through a lot today. Probably best to get some sleep," my dad said.

"We'll be right here if you need us," my mom added. "You can call us for anything. You can talk to us about anything, and I can make up the futon on the floor of our room if you want to sleep there."

I smiled. "I'm okay. I think I'm going to crash." I hugged both of them. My dad had to gently tug at my mom's arm so she'd let me go.

My body was bone tired as I dragged myself from the table to brush my teeth and pull on my flannel boxers and a T-shirt. Even in winter, I wore boxers to bed. Weird, I know. But wearing long pj's made me feel constrained. I hated that feeling.

I turned off the lights and pulled up the blankets. But whenever I tried to close my eyes, my brain revved into motion. Like one of those plastic toy cars you pull back on the carpet and then let go to see it race across the room.

I sat up and grabbed my phone off my nightstand. It was on silent, but the screen flashed a million missed texts and calls. Almost all from Asma. Usman had checked in, since he thought I was feeling sick. A couple from Richard, which I didn't read. Didn't have the energy. I felt hollow. Like even looking at all the texts was too exhausting. Every part of me was tired.

I'd told Asma that I'd found Jawad, but only because she'd gotten my text after her ortho appointment and had called to check on me. I'd picked up and couldn't hide how broken I felt. It was probably a mistake to tell her, to get her even more involved. The detective at the scene warned me to not speak about it to anyone. I was a witness.

With the murderer still out there, it could be dangerous. For me. Or for anyone I talked to. No way I'd risk endangering my friends. I was the one who'd dragged everyone into this in the first place. But at this point Asma knew almost the whole story. None of the news reports had mentioned me by name, stating only that "an individual on a walk had come across the body." I'd asked Asma to keep my secret. I trusted her, and I'd do what I needed to protect her.

I shot off a quick text to her: I think it was Nate. My phone rang immediately. I barely got out a syllable before Asma jumped in:

"What do you mean, you think it was Nate?" she asked. "And holy hell, are you okay? I kept thinking about you when I was scrolling through the news."

"The answer to the second question is, I don't think so. I mean, I saw him. Jawad. His body. I don't know if I'll ever be able to forget that," I whispered. "I don't think I should forget it."

"I'm so sorry. I wish you hadn't been alone."

I took a deep breath. "I think Nate's glasses were at the scene. You know, the green ones?"

"The *signature* glasses he bragged about on his YouTube videos? That he got in London?"

"Yeah. Those."

"Holy crap." Asma paused for a second. "But I guess it could still be a weird coincidence? I mean funky-shaped, emerald-green, translucent frames are unusual, but there have to be other people in Chicago with those same glasses."

"I dunno. Too many coincidences. Eventually circumstantial evidence can actually point to the guilty person, right?"

"Do you know for sure if they're the same?"

"Hang on," I said, and scrolled through my photos. "I sent you three pics I took."

"Oh my God, you took crime-scene photos?"

"No! I mean. Only the glasses and the area. Not of…"

"It's okay. Hang on. Here they are. Let me pull up his YouTube channel."

While Asma did that, I grabbed my laptop from my desk. It was a little banged up at the corners, but it got the job done. I put in my earbuds so I could talk to Asma hands-free and then zoomed in on the writing on the inside of the glasses.

"They look a lot like the ones he's wearing in the videos," Asma said. "I wonder if we got any photos of him at school while he was wearing them. Or maybe yearbook staff did? They were in class-rooms taking candid shots last week. I'll check tomorrow."

"Sounds good," I said absentmindedly. Part of the picture was a bit blurry, and I couldn't make out all the words. I was hoping it was the name of the manufacturer or store where the glasses had been made. Maybe the brand. "Asma, can you tell what the last two letters of that word on the inside of the frame are? It looks like it says *Chelsea Opti*—I can't quite make it out."

"I think it's two *x*'s, like *Optixx*?"

I Googled and got hits right away. "It looks like a fancy eyeglass shop in the Chelsea neighborhood in London."

"I'm pulling it up, too. Oh, this definitely looks posh, as the Brits say. Look, it says they do custom frames. Do you think…?"

My heart pounded in my chest. The puzzle pieces were almost clicking into place. "What's the time difference between here and London?"

"Dude. It's, like, 4:00 a.m. there. It says the shop opens at 10:00 a.m."

"Ugh. I'll call tomorrow." I bookmarked the page, closed the lid of my computer, and crawled back into bed.

"Listen, are you really okay?" Asma gently asked.

"Honestly, no. I think I need to go to bed. See you tomorrow?"

"Wait. You're going to school? No. Don't you think you should take the day off?"

"Ugh. My parents want me to stay home, too. And I feel like I could sleep for a month, but I'd rather be at school than home alone," I said. I didn't add *with my thoughts*. Which is exactly what I was afraid of. Thinking.

"Jesus, I can't believe you discovered the vandalism at your store *this* morning. It feels like a million years ago. Look, stay home tomorrow, okay? Maybe we can grab breakfast before I go to school—I can miss first period."

"Fine. I can't fight both you and my parents."

"Great. I'll swing by and pick you up."

"Please, please, keep everything between us. You can't even tell Usman. The police made me swear I wouldn't tell anyone else. I shouldn't even be talking to you about it. It could be…dangerous, especially with Nate so close.

"I get it. And I won't tell anyone, but…your friends love you. We got your back. Okay? Always. G'night."

I was beyond exhausted, but images of those glasses tugged at my brain. I popped back over to my desk, opened my laptop, and fired off a chipper email from my secondary email account with a fake name to ask about Nate's glasses, but sneakily.

I staggered back to bed, pulled up the covers again. This time when I closed my eyes, all I saw was darkness.

JAWAD

Once when I was little, like three or four, Mama and I were walking down a sidewalk not too far from the new neighborhood we'd moved into. I remember my mom was excited because there was a small grocery store that she hoped would maybe have some spices that she liked to use in her cooking.

(I miss my mom's food so much.)

I was so excited to ride on the bus and pull the cord to ding for our stop. When we got off and headed toward the store, I heard fast steps behind us, like someone running, then a loud voice: "Go home, terrorist! Ragheads!"

My mom didn't even turn to look; she grabbed my hand and hurried toward the store. That's when a white man—maybe he was a teenager—ran up along the street side of the sidewalk and tried to pull my mom's hijab off her head. She screamed and jerked away, pushing me toward the store. An uncle inside saw us from the big window and came hurrying out, and the guy who'd attacked us darted across the street and down another block. My mom was crying.

The uncle helped us into the store, and his wife came out to help. I remember she had a bun wrapped up on her head and a kind smile. The nice lady handed Mama a tissue, and the man got on the phone. I think he was calling the police, because a cop came by a little later. Mama was crying, and it made me sad and scared, so while the adults were talking by a cash register, I wandered down to a table along the big storefront windows. There was a girl there. She was older than me. Maybe seven or eight? Her nose was in a book. She wore two braids and had the same smile as the nice lady, so I guessed that was her mom. I didn't say anything. Just stood there.

And then I started crying. I could hear my mom telling the story of what had happened. Heard her repeating the mean words the man had yelled at us. My mom never said any mean words. It felt scary to hear them come out of her mouth with her soft voice when the words were so hard and ugly.

The little girl looked up at me and told me I could sit down. She got me a napkin from a dispenser that was on the table. I remember she tried to talk to me, asked me my name. I don't know if I answered. I was so scared—I couldn't find any words. "It's okay," she said in a quiet voice. "Sometimes people are mean."

On the table was a small blue purse with a pink butterfly on it. The girl reached into her bag and pulled out a charm, a key chain. I knew it was a palm of Fatima. I'd seen them before. A tiny silver hand with a blue-and-white circle in the center. "I got this in India," she said. "From my aunt. It's for protection." Then she pressed it into my hand. "You can have it," she smiled. "It will keep you safe."

A gift. She was giving me a gift.

I wrapped my fingers around the charm and brushed away some tears with the back of my hand. "You can put it on the belt loop of your jeans," she said. "Since you don't have a purse." She giggled. And then offered to show me how it worked—pushed back a little arm in the metal loop and it opened, like a tiny gate. It was shiny and small, so I could attach it and tuck it into my pocket.

I looked up at her and smiled. I'd never gotten a gift from a stranger before.

"Do you want to color?" she asked.

I nodded and took a seat across from her. She pushed some blank paper and a pack of colored pencils toward me. She read. I colored.

When my mom called me to go, I ran to her but looked back at the girl and waved. As Mama and I stepped out the door into the sun, I heard the girl's mom say, "Safiya, time for lunch, beta."

Safiya. She was the girl who had been kind. Who made me feel safe.

From: Hillary312@geurmail.com
To: Help@chelseaoptixx.com
January 18 at 11:33 p.m.

Hi,

I wanted to ask about getting some glasses that I saw on a bird-
tuber channel: *Fowl Play*? The guy who runs it had a translucent
green pair on in some of his recent videos and said he got them
at your store. I think they're funky and awesome and wanted to
get a pair. Do you have them in stock? How much do they cost?
I'm attaching a screenshot from his video with the glasses on.

Thanks!
Hillary

From: Help@chelseaoptixx.com
To: Hillary312@geurmail.com
January 19 at 4:55 a.m.

Hello, Hillary,

We hope this finds you well. We are happy to answer any questions about our products. Yes indeed, the translucent green
lenses you mention from *Fowl Play* were purchased from our
store. So pleased they made an impression!

As each pair at our store is custom made to exact
specifications after customers meet with our design team, we

are not able to exactly replicate the ones you saw. Our store truly offers a one-of-a-kind frame. Customers are able to choose from our large catalogue of materials, hinge springs, adornments, and shapes.

We would be delighted to work with you to create your own signature look. Our pricing for the design prototype begins at £500.

We very much look forward to guiding you on your journey to a custom frame as unique as you are.

Best,
Hugh Jameson
Customer Experience Specialist

SAFIYA

JANUARY 19, 2022

Lie: Hindsight is 20/20.

Truth: We see our past how we want to see it, to frame ourselves in the best possible light.

"Nate was there. The glasses put him at the scene of the crime! They probably won't even bother questioning him." I shook my head. While Asma drove us to a coffee shop, I filled her in on my early morning call with Detective Diaz. I was still exhausted but was up at the crack of dawn, too jittery to sleep in. "When I told him what I'd found about the glasses, he said they were looking into every possible lead. Kinda cut me off."

"Can I believe the police are giving you the brush-off? Yes. Can I believe that Nate is a white supremacist? Yes. A murderer, though? That is terrifying. He's freaking in school with us." Asma's face blanched as she spoke.

"Allegedly. Allegedly a murderer." I'd never said that word out loud, not in that way, about someone I knew. About someone I was in class with. Someone who seemed incredibly pissed off at me.

"Listen, did your parents or anyone suggest that you talk to someone? Like a therapist?"

I wondered if a therapist could help me understand whether the empty feeling inside my body would ever go away. If the sudden gaping hole in my middle would ever fill up. "Yeah. The nurse mentioned it to my mom. She called a few people. But right now...I think finding the truth—all of it—is the only thing that can help me." My mouth went dry as sawdust. I needed to know if all my fears were true. Even the ones I wasn't ready to say out loud yet, not even to Asma.

"I still can't believe the detective didn't seem interested in the information about the optical shop. It's a major lead! All he said was I should leave the detective work to them," I scoffed.

Asma shook her head. "Maybe you should send anything else you know to the anonymous tip line?"

"What's the point? They'd probably know it was me, anyway." I shrugged and leaned back into the soft leather seats of Asma's BMW. It was nice of her to drive, but every time I was in her car, it was a reminder of exactly where I went to school and how I didn't belong. We'd ordered from the drive-through of the local coffee shop and were sitting in the parking lot with our lattes and breakfast: a croissant for me, an egg-white-with-spinach English muffin sandwich for Asma.

"No one is taking this seriously," Asma said, taking a swig of her coffee. "I scanned the local news, and only Channel 13 did a full segment. The rest were tiny updates, like they were adding a footnote to a tragedy. A kid was kidnapped and murdered! And that's not interesting enough to cover?"

"It totally sucks," I said, my entire body feeling unsteady. "His story can't get them enough clicks, I guess. No one cares about a murdered *Muslim* kid. A *refugee*. An Iraqi…"

"Well, his family wasn't connected. Or—"

"Rich. They weren't rich. Immigrant and poor is not a good lead story." I saw Asma bite her lip as she tightened her grip around her coffee. When you know, you know.

I scratched my head through my knit cap. "If Nate had anything to do with it, it means he's dangerous. He could hurt someone else. I don't want to wait and see if the police actually do their job. Jawad deserves justice."

"Jawad…deserves…justice," Asma repeated slowly, tapping the pads of her fingers against the steering wheel. "Justice for Jawad… That would be a good podcast name. Good podcast material."

Justice for Jawad. Those words hung in the air. "That's it," I said.

"You want to do a podcast?"

"No. I want justice for Jawad, and if the police are moving too slowly, then we have to force them to move faster. Make people care. Get the word out on social. It happened right here. In this neighborhood. In Chicago. Someone has to know something."

"#JusticeforJawad. Yes! I can make accounts with that handle right now—it all has to be anonymous. Oh! Some crime podcasts get info from Reddit boards and set up their own anonymous tip lines."

"Reddit? I thought that was for, like, weird old men and conspiracy theorists."

"It is. But there's, like, multiple subs for missing people and unsolved crimes. That's how police figured out cold cases like Grateful Doe and the Strongsville Skeleton, tips from Reddit users."

"Seriously? Whoa. Okay, let's do it. We can't upload the photo of the glasses, since the police would know it's me, but we can give details about the murder that have been in the news already. Maybe I should write an article?"

"No way is Ms. Cary going to let you write a piece accusing Nate of murder."

"Obviously. I'm going to write it anonymously and post it on Medium. I can pull this all together, since I'll be home anyway. I need something to keep my mind..." I trailed off.

Asma reached over to grab my hand. "Send everything to me when you're done, and I'll link it on social."

"We have to be careful. No information connecting us to it. And we can't tell anyone else. Even Usman or Rachel, okay? In case... anything goes awry." I still didn't like dragging Asma this far down the murder rabbit hole, but I couldn't do it all alone. I didn't like hiding things from my friends or my parents, but it felt safer for everyone. "Maybe we can get Nate to trip himself up?" I suggested, then paused to take a deep breath.

Asma looked at me. "I dunno, maybe it's a bit of a stretch. It seems foolish and—"

"Dangerous," I whispered. "I know, but sometimes you need a hail Mary pass in the last seconds of the fourth quarter."

Asma glanced at me, her eyebrows scrunched together. "Did you correctly use a sports metaphor? Hanging around Richard has had a heck of an effect on you." She gave me a small grin.

I didn't tell her, but her words kind of winded me. My hands got shaky. I steadied them around my coffee cup. I'd been wondering how well I knew Richard. But I wasn't ready to share my questions, and that's all I really had. "Look, maybe we can get people to pay attention. To remember Jawad. The actual him, not #bombboy. People should know his real name. Jawad deserves that. It's the least we can do for him."

TRUE CRIME, JUSTICE

JUSTICE FOR JAWAD

BY GHOST IN THE MACHINE · JAN 19 · 4 MIN READ

Jawad Ali died without anyone he loved holding his hand or whispering final blessings in his ear.

Maybe he cried out. *Help me.* Maybe he pled for his life. *Please. No.* Maybe he thought of his parents as he gasped for his last breath. Maybe he clawed out at his murderer, leaving his final mark. Maybe he looked his murderer in the eyes and thought, *Why me?*

I know we'd all like to think Jawad felt peace at the end. That's what movies sell us, right? That he saw a bright light at the end of the tunnel? Saw his loved ones calling him home? Flights of angels? Those stories are for the comfort of the living.

Jawad's end wasn't soft like that. It was violent. It must've been terrifying. And the last thing he saw was the cruel, cowardly face of his killer. If he was still alive when he was dumped and abandoned, the last thing he would've felt was the cold corrugated steel of the inside of a culvert in Jackson Park. How could there have been peace in that?

A lot of you probably already know the story. Jawad wanted to make a fun costume for Halloween that included a cool-looking jet pack with materials from his school's makerspace lab. Jawad asked his teacher's permission, sketched it out, gathered recyclables, imagined new uses for trash. He was sure the kids in his after-school makerspace club were going to love it, that his teachers would be impressed by his ingenuity.

What he didn't count on was Islamophobia. He couldn't imagine the ingrained racism of the English teacher he trusted. He couldn't imagine the deep-rooted, constantly suspicious type of Islamophobia that would lead an adult to assume that a cosplay jet pack made of plastic soda bottles, old knobs and switches, and paint was a bomb. The kind of "bomb" that a high school freshman would walk into school with, through the metal detectors, and show off to everyone. But racism isn't logical.

Jawad was arrested *and* cleared. But his school still suspended him. His classmates still hounded him. Mocked him with the moniker Bomb Boy. Taped Islamophobic messages to his locker. His parents' dry cleaning business got prank called. People drove by hurling epithets at them. They lost customers. All that notoriety grabbed the attention of haters, probably caught the eye of a murderer. Actions have consequences, but not always for the person who deserves them.

The killer is likely walking among us. That ghost skin is going to be uncovered, his mask ripped off. You know, the white supremacist who takes advantage of the system to blend in, to hide in plain sight, because the system was built for him? That's a ghost skin. Like that Chicago cop who was busted for torturing prisoners. Or like the police academy in Kentucky that used quotes from Hitler and advocated violence in a slideshow it used to train new cops—they were revealed by high school journalists, by the way, and their story led to the resignation of the commissioner. (Imagine Hitler quotes in a police training program. HITLER!) Racists are all around us. At work. At school. At the playground. It's our job to find them, to name them.

Those racists and Islamophobes continued to be in Jawad Ali's life even after the #BombBoy dust settled. He got Islamophobic texts, some weird ones that quoted Nietzsche. Structural racism didn't kill Jawad. His murderer did. But that racism sure put a target on his back. And we don't believe the police are working fast enough to find who took aim at Jawad.

There are sides. Time to choose one. No matter where you are, help us get #JusticeforJawad by keeping this tag and his case front and center in the news, which is already starting to forget about him. Help us make sure another brown boy's murder doesn't become a cold case. If you're in Chicago and might have any clue, even if you don't think it's useful, email us at justiceforjawad@geurmail.com. Supposedly Jawad was last seen not far from Bethune High School on January 9th as he got into a dark blue or black car, possibly four doors, somewhere between Bethune High School and the Greener Day Dry Cleaner.

Jawad deserved so much better. He deserved a full and long life. Let's make sure he at least gets justice.

#justiceforjawad

JAWAD

Except for that incident outside the Mirzas' store, I only remember seeing Mama cry one other time. It was after I got suspended and "Bomb Boy" became a thing. She didn't know I saw her. She and Baba were talking after they thought I'd gone to bed, but I came back out to get a glass of water. They were in the living room, whispering to each other, Mama softly crying, saying that I was a good kid, a kind boy. Saying she didn't understand how the school could be so callous. How the other kids could be so cruel.

A lump swelled in my throat. I went back to my room without getting that glass of water. Hours later, I was still awake, so I tiptoed to the kitchen. I sat at our small, round wood table, another hand-me-down from a neighbor who was throwing it away, another thing Baba fixed and made beautiful. For a long time I sat there, staring at an empty glass.

Now my mom cries all the time. All the time. Her eyes are permanently red and swollen. Even when she's in their dry cleaner's shop. I wish she didn't have to be there. Sometimes Baba tells her he can manage by himself. I stay with her at home so she's not alone, even if she can't see me. But I think it's worse. For her and for me. It makes me miss her even more. Maybe she senses me and it makes her miss me even more, too.

I heard her saying to my dad, "I just want to bury him. To have the funeral prayer and our three days of mourning, like we're supposed to. We can't even give him that. They took everything from us."

Tonight she prayed right after she got home from work and then went to lie down. Baba called for her, but it's like she couldn't get out of bed. Baba was warming some soup in the kitchen. He looked sad, too. His face drooped and he hadn't shaved. Baba can't cook. At all. Mama and I would make fun of him about it sometimes, but he knew we were joking. There are lots of other things Baba is good at. People from the mosque and old friends from the refugee relocation center keep bringing food. So much food, the fridge and freezer are full. They don't know what to say when they drop it off. No one knows what to say.

Mama was lying there. So still. Her eyes open, staring out the window into the dark. I stood next to her, so close. I put my hand on hers. And when I did, her muscles twitched. So slightly. Mama gasped. "Jawad?" she whispered. I tried to say something, tried to touch her again. I tried so hard. But I couldn't make it work. Maybe I wanted it too much. Maybe it would've upset her even more.

My dad called for her to come eat something. She sighed and sat up in bed, moving her legs slowly over the edge with a lot of effort, like they were really heavy. She stood up but paused at the door before walking out. "I love you," she whispered. So soft. So low. It felt like a dream. Like a memory. Like a tiny bit of hope. Hope is her gift.

Reddit

We are looking for Justice for Jawad. We will keep posting everywhere until his killer is found.

Fourteen-year-old Jawad Ali's body was found yesterday in Chicago's Jackson Park. He'd been missing for thirteen days. At first, the police thought it was a kidnapping, but later, alleged texts from Jawad indicated that he had run away, so the police reclassified the case as a runaway and the investigation was redirected, mostly to nowhere. The only other clue the police had besides text messages was an anonymous tip that someone who fit Jawad's description was seen getting into a dark blue or black car near his school.

A hiker found his body in a culvert in an abandoned part of the park. There were clues at the scene that the police have not yet released to the public, but so far no arrests have been made. "We hope to find a witness," the police said on the local news. But it doesn't seem like anyone has come forth.

Some of you may be familiar with Jawad's name because last October he was in the news as "Bomb Boy," the kid arrested for having a jet pack at school that he made out of plastic soda bottles but that his teacher thought was a bomb. Even though he was cleared, he faced a lot of anti-Muslim sentiment at school and in the right-wing press. We think his name being splashed in the news is what drew the attention of the murderer. Shortly after his arrest and release, Jawad got Islamophobic texts, including one that was a Nietzsche quote. The weird thing is, his parents got Islamophobic texts, too (well that part isn't weird because, hello, racism!), but one of them was a Nietzsche quote as well.

Nietzsche quotes have turned up in other recent crimes on the South Side, including in a threatening letter to a local mosque. And the newspaper website at DuSable Prep was hacked by someone calling himself "Ghost Skin" who quoted...wait for it...Nietzsche. The police don't seem to be moving on this, but we think there is obviously a connection. I mean, how many people are quoting Nietzsche in their racist screeds? We think the killer clearly has a Nietzsche obsession. And he *might* also wear glasses.

Look, Jawad was a brown Muslim kid whose parents are refugees, and the police don't seem as interested as we think they should be. This case is only two weeks old, and the murderer has to still be out there, probably close by. Maybe you know something. Maybe you saw something.

Help us get #JusticeforJawad.

Link: <u>Muslim Teen Arrested on Suspicion of Terrorism for Bringing Homemade Jet Pack to School</u>

Link: <u>Search Continues for Jawad Ali, Teen Who Drew Notoriety for "Bomb Boy" Arrest</u>

Nietzsche quote sent to Jawad: If you want me to believe in your Redeemer, you're going to have to look a lot more redeemed.

Nietzsche quote sent to Jawad's parents: Dead are all gods: now we want the supermen to live.

Nietzsche quotes from DuSable hack: 1) I am the herald of lightning. 2) Swallow your poison, for you need it badly.

Squishy1776 782 points

The kidnapping caught my attention because I remembered the #bombboy thing. Sounds like he got more attention for being falsely accused than for being murdered. I did some digging, did you know that Hitler loved Nietzsche? So do some of the Q white supremacist groups. Might be a connection to see if there are any in Chicago that use one of those quotes as a motto, maybe?

Rebecca_sunnyrbrooke 1672 points

That case is so sad. Poor kid. Never got a break.

Anemone_Sea 1305 points

Did the police release anything further on the make of that car? Four-door? Did they release surveillance footage? Or follow up at all?

Coopted_57 1001 points

I'm local-ish. Have you looked at the Good Neighbor Facebook page for the area? I popped in and found this from around the time of the kidnapping: "Hey neighbors! Noticed a black Chrysler 200 circling through the neighborhood a few

times. Seemed kind of fishy. Probably a rental. No one would *buy* one of those, amirite? LOL. Am I being paranoid???"
Maybe check it out?

NutsnBolts12 2117 points
A Chrysler 200? Definitely a rental. Have you looked at local car rental agencies? Probably won't give you any customer information, but good to at least find out which cars they have?

RyngofFyre 7501 points
I might have something for you. DM.

SAFIYA

JANUARY 20, 2022

Fact: Lies can hide the truth. But they can't change the truth.

Truth: The safest place to hide is in plain sight.

"Are you avoiding me?"

The sound of his voice made me jump. I slammed my locker to see Richard, wearing a cream-colored fisherman's sweater, leaning on the locker next to mine. My heart raced, but not for the usual reason it did when I was around him. Even though I'd spent most of my day off yesterday putting together the Medium and Reddit posts, I'd also spent a lot of time going over everything that had happened the last two weeks. Richard had lied to me about London. I wanted to find out why.

"What do you mean?" I asked. *Act casual. Be normal.* Richard was wearing his usual charming smile and gazing at me with soft eyes, but for the first time, it felt strained. Was I the only one who felt this weirdness? Dammit. What if I was seeing connections where none existed? I didn't like constantly questioning myself, but everything was so messed up right now, it was hard to know who or what to trust.

"Only that you didn't respond to my texts and I think I know why," he grinned.

The text from the day before yesterday, when I'd found Jawad's body. I hadn't responded to that or one from yesterday when he was checking in to see how I was feeling. My throat went dry. Richard didn't know about anything besides the vandalism at our store and that I stayed home because I was a little under the weather. I had to keep it that way. I shrugged, painting a confused look on my face.

"It's because of what Dakota said, right? The scarf I got her? I swear it didn't mean anything."

"Oh!" I said, relieved but still on guard. "Yeah. No big deal."

"Cool. I was getting worried." Richard pretended to wipe sweat off his brow.

"I've been distracted is all. You know with everything…the vandalism at my parents' store. And now about Jawad. It's so scary. There could be a murderer in our neighborhood."

"Yeah. I wouldn't worry about it, though."

"There's a dead Muslim kid and I shouldn't worry about it?" I couldn't hide the shocked look on my face. Richard clearly noticed.

He stepped closer to me and took my hands in his, his eyes full of concern. "I meant that you're safe. Jawad attracted attention because of the whole bomb thing."

"It wasn't a bomb, though. It was a costume jet pack. And he didn't *attract* anything. A racist teacher called the police on him, and a racist murderer killed him. None of it was his fault." I pulled my hands away from Richard's and stuffed them into my pockets.

"I get it. It's super upsetting. Especially after what happened at your parents' store. But getting all fixated on it isn't going to help, you know?"

"You knew Jawad, right? That's what you told us at the bench." I could feel the bile rising in my throat. I'd been so tired the last day and a half. But I'd woken up full of rage, and I didn't know where to put it.

"I saw him, like, once or twice when I was volunteering. That's all."

"So a dead kid doesn't bother you?" I snapped.

"Of course it does. All I'm saying is, I'm not shocked. People get murdered in Chicago every day. It sucks, but he was probably in the wrong place at the wrong time. You're too smart to let that happen to you." Richard smiled and rubbed his knuckle against my cheek. It made me flinch. His hands, which were always so warm, were ice cold.

"So charming Richard is turning out to be an unfeeling asshole? Ugh. That's doesn't seem like him," Asma said as we ate our lunch at the bench, our fingers freezing. It was cold, too cold for everyone else, but it was dry, and the bench across the street was the only place we could make sure no one heard us.

I nodded, distracted, and crunched into my chutney, chips, and kheema sandwich, thinking about the exchange I'd had with him earlier. Asma winced as she watched me take another bite. "What?" I asked. "It's my leftover fave."

"Kheema with rice, lentils, and mango achar? Yes. But ground beef, cold, on sandwich bread with potato chips? Uh, no. Hard pass."

"That's salt-and-vinegar potato chips, miss. It's the perfect balance of flavors, salt, and crunch. You clearly have no sense of culinary adventure." I laughed. And immediately felt horrible about having the privilege of laughter. My smile faded.

"So…how are you dealing with everything? Does it feel okay to be back at school?" Asma's tone shifted.

I sighed. "I'm relieved that Nate is absent again today. I don't know if I could spend a whole class looking at his face." Asma told me he'd been a no-show yesterday, too, which only made him more suspect in my book. "And as far as Richard? I don't know. Maybe I'm misreading it? Or maybe he's having second thoughts about getting involved with someone who is obsessed with a murder." I shrugged.

I didn't tell her that I kept seeing Jawad's body in my mind. Kept replaying that moment when they'd placed him on the stretcher. I chewed for a bit, letting my mind drift to my conversation with Richard again. I hadn't told Asma about his being in London, and I wasn't sure if I was ready to. None of it made sense. "Richard was all nice and chivalrous, stepping up when Nate was harassing me. And now he's super insensitive about Jawad, and he called Dakota a bitch the other day."

"Whoa! Misogynist alarm!" Asma drew back and raised her eyebrows. "That's some creepy Jekyll and Hyde crap. Red flag! You didn't tell him about finding Jawad, did you? Or your suspicions about Nate?"

I inadvertently knocked over my bag of chips and watched as

they scattered over the ice-crusted, dirty snow. I squeezed my eyes shut. There was so much I wasn't saying. So much I wasn't admitting to myself. I could barely comprehend that I'd seen Jawad lying facedown in that culvert. My whole life felt like the most precarious Jenga tower, ready to topple if I even breathed wrong. I thought about Richard being in London. I racked my brain trying to remember if he was in the crowd shots on the day of the smoke bomb. I shook my head. It was all too much. "No! I told you, no one else can know. Besides…I…I mean…I'm not even sure. Everything points to Nate. He has all the Ghost Skin characteristics. He confronted me. He's obviously obsessed with Nietzsche. And the glasses…"

Asma bit her lower lip. "Listen. Hear me out for a sec. There are a lot of things we don't know. There could still be a plausible explanation for everything. Let's say Nate is the hacker and the vandal. Does it mean he murdered Jawad, too? What if someone stole his glasses or he lost them? He goes birding around there, right? What if he actually has been sick the last two days. Maybe this is, I dunno…too much for us?"

"So you're saying I should drop it? That Richard is right, that I'm obsessed? Jawad is dead! Someone has to do something!" I could feel the anger in my voice, but I was having a hard time controlling it.

"I know. I get it," Asma said in a soft tone. "I'm on your side. But I'm saying you need to be careful. And—" Her phone buzzed. "Hang on. I set up notifications for if we get any bites on our Reddit post."

I scooched over to peer at her phone as she scrolled through the post, which we'd uploaded last night. A lot of the responses were condolences. Some had good questions. "I can't believe we didn't check South Side neighbor pages on Facebook. Duh," I said.

"Of course we didn't. We're not middle-aged parents."

I gave Asma a small smile. We weren't exactly Redditors, either. And if we wanted to bust Nate, we had to think outside the box, as Ms. Cary loved to say when we were brainstorming story ideas. "Oh my God. Look at that." I pointed to the screen, a message from someone with the handle RyngofFyre with info about a car rental. My palms got sweaty, and I wiped them against my jeans. Asma clicked through to the DMs.

> I can't say how I know this, but about two weeks ago, a black sedan, a Chevy 200, was rented at Anderson Car Rental to a guy named Fred Nietzsche. You said your boy was obsessed with Nietzsche. Seems kinda sus to me. Maybe check it out. Investigate every angle. Like, today. Don't dismiss any coincidences in a crime. Right? Good luck. Hope you nail that asshole.

Asma and I looked at each other. My jaw dropped. My heart thudded in my ears. This had to be it. "I'm going after school," I whispered. My mouth was dry as sawdust as I Googled the location and hours of the agency.

"I can't go. I have a final fitting for the gagra choli I'm wearing to my cousin's wedding reception. It's a whole thing—we're all going to Devon for the last big pre-wedding shopping trip and dinner; it's a caravan of cousins and aunties. There's no way I can miss it. Wait 'til tomorrow. I'll drive. Safety in numbers."

As Asma spoke, I could feel my agitation growing. If there were any answers out there, I had to find them. Now. By tomorrow someone else could be hurt. I'd already lost a day by staying home yesterday. Asma's extended family was super tight, and I got how important the wedding planning was. And I would never say this out loud to her, but I couldn't see how she didn't want to find answers about Jawad's murder right away, too. I couldn't wait. I wouldn't.

"This place closes at 6:00 p.m. today," I said. "I can go myself. It's an easy bus ride there and back. I'll be around people the whole time. No worries." I tried to sound confident, but I was nervous. I had no idea what I was going to ask or find out. I had no idea who RyngofFyre was or whether any of this was even real. Or safe. But I also knew I couldn't wait to check it out. Jawad was with me all the time now. Even when it wasn't his voice. It was him. His cold face. Rigid, bent fingers. The damp shoes. It was like he picked me to be his guardian. I couldn't let him down.

Asma sighed. "I know how important this is to you. But I wish you'd wait until tomorrow. Or take someone else with you."

"No! I told you what the police said. You're not even supposed to know. Telling Usman or Rachel at this point could get them in trouble, too. It's better for everyone this way. I'll be fine. Seriously. Look." I showed Asma my phone. "The bus stop is directly in front of the car rental. I'll be there and back before dark."

"Okay, if you're sure," Asma said, but the look on her face was pure worry.

Even Asma didn't seem to understand how desperately I needed answers. It was my parents' store that was vandalized. I was the one the hacker targeted. And I was the one who'd found Jawad's body. He was counting on me. I nodded, trying to reassure her. I was one-hundred-percent *un*sure. But I still had to find the truth.

JAWAD

What do I do now? What happens next? Can they finally bury me? Can we finally have peace?

I can't watch my mom cry all the time. Or watch my dad's sad face as he makes tea. There is already a big hole in me, and it keeps getting bigger. Soon the hole will be all that I am.

I sat on the big rocks by the lake for a long, long time. Maybe hours. Maybe days. I don't know. I thought I heard something. A voice like mine. Praying melodically, so it sounded like a song and I kept it in my heart.

There's no one to tell me what to do. No explanation I can find for why all the events in my life—and in my death—are happening this way and not the way I thought they would. Is this all there is? Am I only ever going to be #bombboy?

Not a lot of things make sense right now, but maybe one thing I can do is help. I'd like to help. Safiya is so close to danger. When I'm nearby, though, I think I give her bad dreams. Dreams that haunt her. I'm sorry. That's not what I wanted. Nothing is what I wanted.

She's the only one who notices me. The only one besides my parents who seems to remember me. Everyone is forgetting. Everyone will forget. Please don't forget.

SAFIYA

JANUARY 20, 2022

Fact: Women are socialized not to show their anger.

Lie: Anger is unbecoming in a woman.

Truth: Don't underestimate the power of your rage to get things done.

The late-afternoon bus was mostly empty. A few students from a Catholic girls' school, their noses buried in their phones, sat with their backpacks between their navy-blue slacks or green-and-blue-plaid skirts with dark tights. The farther west the bus headed, the more white people got off at their stops, until there were none left. Only the Black and brown schoolkids and a few adults who looked like they were maybe leaving work. One of them leaned her head back on the seat and closed her eyes. One man flipped through the pages of a book, his finger underlining the words as he read. We rolled along, hitting each new Chicago winter pothole with a thud, each one jolting me with the reality of what I was doing.

At breakfast my mom had asked me if I was okay. I'd assured her I was. I lied. I didn't think she believed me, but she nodded anyway. She subtly suggested talking to one of the counselors at school. I said I would, but I lied about that, too. I didn't trust the adults at school. She'd looked so worried, but I hadn't been ready to admit that I was running on fumes, pushing images out of my mind, hearing Jawad's voice. And believing so hard that I had to keep going forward. I didn't have a choice, like how a great white shark will die if it stops moving. Except I didn't feel like an apex predator at all. More like bait. Still, if I paused too long, thought too hard, all I'd see would be images of Jawad, and of Nate's angry face, the *Swallow your poison* text, the swastika, the threatening letter to the mosque. If I stopped moving, I'd drown. In fear. In sadness. In rage.

Anderson Car Rental was not a chain. It was a small agency in a strip mall next to a place called Speedy Cash, which, judging from the signs in the window, was a money-transfer spot that also sold lottery tickets. On the other side of the rental place was a sandwich shop. If Nate was the one who'd rented a car under the name Fred Nietzsche (did he think he was being clever?), then it would make sense for him to come all the way out here. It was far from his neighborhood of gated mansions with wide lawns and old money, and unlikely that anyone would recognize him. It also meant it was premeditated. I shivered.

A cheerful bell rang as I walked in. A tall, skinny Black man in a red sweater and with gray hair around his temples greeted me with a warm smile. Next to him, a younger Black man with short locs was busy entering information into a computer.

"Good afternoon. Can I help you, miss? Do you have a reservation?"

"Oh, hi," I muttered, somehow caught off guard with the simple, kind greeting. "Well, um, I have a couple questions, actually." I'd planned out what I was going to say in the bus, but now as I stood here, I realized how ridiculous it all sounded.

"I hope I can give you some answers." He grinned.

"I'm a reporter from the DuSable Prep *Spectator*," I said. The young man at the computer paused his work but kept his eyes glued to the screen.

"The private school? That's a bit of a ride, isn't it?"

I chuckled nervously and edged closer because I felt the need to whisper. My hands were sweating, so I took off my mittens and placed them on the counter, leaning my elbow on them to steady me.

"Well…," I continued. "We are doing an investigative report into a possible crime, and we think the criminal—uh, the, um, alleged criminal—might have rented a car here."

The man jutted his neck out toward me and scrunched his eyebrows like he heard me but couldn't believe what I was saying. The young man next to him sucked in his breath. There was a very long, painful pause. So I kept going. "You see, sir, we believe that a black Chevy 200 might have been rented here under the name Fred Nietzsche and—"

The guy entering info into the computer dropped a bunch of receipts and bent down behind the counter to get them. The older gentleman shook his head. "Now, miss, I'm certain the journalism teacher at your very fancy school has talked to you about rights to privacy. And subpoenas? I'm sure you also know that we would never give out any client's personal information. And because I'm sure you've done all your homework, you are likely aware that the Graves Amendment bars vicarious liability claims against car rental agencies."

"I…uh…" *Dammit*. What was I thinking? I'd broken all the journalist rules: research, prepare, don't make it personal. This whole thing was a mistake, and I'd been presumptuous on top of it all. The gentleman didn't even look mad, but he was staring at me like I was wearing a hat made out of stuffed parakeets. And I didn't blame him. I was acting like the stereotype of a privileged private-school kid. "Of course, sir. I…I am sorry. I didn't mean to imply…" I turned to the young man, who had finished picking up the papers he'd dropped. He caught my eye and gave me the slightest nod, a look that was almost imperceptible. "I didn't mean to waste your time. I…I'm truly sorry," I said, backing away from the counter.

"That's all right, young lady. Live and learn. I'm sure you'll do your homework next time," the man said before turning from the counter and heading through a door marked OFFICE.

I locked eyes with the young man who was rearranging the receipts. He gave me a small knowing smile.

I headed out, the bell jingling again as I stepped through the door. As I slowly walked past the sandwich shop, I heard a voice behind me. "You forgot your mittens." I smiled to myself and turned around. The young man was holding my mittens out for me. He stepped closer. "Did you leave them on purpose?"

I shrugged. "Maybe?"

"You're #JusticeforJawad?"

I grinned. "You RyngofFyre?"

"Maybe?" He grinned back.

He took a step closer to me. "That Fred Nietzsche thing you mentioned? I remember. I'm not supposed to say anything, but I can't let this go. I remember because it was weird. We almost never get rich white guys like that in here. Especially not ones who pay with AmEx gift cards."

"Wait. Did you say guys? As in more than one?" My heart stopped. My fingers went numb. I couldn't even tell whether I was breathing anymore.

"Yeah. There were two guys. I remember. One of 'em was thin and had some funky glasses. He kept glancing around like he was about to get jumped. So ridiculous." The boy shook his head. "The other one was bigger, had on a hoodie from your school. It said *Captain* on it. Which made me laugh. Like, who wears that around like it's a big deal? That kid definitely thought he was the shit."

I reached into my bag and pulled out my phone with trembling fingers. "Is that one of them?" I asked, showing him the screenshot I'd taken of Nate from one of his birding videos.

He nodded. "Think so. Those green glasses. He kept adjusting them like a nervous tic or something. He also asked for our most expensive vehicle, the newest one we had. For real." He rolled his eyes. "The Chrysler we gave them was the same as the rest except it had a heated steering wheel, satellite stereo, and beverage warmer. No one ever wants to spend the extra seventy-five bucks for that package. I don't think anyone's taken it out since, either. January is our slow month."

I tightened my sweaty grip on the phone, searching for the selfie Richard had texted me that day he visited me at the store. I was afraid of what the answer was going to be. But there was no turning away from the truth now. This was way beyond the power of denial. I turned the screen back around to show the young man. "And this guy: Was he the other one?"

319

"Yeah! That's him. I'm pretty sure. How many captains does your swim team..." His voice trailed off. He looked up at me, then back at the photo. He was starting to understand what I was trying to wrap my mind around. The smiling kid in that photo was definitely a liar. And maybe a killer. And was a guy who was sending me selfies. And getting me garbage cookies. And taking me to the dance. I went numb.

All the things Richard had said to me played over and over in my head like a twisted montage now that I was seeing them with a new lens. *God.* When we thought Usman had seen Nate arguing by the loading dock...It wasn't Joel he was fighting with. It was Richard. *"You're having second thoughts now cuz of her? She doesn't scare me."* How was this real? Bile rose in the back of my throat as my body went cold and clammy all over.

"Thanks," I whispered, my mind shifting into some kind of automatic-response mode. "I...I'm going to have to tell the police."

"Yeah. Yeah. But you can't say where it came from, okay?"

"No worries. I'm a journalist. Even if I didn't sound like it when I was talking to your boss. I swear, I protect my sources."

The young man raised an eyebrow. "That applies even for high school papers?"

I nodded. "Of course it does. At least for me."

"Check your Reddit DMs in a minute. I'll send the receipt," he said as he started to walk back inside.

"Hey!" I called. He stopped and turned around. "What made you decide to help us?"

"I felt bad for that kid...Jawad. All he did was try to live his life. I couldn't stand by and stay quiet. Wanted to help if I could."

An ache grew in my chest. Jawad deserved people looking out for him. I wish he'd had that when he was alive. I waved at #RyngofFyre as he slipped back inside. My phone buzzed, a voice text from Asma: "#JusticeforJawad is trending in Chicago. Your article got picked up by a news outlet and is blowing up. It's got fifteen thousand views! Uh…I gotta go. There's a haggling situation going on with aunts and the tailor. I'll call when I get home. Be safe!"

I rubbed my thumb over my screen as I contemplated what to text Asma. What I should do next. The thought occurred to me that maybe we shouldn't be texting this stuff anymore. We needed to talk IRL. My phone buzzed again. This time it was Richard: Can we meet up? Need to talk.

My heart leaped to my throat. Richard had played me. He'd been in on it with Nate the whole time. Had they planned it all? The murder? Everything at school? Had all of it been a ruse? A sick joy ride? I plopped down on the curb. Tears I'd been holding back flowed down my face. My phone lit up with another text from Richard: Park across from Medici? 30 minutes?

I felt stuck, like a fly in amber, as I sat on the edge of the sidewalk. Every moment with Richard since we'd gotten back from break played like a jagged patchwork of scenes in my mind. Every look, every gesture, every word: a toxic lie. He'd been feeding me the poison they wanted me to swallow. And I'd fallen for it.

How had I not seen who he was? A fireball whirred in my chest. Guys like Richard and Nate—rich, connected, from "good families"—always got away with everything. I remembered the words of the former president, one who was from the same club as Nate and Richard—the silver-spoon, always-get-out-of-jail-free

321

club: *I could stand in the middle of the street and shoot someone and I wouldn't lose any voters. I'd still win.*

I wiped my tears on the back of my coat sleeve, stood up from the curb, and brushed myself off. I texted Richard back: Make it 45 minutes and bring cocoa.

I was terrified. I was angry. My body felt like it had shattered into a million pieces of blood and bone. I wasn't sure if I should be doing any of this, but I had to find the truth.

WCHI Radio News Roundup

This evening, a viral development in the murder case of fourteen-year-old Jawad Ali. A person or persons going by the name Justice for Jawad has penned an anonymous article linking the murder of Ali to acts of white supremacy in the area, including Nazi graffiti at DuSable Prep and a threatening message sent to a local mosque. The common thread? A seeming obsession with Nietzsche.

The group implored the public to reach out with any clues that might lead to apprehending the murderer, while decrying what they claim is insufficient action by Chicago PD.

Reached for comment, lead detective Will Diaz assured us the Chicago PD is working hard to solve the case. "We will find and bring the murderers to justice," he said. "We appreciate any tips from the public that can be called in anonymously to the Chicago PD tip line. But I must warn any armchair detectives out there—you know who you are—to leave the actual work to trained police. I am following up on a number of solid leads. We believe whoever murdered Jawad may still be in the area and they are highly dangerous."

A DM to the Justice for Jawad group asking for a comment received a short reply: "We know who did it. In a short time, the rest of the world will, too."

SAFIYA

JANUARY 20, 2022

Truth: Toxic behavior hides behind civility.

Lie: If you let yourself get manipulated, it's because you're weak.

On the bus ride back to my neighborhood, I texted Asma, even knowing she might not be free for a while. I told her I was meeting Richard but hadn't told her that maybe he was a murderer, too. I couldn't type that in a text. My fingers were so shaky as it was.

I quickly texted my parents that I'd be out late studying at the library. I hated lying to them, but I couldn't exactly tell them the truth, either. Not after everything that had already happened. The guy from the car rental DM'd us the receipt, and I forwarded it to Detective Diaz. I tried calling him, but it went to voice mail, so I left him a message.

Hi, um, Detective Diaz? This is Safiya…you know the one who found…the one from Jackson Park. I texted you a receipt from a car rental agency for a Chevy 200 rented the day before the murder to someone name Fred Nietzsche. Remember what I said about all the

Nietzsche quotes? And, uh, someone at the agency ID'd the two people who rented the car...Nate Chase and...Richard Reynolds. Look, I know you said to let the police handle everything but...[long pause] but I'm scared they'll get away. Richard and I were supposed to go to Winter Ball together and...and...I'm going to meet him at the park across from Medici. Now. Can you—

The bus dipped under the tracks, and I lost coverage toward the end of my message. I hoped he heard it all. I couldn't stomach calling back. If I called back and Detective Diaz answered, he'd try to talk me out of it. I was pretty much trying to talk myself out of it, too, but my body was moving forward. I couldn't let it go. Besides, it was still light out. And I was meeting him in public. I would be okay. And I couldn't let Jawad down. I needed to know the truth. To know why. There were so many whys. And the only one who could answer was Richard. And maybe the only one who could get him to answer was me.

January was the cruelest month. That was my most steadfast belief about winter. And this January was proving to be more horrible than I ever could have imagined. The park across from Medici was mostly empty; still, it was outside, in a public place. A few people hurried through, their heads down and collars up against the wind. Dark clouds had rolled in. The tot lot playground, usually so colorful and bursting with laughter and noise, was deserted. One of the kiddie swings moved back and forth listlessly, pushed by an invisible hand. Its chains squeaked. The breeze kicked up, blowing some loose strands of hair in my face. I sat down on a weathered red bench. It was the closest to the street, right under a lamp. It felt safe-ish. I closed my eyes and took a deep breath. That incense smell, that woodsy, smoky musk, swirled in the whispers around me.

Be careful, Safiya. He hurt me. He'll hurt you.

Richard was across the street, two takeaway cups in his hands, a blue scarf wrapped around his neck, the collar of his pea coat up. Looking at him, I felt the bile rise in my throat. When our eyes connected, he smiled. The wide charming smile that had fooled everyone. That had fooled me, sucked me in, made me believe. I tried to smile back. I couldn't give it away. Not yet. I had to act normal, happy to see him. That's what would keep me safe. But I'd always had the worst poker face.

He took leisurely strides over to me, making me wait. As if he could feel the tension in the air and wanted to draw it all out. The moment felt like a car crash. Like I was inside the car and time totally slowed and I was helplessly watching a truck barrel toward me. But it was also like I was a passerby on the sidewalk, witnessing everything happen in real time, in the seconds it took for the truck to T-bone the car. Time felt both too fast and too slow. I was in the moment and outside the moment, occupying two spaces at once. His footsteps boomed in sync with the thudding of my heart. I heard the swoosh of the blood rushing through my veins. I closed my eyes for the barest second to try and collect myself.

Then everything stopped. My heart. The blood in my veins. The creak of the swing. The clink and thud of cars going over the sewer cover in the middle of the intersection. I took a breath and forced myself to open my eyes. However confused I was, this was real and I had to face it.

"Extra whipped cream for you," Richard said, handing me one of the cups as he stood above me, a huge grin on his face.

His voice sounded so normal. He still wore that charming smile. Looked at me like I was the most important person in the world. It was chilling.

"Uh...sorry, spaced out for a sec. Thanks," I muttered, reaching out to accept the cup. Too hot to take a sip, so I wrapped my unmittened hands around it to warm my fingers and to bolster my courage. In the dark, with only the streetlamps for light, Richard looked menacing towering over me, but a second later, he plunked down beside me, scooting in closer than I wanted him to. I was almost at the edge of the bench. I couldn't move over without running out of seat. Last week, this is what I would've wanted. Us, smashed together, having cocoa on a winter night. It's weird how the thing I once hoped for was now freeze-my-blood terrifying. My God. He'd duped me so easily. He'd fooled us all.

Richard's shoulder leaned into mine. He looked out across the street and took a sip of his cocoa. It was silent for a long time. Not the companionable type of silence like when Asma and I were at the library studying together or when all the newspaper staff were sitting at a table editing stories. It was a silence that held the weight of secrets. Dangerous ones. And I think the reality of the situation was starting to press on me. What the hell was I thinking? I could imagine Asma screaming at me right now. The skies were darkening, the clouds getting heavier. This was a stupid, risky decision. I'd moved

327

my phone to my coat pocket and I snuck a look: 15 percent battery left. No new texts.

"Expecting someone?" Richard asked with a sidelong glance. "I was hoping I'd finally get you alone." It was a casual enough remark, and under different circumstances it might have even played as flirty, but right now every word he spoke felt like a con. Like his game of cloak-and-dagger was finally transparent.

"Asma said she'd swing by and give me a ride home." Asma and I hadn't connected before I got here, and I was wishing we had because this lie would become apparent pretty soon.

"I can give you a ride home. Happy to be alone in my car with you," Richard said as he gently moved a stray hair from my cheek. I held my breath as the tips of his fingers brushed against my skin. Being alone in his car was absolutely the last place I wanted to be. I couldn't shake the feeling that he knew how his words seemed innocent but sounded sinister. Like he was toying with me. Enjoying the game. Enjoying seeing me so nervous. It gave him control. He still hadn't dropped his smile.

I took a deep breath. Then another. The empty playground swing creaked louder. For a second there was the echo of dull footsteps behind us, but when I glanced over my shoulder, the park was empty.

Then I heard Jawad's voice:

His kindness is a lie. His words are hollow. He likes it when you're scared.

I drew my phone out of my pocket again, began typing out a text to Asma. "I'm telling her we're here," I said in as singsongy a voice as I could. By Medici is all I managed to type out before Richard reached over and gently nudged my phone away. So casual. Like it wasn't aggressive. Like it wasn't all about him wanting control.

"I said I'd love to give you a ride." His face broke into a wide grin.

"Sure, yeah," I said, slipping my phone back in my pocket, fumbling to try and send off the text. I couldn't even check to see if it had been delivered. "Asma and I have a few things to finalize for a spread we're doing for the *Spectator*." I was working so hard to unclench my jaw when I spoke, I was sure he could tell I was lying.

"Cool. What's it about?"

"Huh?"

"The spread you're working on. What's it about?"

"Oh, umm, pizza." Wow. Could I possibly have chosen something less believable. At least I didn't say rainbows and unicorns. Where was my brain?

"Pizza. You are doing a spread on pizza? That's not exactly your usual."

"Well, Hardy clamped down on freedom of the press at school, so…"

"Yeah. Like I said, he really has it in for you. Guess he's sick of your liberal rag."

I paused. "Huh?"

"I'm saying that's how *he* thinks of the paper. But I'm surprised you're not trying to write about Ghost Skin. Or about that kid's murder. Aren't you kind of, like, obsessed with getting justice for Jawad?"

There it was. He knew. It was chilling how nonchalant he could be. He wore a mask like a second skin.

Every muscle in my body tensed. I took a deep breath in. Tried to calm myself down, which felt impossible since my heart was like a jackhammer in my chest. He was opening a door. Fine. Time for me to bust it down. I turned away for a second and pretended to spill a bit of my cocoa on myself. "Dammit," I said as I handed Richard my drink, then reached into my pocket. "I think I have a tissue. Hang on." I fumbled around but managed to click the side and volume buttons on my phone to make the SOS bar appear. I quickly slid right. I'd never used that phone function before, but it was supposed to send 911 your location and ping your emergency contact, too. Mine was Asma. We'd set up that function together, and I'd meant to add other contacts, like my parents, but had kinda forgotten about it. Never thought I'd need it.

Since I didn't have a tissue, I made a big deal of pulling my mitten from my pocket and using it as a napkin. It was ridiculous, but it was buying me some time.

"Why wouldn't I want his murderers brought to justice? It's what any decent human being would want." My chest tightened as I spoke. Richard looked straight ahead, then glanced down the street.

"So you think it was more than one murderer?"

"Is there a reason you'd know different?"

Richard chuckled. Then placed the cups in his hands on the sidewalk in front of him. "It's logical, isn't it? Only one person could have killed him. The other person would be driving the car while the murder occurred. Hypothetically speaking."

The blood froze in my veins. I bit the side of my cheek and felt a trickle of blood in my mouth. "Yes, they would be," I said slowly. "If you assumed they'd killed him in the car. And then dumped his body after they murdered him. Hypothetically speaking."

Scream, Safiya. Run.

He was here. Jawad. I couldn't explain. I didn't understand it. I had no idea how it was possible. But that potent woodsy, musky incense smell caught in the breeze and swirled around us. It was in the bare branches that swayed in the trees behind us. In the few dry leaves that formed a tiny tornado at our feet. There was the thunderous sound of a branch falling in a gust of wind near the playground. The chains of the empty swing creaked louder, like they were screeching into the night.

I stood up abruptly, peering down the street, looking for help that didn't seem to be coming. "Crap," I said louder than necessary. "I... uh...bet our drinks are ice cold. Cold cocoa is the worst! Let's get refills at Medici." I started bouncing on my toes. My body was saying to run, but part of me was saying to stall, maybe Detective Diaz would come. I should've tried calling him again. I began inching away from the bench, my brain spiraling. The ground under my feet started to sway.

Richard grabbed my left hand. Hard. "Hang on. I wanted to talk, remember?" His voice was still so calm, almost sweet.

"Cool. We can grab a table and chat inside." I tried to pull my hand away, but he squeezed it, twisting my wrist.

"No. I think here is good."

"Let go of me." I wanted to scream those words but they came out like a raspy whisper. I couldn't even tell if I was breathing anymore. I couldn't feel any air moving through my lungs.

Richard was still smiling up at me. Smiling. As he twisted my hand, sending sharp pains shooting up my arm.

Run, Safiya. Fight for yourself.

And then, for a split second, the scene distorted, like I was looking at us—at myself—through a glass of water. I muttered a prayer as I clenched my right hand into a fist and swung at Richard's face. He didn't see it coming, and when I connected with his nose, bone hitting bone, there was a horrifying crunch as an electric shock reverberated through my arm. He yelped and pulled his hand to his face. I drew back, stumbled a few steps toward the sidewalk, and righted myself. My mouth opened to cry out, scream, but I couldn't hear my voice.

"You dirty raghead!" he howled.

I glanced over my shoulder and saw him stand up, sway a bit as he stepped into a pool of light from the streetlamp. Blood smeared his face; his eyes filled with rage. My legs felt like lead, my hand throbbed, but I forced myself to move. A car sped down the street, and I jumped off the curb, waving my hands, trying to flag it down, but the driver laid on the horn and swerved around me.

No! Dammit!

I heard the rumble of an engine starting from a car that was parallel parked, and then the headlights flipped on, blinding me for a second.

Behind me I heard Richard laughing. "It's. All. Happening," he mocked, drawing out the words.

I squinted at the car that screeched as it reversed to get out of the spot. A white Mercedes. License plate FWL PLAY 60615. My heart exploded in my chest. It was Nate. I ran across the street to the other sidewalk and headed in the opposite direction from where Nate's car was facing, but that meant I was moving away from Medici and my chance to run inside for help. The sidewalk was empty, lined with large apartment buildings. I ran to one and slammed my hand against every buzzer, hoping someone would let me in. *C'mon. C'mon. Someone.* I glanced back to see Richard motioning to Nate to turn the car around. Richard caught my eye and sprinted down the street toward me, slowing to squeeze between two parked cars.

My panicky breaths came hard and fast. I left the apartment building and raced down the sidewalk. I saw Nate's headlights barreling toward me, the wrong way down the one-way street. Richard was so close, I could hear his heaving breaths. I stumbled off the curb, but he grabbed at my collar, yanking me toward him. I slammed into him and we both fell backward onto the grassy strip by the sidewalk. I tried to scramble away, first on all fours and then standing, but Richard pulled at my leg and I went down hard on my right side. Pain blasted through my shoulder and hip. He grabbed for me and I kicked at him, making contact with his shin as he dropped down closer to me. I tried to push myself off the ground with my left hand, but Richard shoved me back, straddling me to keep me pinned down.

Icy drizzle began to fall. The drying blood under his nose and cheek mingled with the rain and streamed down his chin. He wiped it away with the back of his hand, and it was only then that I saw his fingers curled around a rock. I heard a voice in my ear, barely a whisper, a breath against my skin.

Fight, Safiya. Fight. Help is coming.

But how? How was I supposed to fight? I could barely muster the strength to breathe.

"Is that what you did to him?" I forced myself to speak even as I started to shiver and felt my knees and legs grow weak. "To Jawad?

What did he ever do to you?" In the distance I heard a siren. So far away, I couldn't tell where it was heading. In my ear, the whisper. Swirls of incense rising like smoke in the rain.

"It wasn't personal. It was necessary. Can't let you all steal everything."

"What are you talking about? I'm not stealing anything. You don't have to do this. Let me go."

Richard grinned. Nate's car pulled up next to the curb. If they pulled me into that car, I knew it would be the last place I'd ever see. I clawed at the dirt, trying to find a rock, a shard of broken glass, anything. The freezing rain started to fall harder now; it felt like tiny pellets of ice on my skin. I couldn't breathe. I was too terrified to look at Richard, but I was also too scared to turn away.

A glassy-eyed look fell over him, his face almost serene. Richard's voice was so even again. Collected. "It was always Us against Them. And you're a Them. Every single one of your SJW Be the Change pleas? Your bullshit talk about justice? About affirmative action leveling the playing field? What's fair about you people taking our spots in college, places you haven't earned? You want special treatment. You want to eliminate our rights. Erase us. That's the real racism in this country, right there."

"What? This is about you not getting into Harvard? I don't... Why...why did you even ask me to the dance? Act like you liked me? Like you understood me." The sirens were getting closer. I prayed they were for me. I didn't know if Richard could even hear them; he seemed like he was in his own world. Nate was in the car, motor running, waving frantically at Richard.

"Infiltrate. Keep your enemies close." He grinned, then shook his head. "You're so weak. So blind. You never saw me watching you when you broke into Nate's locker, overhearing you and your stupid friends wonder if that chump Joel was in on it. Or Hardy?" He paused and let out a little laugh. "You and your cute Justice for Jawad article? What a joke. At first toying with you was fun, but now I'm bored."

All along I'd thought it was Nate masterminding the whole thing, getting Joel's help. But Richard was right. I hadn't seen what was right in front of me. I hadn't seen how he'd set it all up, lied, manipulated me, made me doubt myself. How he'd hidden in plain sight. The passenger-side window in Nate's car rolled down. "Hurry up! Get her in the car. Someone is going to notice," he hissed.

I was not going to get into that car.

I dug my nails into the cold, wet earth and grabbed a fistful of dirt and flung it into Richard's eyes. He reeled back and I pushed myself away from him, my body screaming in pain as I struggled to stand. He lunged for me, grabbed me, shoved me against the hood of Nate's car. There was a rage in his eyes as he raised the rock above me.

"Not here, dude!" Nate yelled from inside the car.

Richard didn't seem to hear Nate, because his eyes were laser focused on me. "Please don't," I begged. "Please."

"You must have chaos within you to give birth to a rising star." I recognized Richard's words. They were from that Nietzsche book, and he was reciting them like a prayer.

A car careened around the corner, its headlights dipping as it turned, then flashed at us, its bright beams on.

Move. It's not over, Safiya. You're still here. Fight.

Richard raised a hand to shade his eyes as the driver laid on the horn. A light came on inside the car. Asma. The window rolled down. "Move!" She screamed as she sped up. The sirens were louder now. They were right here.

I rolled off the hood and onto the ground, clawing away, a second before Asma steered her car and crashed it into Nate's. There was a crunch of metal on metal. A shower of broken glass. Screams. Red and blue lights flashed along the street as my body fell limp into the mud. As my eyes were closing, I heard a whisper on the wind…

JAWAD

You're okay, Safiya. You'll be okay. Breathe. You're not alone. They're all coming.

You were the only one who saw me. Who reminded me I was a real boy.

You are the girl who made me feel safe. You are the girl who remembered me. Who wouldn't let them forget.

Thank you.

Thank you.

Thank you.

PART VII

ETERNAL RETURN: FALLOUT OF A MURDER

SAFIYA

JANUARY 25, 2022

Truth: Sometimes, in real life, the bad guys win. But being a good guy means you keep fighting, anyway.

On a bright afternoon, when I was seven, maybe eight, I was reading at the table by the window in my parents' store. I loved sitting there on sunny weekends while my parents worked; sometimes my nose was buried in a book, sometimes I colored. Sometimes I did both. There was always this cheery din of customers, the old-fashioned bell ringing as they came in and went out. My parents chatting with them in Hindi or Urdu or English. Sometimes my mom would even bust out her rusty Telugu or Bangla. Every weekend there would also be someone new, a family or maybe a couple, who would come in, really excited, thrilled that they found a local desi grocery store. They would ask, almost breathlessly, *Do you carry Patak's mango pickle, extra spicy?* Or *Lamsa chocolate tea?* Or *A cast-iron tawa like my nani used to make parathas?* I especially loved listening to my dad respond to them: *My dear madam, our store has the answer to your dreams.* I always giggled when I heard him talk like that.

My mom would check in on me, and when my parents were having afternoon chai, she would bring me a very milky version in my own small mug. My parents never drank chai out of foam cups or coffee tumblers. They were snobs for actual mugs, even in the store. And if there were customers around, my mom always asked if they wanted chai, too, and then would disappear into the back, re-emerging with a steaming cup. I couldn't remember how many afternoons I'd spent like that.

But one old, forgotten afternoon finally floated back to me. I heard a loud voice outside: a man, with a face full of hate, teeth bared, yelling at an auntie in hijab and her little boy. My dad rushed out of the store; my mom was in the back making tea. My dad urged them into the store for safety. The auntie had an accent, but it wasn't Indian; I wasn't sure what it was. She was crying. The wavy-haired little boy with light-tan skin was clutching his mom's hand.

When my mom heard my dad calling her, she rushed out. I couldn't hear everything the adults were saying to each other. I remembered turning back to my book because when I made eye contact with my mom, she gave me one of those reassuring mom smiles, telling me everything was okay. I always believed her because she told the truth. Because little kids believe the things adults tell them, until at some point they grow out of it. I went back to my book—a fantasy. I loved reading fantasy when I was little. I loved how the worlds drew you in. How sometimes things got scary, but there was a hero my age, a kid, who could change the world. And the bad guys always lost.

I was so engrossed in the story, I didn't notice the little boy who was standing by my table until I heard his sobs. They weren't loud, but they were deep. Fat tears slowly rolled down his cheeks. I remember feeling bad for him. He looked like he was in nursery school. I handed him a napkin. I asked him his name. He didn't say anything. Just stood there, wiping tears away. Rubbing his eyes. I waited for him to answer, but he didn't. Maybe he was too scared. Maybe we didn't speak the same language.

"It's okay," I told him. "You're okay now. It's safe in here." I don't think he believed me because when I said those things it made him cry again. And then, I don't know what made me do this but I reached into my little purse—I used to carry that butterfly purse everywhere—and pulled out my hand of Fatima key chain. An aunt in India had given it to me, right before we got on the airplane to leave, last time we were there. *It will keep you safe*, she'd said as she pressed it into my hand. *Keep it with you always, for protection.* It was a tiny silver hand with a blue and white bead in the middle. I'd tucked it away in a small pocket inside my purse and pretty much forgotten it was even there until I saw that scared little boy, crying. He needed it more than I did, so I reached into my purse, dug it out, and handed it to him, showed him how to hook it onto the belt loop of his jeans. I echoed the words my aunt had told me: *It will keep you safe.*

He looked up at me and smiled. One of those giant grins that take up most of a little kid's face. Then he sat with me at the table and colored until his mom called to him and they left. I waved as they stepped out of the store.

I'd forgotten about that moment.

343

Until I saw that key chain attached to Jawad's belt loop as they lifted his body onto the stretcher. He'd kept it this whole time. That broke my heart.

It's weird how memory works. How it's impossible to know what you've forgotten until a cobwebby string of the past gets plucked. *It will keep you safe*, I'd said.

I was only a little kid myself, but I knew how to make someone feel better. I repeated things adults told me when I was sad. What if all I'd sold him was a lie? But sitting there, body bruised, heart shattered, I knew I couldn't change the past no matter how badly I wanted to. Richard and Nate murdered Jawad. They stole his whole life. I couldn't wish that truth away. What I had to do was make sure Jawad was remembered as more than a victim. What I could do was remember him, always.

January 20, 2022

ARRESTS IN MURDER OF REFUGEE STUDENT

Breaking: Chicago police arrest local teens suspected in the kidnapping and murder of fourteen-year-old Jawad Ali, whose arrest at school for bringing in a jet pack mistaken for an explosive garnered him the moniker of Bomb Boy. Detectives were later seen entering two homes in the Kengrove neighborhood, an area of gated mansions, home to some of Chicago's most connected and wealthy families.

This story is developing.

Here are Jawad's own words, a transcript of his recording for Bethune High School's *Voices Carry: Oral Histories* pop-up. I'm not going to lie. I didn't want to listen to his voice. I thought it was going to be too much. That putting a voice to his face, the open eyes, the scratches on his cheeks, the trickle of dried blood by his lips, would give me nightmares. Keep me up at night. The truth is, I haven't slept well in sixteen months. The truth is, I already knew Jawad's voice. Besides, I've been haunted every night since the day I found his body in Jackson Park.

An American Dream

BY JAWAD ALI

When we decided to move to this country...No, that's not it. "Decided" isn't the right word. It's not like we had a choice. I definitely didn't—I was only two years old. Mama and Baba had to flee the war in Iraq that no one asked for but that came anyway. It was home, but home was one war after another, my dad says. Until they all bled into one, my mom says. So much blood. People were hungry. Kids were dying. And the explosions sounded louder and every day came closer to what was left of our town. Bombs and drones weren't the only danger, though.

Baba was an English professor at the university before it shut down, and when the coalition forces came, he took a test and became a translator and got paid $300 a month. It doesn't seem like a lot in this country. But it was enough for our small family to live on while we also helped out my grandparents and my two aunts. All my dad wanted to do was help people understand each other. To not get killed for stupid reasons, for the wrong words. Words matter, he always says. Words are what we are.

Mama says they lived in fear all the time, especially after I was born. There were rumors that Baba was a spy for the Americans. But he wasn't telling on his friends or neighbors or imprisoning them. He just wanted people not to get killed. Sometimes he would disappear for days, weeks at a time, on a mission with the Americans in some secret location. And Mama couldn't be sure if he was even alive. But she always held out hope. Hope is what kept her breathing, she told me. One breath after another. Hope is her gift.

One day, Baba came home in the middle of the night. He told my mom to grab whatever she could carry in a backpack. They bundled me up. Left Iraq forever. Then we went to Jordan. For six months, we waited for a special visa to the United States. Baba hoped we could live free from fear here. From grenades. From drone strikes. From the war that was our everyday lives. It seems weird to go to the place that was bombing our country, but Mama says we didn't have any choices left. We were down to our last dollars when the paperwork finally came through. When we finally got to America, all we had were the clothes on our backs, the shoes on our feet, my small elephant stuffie, and my mom's never-ending hope.

I don't remember anything about Iraq. About the bombs or the screams that my parents still have nightmares about. We've never been back. Not even when my grandparents died so close together and my dad wondered if the sacrifices had been worth it. I heard my mom whisper to him once in Arabic: *Look at Jawad. What life could we have given him there, running from drones and their bombs. Here he goes to school every day and I don't fear he'll never come home as I feared so many times for you. Here he isn't human collateral.*

Then their voices got quiet.

My mom was a nurse in Iraq. My dad, a professor. Here, they just bought the dry cleaner shop they've been working at since we arrived. Six days a week. Every week. Every month. Every year. When they come home, they smell like Greener Earth cleaner and plastic and stale steam. Every night, Mama soaks her hands in oil she scents with rose water. On weekends and holidays now, I help at the store. But my parents don't want me to take over the business. They want me to go to college. To live a different kind of life where I don't work with my hands. But I like working with my hands. I like tinkering. Inventing. But I think I get what they mean.

They tell me over and over again that I am their American dream.

Dream big.

Work hard.

Don't let the hate others feel for you into your heart.

In America, they say, anything is possible.

A Knot of Lies: The Truth about the Murder of Jawad Ali

Section 2, Confessions and Other Statements: Nate Chase

January 20, 2022, 9:35 p.m.

Detective Diaz: To begin, this conversation is being recorded, as per Illinois statute. Please state, for the record, your name and age.

Nate: Nathaniel Chase Jr. But I go by Nate. I'm seventeen. I turn eighteen next week.

Diaz: The arresting officer informed you of your Miranda rights and you have agreed to speak to me and Detective Crowe without a lawyer present.

Detective Crowe: Attempts have been made to contact your parents.

Nate: You know who my dad is, right? Alderman Chase.

Crowe: We are aware.

Nate: As my dad always says, the innocent have nothing to hide. [*smiles*] Go ahead.

Crowe: Your parents are at your second home in Michigan, it seems.

Nate: I'm sure they're on their way and heads will roll when they get here.

349

Diaz: [*clears throat*] You're wearing glasses. Do you wear them all the time?

Nate: Starting with the tough questions, huh? [*chuckles*] Yeah, pretty much all the time.

Crowe: Do you have more than one pair of glasses?

Nate: I mean, yeah. I've got like four, maybe five. Who only has one pair?

Diaz: And you're a...um...birder? Is that correct? You have a YouTube Channel.

Nate: [*scoffs*] With over a hundred thousand subscribers. I'm not *just* a birder. The *New Yorker* called me "Audubon for the Gen Z set." I'm published in major nature journals. The *Tribune* did a whole spread on me.

Diaz: And do you wear your glasses when birding?

Nate: I said all the time. Except for when I'm sleeping and in the shower.

Diaz: Why don't you get contacts? I'm sure you can afford them.

Nate: Obviously. But my glasses are, like, my signature look. My prescription's not strong, and I barely even need to wear them. But it's part of my birder uniform, my brand.

Diaz: Do you ever buy custom frames? Frames made solely for you?

Nate: [*rolls eyes*] I know what "custom" means. And yes, I said they were my signature piece. You can't have a signature piece if you're a lemming. Each of my frames is unique.

Diaz: And did you ever purchase one of those, um, *signature pieces* from Chelsea Optixx in London?

Nate: Yes, I bought a pair from there. But you obviously know that or you wouldn't be asking me these asinine questions.

Diaz: A green pair? Ones you wore in some of those birding videos?

Nate: [*nods*]

Crowe: Please answer, yes or no.

Nate: Yes.

Diaz: And where is that unique, one-of-a-kind green pair of glasses right now?

Nate: Probably my bathroom? My bedroom? I don't know. Not like I keep a log of where I left them.

Crowe: Detectives are searching your home right now.

Nate: [*fidgets in chair, stays quiet*]

Diaz: Are these your glasses?

Crowe: [*pushes photos across table of glasses in evidence*]

Nate: I can't say for sure. I mean, they could be. They look...uh...similar. But no. I don't know.

Crowe: But aren't they unique to you? Yours alone?

Nate: Yeah, but I don't have a photographic memory or anything. They could be any green glasses. Maybe they look like mine, but so what? They're glasses. Not fingerprints.

Diaz: So...they were found at the murder scene by Jackson Park and we were able to lift prints off them. Did they fall off when you were dumping the body or did you lose them when you went back to the scene of the crime?

Nate: [*looks down*] Can one of you get me some coffee?

Nothing But the Night Podcast

May 2023

Interview Excerpt: Safiya Mirza

Host: Can you tell us what was going through your mind at that moment, when you confronted Richard?

Safiya: Honestly, some of it feels like a blur—especially now, nearly a year and a half later. Sometimes when I look back, it seems like it happened so fast. Other times, I see it like it's in slow motion. Like I'm watching it outside of myself. Mostly I remember his face—Richard's—it changed in a split instant. He pulled off the mask, the one he wore all the time, I guess. He convinced everyone that the fiction he created was real.

Host: But you didn't feel Nate was wearing a mask? Hiding things?

Safiya: Oh, no. No. I mean, he definitely was hiding things. That's the whole ghost skin philosophy, right? Hide who you are, blend in, be insidious, spread your toxicity, but be charming, be perfect. And gaslight anyone who sees through you. Nate did that, too. He used his friend Joel that way, like a decoy. But Richard was better at it. An expert. He got along with everyone. Was super popular. Teachers loved him. He's the devil we all knew but didn't recognize. He's still working that charm even now. I mean, look at the press coverage, all the people fawning over him after he was arrested. He gets love letters in jail. It's sick.

Host: You think that was because of his charm? Good looks?

Safiya: That and the fact that rich, connected white boys couldn't possibly be the bad guys, right? Even when they were clearly guilty. Even when they admit it, they're still given another chance. Kid of an alderman and another from a major philanthropist family? C'mon. They get a thousand chances, really. Remember that rapist from Stanford? Newspaper headlines referred to him as the "Swimmer from Stanford," even after he was found guilty. Honor students, athletes—that's how the press talks about Nate and Richard. It's not their mugshots you see everywhere. It's their airbrushed senior photos, their posed varsity team pics. But if you're Black you get blamed for your own murder because you're a "thug," even when all you were doing was wearing a hoodie or holding your own cell phone or sleeping in your own bed. If you're Mexican, people call you "illegal." When you're Muslim, everyone assumes you're a terrorist. That's what happened to Jawad. The media doesn't want to investigate its own bias, its own culpability.

Host: Is that why you're going to journalism school?

Safiya: Partly. Look, a free press is foundational to our democracy. But it's an institution and racism is built in. Also, I love finding and telling stories that are forgotten—being a journalist gives me power to do that.

Host: Before the trial, both Nate and Richard pointed the finger at each other for the actual murder. Who do you think is guilty?

Safiya: Both of them, as far as I'm concerned. Them blaming each other for the actual act of the murder? I one-hundred-percent believe that was part of their plan, too, to confuse the jury, create a shadow of a doubt.

Host: The verdict is about to come down. Do you think you'll get justice for Jawad as you wanted?

Safiya: I hope so...for Jawad's parents. For society, too, I guess. But there is no real justice for Jawad, is there? No matter what the verdict is. No matter how long they would serve. They're alive. Jawad isn't. We might get accountability, but it won't be justice. What's justice for a murdered kid?

A Knot of Lies: The Truth about the Murder of Jawad Ali

Section 2, Confessions and Other Statements: Richard Reynolds

January 20, 2022, 10:01 p.m.

While police were processing Chase and Reynolds, they impounded the
vehicle that the two used when luring Jawad Ali into the car. Police were able
to quickly locate the car rental agency based on a tip that had come in shortly
prior to the arrest.

Detective Diaz: We are recording this interview as per Illinois statute.
Please state your name and age for the record.

Richard: Took you long enough. Now which one of you is the good cop
and which one is the bad cop? Let me guess. Diaz? You're the mean one.

Detective Crowe: State your name and age for the record.

Richard: Richard Reynolds, eighteen years old.

Diaz: Richard, you have chosen to speak to us without a lawyer present
and have consented to this interview. Is that correct?

Richard: Yup. [*leans back in chair*]

Crowe: At this point, I want to make you aware that we have recovered
the rental vehicle—a Chevy 200 rented under the name Fred

Nietzsche from Anderson Car Rental. Are you familiar with that rental agency?

Richard: I have a car. And even a driver, if I want. I don't need a rental from some crappy rental place on the West Side.

Crowe: So you are aware of the location of Anderson's.

Richard: Wow. You got me. I've seen their ads on the sides of buses. Brilliant detective work on your part, really. You should ask for a raise.

Crowe: [*clears throat*] You thought you were being smart, huh? Cleaning up the vehicle?

Richard: I have no idea what you're talking about.

Crowe: You didn't do such a good job though. I guess you're used to other people cleaning up your mess. Our investigators sprayed the car seats with luminol, lit up like a Christmas tree. They found plenty of blood spatter on the passenger and back seats, the seat belts, too. DNA results on the blood should be back soon.

Diaz: We should maybe mention that we picked up some prints, too. They're harder to wipe away than you might think. We heard you hate wearing gloves, huh? Don't even own a pair? Seems like this would be an opportune time to share anything you might know. Before we really start digging around. While you still have a chance to be in our good graces.

Richard: [*scoffs, pushes back chair*] Look...I know how this works. I know what entrapment is. You can say anything you want in here. It's all lies. I don't have anything else to add besides that. I'm going to go ahead and wait for my parents to show with a lawyer.

Crowe: Fine. Fine. But it might interest you to know that Nate confessed to being in the car at the time of Jawad Ali's murder. Further, he contends that he was merely driving the vehicle and that you, Richard, were the one who killed Jawad Ali with a blow to the back of the head and then proceeded to suffocate him with a scarf while Nate drove. He also asserts that you cleaned and returned the vehicle, alone.

Richard: Bullshit.

Diaz: Look, Richard, your friend Nate pinned it all on you. Says you're the mastermind. Says you were the Nietzsche fanatic. Says you introduced him to WRA: White Resistance Army. *Recruited* was the word he used. You lured him in.

Richard: [*slams fist on table*] That is absolute bullshit! I didn't lay a hand on that sand— Nate picked him. Wanted to go after him. Sent those texts after the Bomb Boy thing. The fake ransom? The vandalism? The swastika? It was all him.

Diaz: He says the opposite. Said you called it a game, that's why you toyed with Safiya, wanted her as your plaything, that's why you hacked the school newspaper. He said you bought the burner phones. Said you picked the spot to dump the body and—

Richard: That fucking liar! That weak piece of shit. He did it! All of it! I never laid a hand on that raghead skittle. All I did was drive.

"BRILLIANT," "ATHLETIC," STRAIGHT-A STUDENTS INDICTED ON MURDER CHARGES

Eighteen-year-old Richard Reynolds and seventeen-year-old Nathan "Nate" Chase, both seniors at DuSable Preparatory High School, were arrested Wednesday for the murder of fourteen-year-old Jawad Ali, an Iraqi refugee who gained notoriety for his own arrest when a teacher mistakenly thought he had brought a bomb to his school.

Chase, the son of alderman Ted Chase, and Reynolds, the scion of one of Chicago's wealthiest families, are described as "fine young men" by teachers and neighbors. Both families reside in Kengrove, a wealthy, tight-knit community of manicured lawns and mansions. Many wondered if the police had made a grave mistake. "I refuse to believe either of these outstanding students could have committed such a heinous act," James Hardy, principal of DuSable Preparatory High School, said. "I've known these boys and their families for years, and both of them have bright futures ahead. I truly worry for their mental and emotional health in this era of social media lynch-mob justice and cancel culture." When reached for comment, Felicity Reynolds, Richard's aunt, who recently began a term on the school's board of directors, said, "My nephew doesn't have a racist bone in his body. That's not how he was raised."

Social justice activists are dismayed that initial charges did not carry a hate crime designation. "If you're white and wealthy, this state bends over backward to find you innocent, even if you're guilty. Even when you confess," Regina Thompson, social media director for Chicago Advocates of Color, tweeted.

A source inside the police department tells us that it was another high school student who first raised alarms with police about Chase, connecting him to a newspaper hack and anti-Semitic graffiti at DuSable Prep. Defendants are expected to be arraigned next month.

JAWAD

They finally let my parents bury me. So much later than my parents wanted. So much later than was fair. For them or for me.

They whispered their tearful prayers over me in their choked-up voices. I felt their love. And I felt light. Finally, warmth. I wasn't cold anymore. And I smelled something sweet and soft, like roses. It was the first moment in so long that I felt safe, felt quiet. Like I could rest. That's when I knew I could finally say goodbye:

As-Salaamu-Alaikum, Mama and Baba. Peace be with you. You were good parents. So, so good. I knew I was loved. I know I am loved. Forever.

I promise I will be with you always. In a good way. Like a hug that never ends. The kind that you can still feel even though the person who hugged you isn't there anymore.

I know you're sad right now. More sad than you've ever been. Even sadder than when you left your home and family to come to America. But I hope you smile again.

Do you remember how I would ask if the lake went on forever, if it melted into the sky? Because way far away all the blues met each other? Maybe you can go to the lake and remember how when I was little I loved playing right at the edge of the shore. I'd run away from the waves when they came up on the sand, pretending they were chasing me. I remember one time we all laughed so much when our clothes got wet even though we'd rolled up our pants. I was so little. I think that might be my first memory of laughter. I hope you go to the lake sometimes. Remember me laughing, okay? Remember us laughing.

Twitter

@Chitownnews
Breaking: $2 million bail ordered for Chicago teens accused in "Bomb Boy" murder. Defendants released despite strong objection from state's attorney, parents of victim.

@WindyCityTrending
#FelonCrushFridays #hotconvict trend as mugshots of Richard Reynolds and Nathaniel Chase go viral after their arrest for the murder of Jawad Ali.

@Grown60614
Talk about #hotconvict did you see the million-dollar smile on that Richard Reynolds. I know he may be a murderer, but damn 🔥 🔥 🔥 #FCF #FelonCrushFridays

@BellowsBae
We have a new candidate for #feloncrushfridays everyone. Look at that pout! Those chiseled cheekbones! *faints* #hotconvict #fcf

@smoakee
Baby boo convict can step on my neck anytime. #FCF #feloncrushfridays #HotConvict

@proudgirl

These hometown heroes are making our nation great again.
And they're hot, too. LOL. #fcf #monga #whitelivesmatter

@chinowdefender

One less cockroach in the world thanks to #hotconvicts. Cry
more, snowflakes.

SAFIYA

JANUARY 22, 2022

Truth: I am my brother's keeper.

"It's disgusting," I said, throwing my phone facedown on my comforter after scanning through all the #hotconvict and #feloncrushfriday posts from the last day and a half that fawned all over Richard and Nate. Mostly Richard. Asma shook her head. She sat at the foot of my bed, her face red and bruised, a part of the bandage on her right arm exposed beneath the cuff of her sweater. After she'd crashed into Nate's car to save me, she'd gotten some scrapes when the airbag deployed. And then when she rushed out to see if I was okay, she slipped and slid into some broken glass, getting a gash bad enough for stitches.

I fared a bit worse. Hairline rib fracture that hurt anytime I took a deep breath. Contusions all over my body. A sprained wrist. A giant scrape on my face that they had to pick tiny glass shards out of in the ER. And a dislocated shoulder, which the doctor fixed with a "closed reduction," basically popping my shoulder back in place. It made a sound that I never ever want to hear again. Holy hell, it hurt. But every bruise, scrape, and fracture, my currently immobilized shoulder, all of it, all of it, was worth it to see Richard and Nate get arrested.

After I woke up in the hospital, my terrified parents at my side, I realized it wasn't like TV shows when the arrest is the end of the episode. The arrest was the beginning in a way. And maybe there would never be an end.

"Jawad's life didn't matter to them," I said. "It barely mattered to anyone."

"It did to you," Asma said. "Enough to almost get yourself…"

She trailed off. We both knew what she was going to say. I saw it in her face when she walked into my room earlier. We both sat on the edge of my bed and cried. And then we were silent for a long time. Asma had saved me. I guessed the weight of that debt would stay with me forever, as much as I knew Asma didn't see it as a debt; she saw it as friendship.

Adults are always saying that teenagers don't have real perspective because we haven't lived long enough to put miles between us and the past. But this was one moment when that would be wrong. We didn't need distance to understand that the knot of secrets we'd started to untangle would keep trying to retie itself, over and over. In different ways. Different people. Same lies.

"I'm scared," I whispered.

"I know. Me too, but even if they make bail, I think you'll be safe."

"I think you mean *when* they make bail. Their daddies could pay all cash, unlike most people, like the ones forced to rot in jail waiting for trial because they stole, like, a backpack and don't have thousands of dollars to pay up. But that's not what I'm scared of. I'm scared they'll get away with it," I said, pulling at loose threads of my faded kantha quilt.

"They already have, in a way," Asma whispered. "They're so connected and—"

"They have the best lawyers money can buy," I finished her sentence. "I can't deal with all the gross tweets about Richard being hot. They haven't even called it a hate crime yet! I wish—" A yawn interrupted my thought. The doctor told me I had to take a few days off. Even if I wanted to go to school, I was too tired to get out of bed. It's like every ounce of my energy had been spent and my body had to rebuild itself from the cellular level up.

Asma gently hugged me goodbye and reminded me to text Usman and Rachel, who were going bananas worrying about me. I still didn't feel ready to see anyone else. I switched off my lamp and settled into my bed, even though it was only 3:00 p.m. My mom would come and get me for dinner. My mom had hovered around me the last two days until I told her it was hard for me to get any rest with her constantly asking me if I needed anything. She and Dad felt helpless. I related.

Detective Diaz had checked up on me when I was in the ER. After he gave me a stern warning to never ever get involved in a police investigation again, he thanked me for sending him what I'd found. "We'll nail them," he promised.

I wished I felt that confident. I told him everything I knew, recounted every detail except one: my ghost. Jawad. He was with me in the creak of that swing, in the wind that kicked up the leaves, and in my ear, whispering warnings, giving me courage. And he was there, right before my eyes closed on that cold, wet earth, pebbled windshield glass raining down around me. I heard his voice clear as a bell: *You're the girl that made me feel safe. You're the girl who remembered me. You're the girl who believed.*

A Knot of Lies: The Truth about the Murder of Jawad Ali

Section 2, Confessions and Other Statements: Nate Chase

January 20, 2022, 10:45 p.m.

Detective Crowe: [*reenters room with coffee*] Here you go.

Nate: That was a long time to get coffee. [*takes sip from cup*] Blech. You need to complain to the manager. [*chuckles to self*]

Crowe: As a reminder, this is being taped.

Detective Diaz: [*enters room*] Sorry for the delay. I was checking on—

Nate: It's possible they could've made another pair.

Diaz: Pardon?

Nate: Chelsea Optixx. They say each design is totally custom. But they could've lied. Replicated it. It could've been that one of my followers begged them to make a second pair. There was a lot of chat about the green glasses in the comments. Take a look yourself. I have lots of admirers. A lot of freaks and stalkers out there.

Diaz: [*nods*] So it would seem. As I was saying, I checked in with your friend, Richard. Although, maybe he's not such a good friend...

Nate: What are you talking about?

Crowe: He put it all on you. Said you masterminded the whole thing.

Nate: What? That accident? That was Asma's fault—crazy bitch driver.

Diaz: Not the accident. The murder of Jawad Ali. Richard claims you chose Jawad because you were obsessed with teaching Bomb Boy a lesson. You're the one that hit him from behind. Suffocated him with a scarf.

Crowe: Richard said all he did was drive. Indicated that you coerced him. [*looks to Diaz*]

Diaz: [*nods*] Absolutely. Laid it all out. Said you wrote it all down in your journal.

Nate: No. No. No. That didn't happen. None of that happened. You're trying to trick me. I've seen how this works on TV. You're lying. Richard would never give me up.

Crowe: He said you found the culvert when you were birding, knew how to drive the back access road to get to it.

Nate: Bullshit.

Crowe: He told us where to find Jawad's cell phone. The shoebox in your closet, right? That's where your journal is, too?

Nate: [*throws coffee cup across the room*] It was him! All of it. He told me to write it all down! Document *his* plan. He even organized how to take down that freak-show editor. He was obsessed. Said we'd never get caught. Said supermen can commit the perfect crime. We were the supermen, him and me. All I did was drive.

"THE RADICALIZED LONE WHITE WOLF,"
BY CLEO PLAUTZ

Nate Chase and Richard Reynolds were your not-so-average prep school seniors. Both came from wealthy, connected families and attended one of the most expensive private schools in the country. At seventeen, Nate had a popular YouTube channel on birding, had been profiled as an up-and-coming young birding expert in magazines including the *New Yorker*, and had already appeared in multiple nature documentaries. Eighteen-year-old Richard was the popular captain of the swim and lacrosse teams and homecoming king and was probably headed to Yale.

What set them apart? They were murderers who'd been radicalized by white supremacists online. In their sophomore year, both boys connected online while searching for gaming videos and tutorials. They were quickly trapped by "filter bubbles," the type of algorithm used by multiple websites to keep users on for longer and longer hours, as they fell down a rabbit hole that began with clips for the multiplayer game *Answer the Call* and led them to recommendations for racist and anti-feminist subcultures; from there it was a short hop to the men's rights movement, Holocaust denial, and Islamophobia. With every video they watched, they continued to get more and more recommendations that took them into the deepest parts of internet hatred and eventually to boards on the alt-right Core Values platform. The algorithm pushed users from nonpolitical content into a hyper-partisan sphere, eventually leading them to the most extremist content in that world.

According to sociologist Jacob Wilson, "Young white men are the most valuable recruitment target for these often anonymous or camouflaged hate groups. They find tiny wedge issues, focus on conflict and exploiting the algorithm, and then fling the door wide open. Soon those young men are using far-right rhetoric in everyday speech. The thinking goes, if we can get the normies talking the talk, soon they will walk the walk."

This appears to have been the case with both Chase and Reynolds, as investigators discovered a virtual treasure trove of online activity on alt-right sites, including Ghost Skkkin America and White Resistance Army (WRA), that could be traced to their IP addresses. Posts included calls to violence referred to as "missions for the motherland," individual acts that organizers hoped would lead to "revolution against the cockroaches who have overrun America."

On the evening before the murder, there was a chilling post from Zarathustra14/88, a single handle used interchangeably by both boys: "About to change the course of history. This is the way the Bomb Boy ends. This is the way the Bomb Boy ends. Not with a bang but a whimper."

A response to their post met with a warning: "Watch your backs. Cover yourselves. Some police on our side. But not enough allies." Zarathustra14/88's response? A quote from Nietzsche: "Behold I am a prophet of lightning…this lightning is called Superman."

State's Exhibit 16

Journal entries of Nate Chase

January 7, 2022

We are in this. No turning back now. R seemed afraid I would turn against him, rat him out, until I pointed out that we both had enough evidence to get the other in trouble. Mutually assured destruction. It goes back before the letter from London, before the hack. Way before. Earlier, to the summer, the graffiti at the mosque in Michigan. At the graves, too. LOL. Everyone is too stupid to figure it out.

So sick of these damn normie automatons. They don't know what's good for them. It's like R says: They need to be told. They're animals, waiting for the supermen to rise and rule them. Not the cartoon who wears a red cape, but like Nietzsche said: "Behold, I teach you Superman. The Superman is the meaning of the earth." We are the supermen. We'll show them our power to wipe out the others, cage them, end them. It starts with the first one.

January 19, 2022

R. Signaled me: *Be ready for the repeat. If that bitchy skittle thinks she can take me down, she's got another thing coming.*

He finally sees it. Sees what she is. She thinks she's smart, but she's a lemming. Like all of them.

January 20, 2022

"You must be ready to burn yourself in your own flame; how could you rise anew if you have not first become ashes." —Nietzsche

The Kayleigh Barr Show

Sharp Channel Radio

If you're a fan of the show, you know I've been following the trial of Nathaniel Chase and Richard Reynolds like a hawk. The trial has come to a close, and patriots, let me tell you, I am absolutely disgusted. Disgusted at the way these two young boys Chase and Reynolds have been treated. These two all-American kids—kids who volunteer in their community, kids who regularly hit the honor roll, have been set up, scapegoated by a vast left-wing conspiracy in this country. Cop-hating, anarchist-loving so-called activists were poisoning the jury pool through the media before the trial even began, before these young men with such bright futures ahead of them even had a chance. SJWs believe these true-blooded American boys are guilty of the crime of being wealthy and white.

I call bullshit.

Crisis actors have organized and incited racist mobs at police headquarters and outside the courtroom under the guise of "vigils" when they clearly mean to intimidate jurors. This is truly anti-American. It disgusts me.

And what about this Iraqi refugee Chase and Reynolds are accused of killing? Unlike Chase and Reynolds, he had a rap sheet. He was arrested at school for suspected terrorist activity. Sources tell me his parents, who we welcomed into this country under a refugee program that clearly needs to be stopped, have been under surveillance by Homeland Security. That the South Side mosque they attend is a known hotbed for sleepers and anti-American activity. Has anyone even considered that Jawad Ali was killed because of a disagreement with fellow terrorists? You see this kind of thing in gang activity all the time. The cockroaches kill their own and then set it up so an innocent party is the fall guy.

And those so-called confessions? Kids being questioned without their parents? I heard that one of the detectives who questioned them—Detective *Diaz*—was alone in the room with these boys for a period of time and has a questionable history of deleted social media posts. So who was corroborating the story?

Has the State's Attorney's office even looked into whether Chase and Reynolds were under duress? Something's fishy if you ask me. How did this suddenly get labeled a hate crime when the police never investigated it as such? Have we looked into who financially backed the new State's Attorney when she won in the last election? My producers tell me there were many donations from the South Side, from groups and individuals who might be on watch lists. There's talk of foreign interference, here at the local level. Why? Would it have anything to do with the increase in Muslim refugees who are resettling across Illinois?

How long are we going to let this go on? We keep letting these people and their Sharia Law into our country. They don't share our values, our faith. They don't think like us. Dress like us. Act like us. They subjugate their women.

This is all a setup. We can't let them win. A verdict is set to come down any minute in the case. We cannot and will not let a false God and false justice be served. I'm calling on all 2A Patriots to be ready. Stand back and stand by. America First. America Always.

TRIAL OF CHASE, REYNOLDS DRAWS TO A CLOSE

The widely followed Jawad Ali murder trial awaits a jury decision as attorneys for both sides presented their closing argument yesterday.

Neither Nathaniel Chase nor Richard Reynolds took the stand on their behalf in what many trial experts are calling a strategic move by their lawyers, who used character witnesses to paint sympathetic portraits of the defendants. Both Chase and Reynolds confessed during questioning and attempts by their lawyers to suppress the confessions proved unsuccessful.

Defendants had been Mirandized but according to the Defense's affluenza argument, the two were not able to understand the magnitude of their actions as they were raised to believe their wealth and privilege superseded the law. The two set out on a "childish endeavor to commit the perfect crime," defense lawyers argued, not realizing the real-world consequences of their actions. In their closing arguments, the defense team characterized affluenza as a mental disorder. It should be noted that "affluenza" is not listed in *The Diagnostic and Statistical Manual of Mental Disorders*—the leading guidebook for mental health professionals. Nor is it designated as a medical condition. However, it has been successfully used in prior cases as a mitigating factor. The Defense further argued that the young men were unduly influenced by writings of German philosopher Frederick Nietzsche, who they first discovered on an alt-right YouTube site promoting a Nazi-like worldview.

Lawyers from the State's Attorney's office balked at the affluenza argument and urged the jury to return with a plea of guilt for 1st degree murder charges in the killing they painted as a hate crime. During the trial, nineteen-year-old Safiya Mirza, a former fellow student at DuSable Prep who first suspected Chase and Reynolds, described how she was attacked by Reynolds when she confronted him.

She and other witnesses described a series of school violations and offenses that prosecutors painted into a timeline of escalating crimes that culminated in the murder of Jawad Ali. Prosecutors presented a mountain of evidence, including journal entries, text messages, and receipts for the murder weapon and rental car that showed the defendants chose and stalked their victim and planned the crime. A guilty verdict in a 1st-degree murder that is designated a hate crime could result in a lifetime prison sentence.

Throughout the United States, the overwhelming majority of criminal cases do not go to trial as defendants often plead guilty and most cases end pursuant to a plea bargain; according to some estimates that includes 94% of all state cases. In the case of Chase and Reynolds, sources say that despite a plea deal being offered by the state, both Chase and Reynolds declined, assured a jury would not find them guilty.

JAWAD

There is no justice.

Not here. Not on this earth. Not for me. Not for my parents.
Not for Safiya. I think justice might be a word adults use to make
themselves feel better. They do that with a lot of words. The ones
they want to pretend are real.

But some of the words *are* good. And pure. The ones my mom
sang to me before I fell asleep. The ones that sounded so proud
in my dad's voice. The ones they whispered over my grave. Their
prayers. Some words we need. Some words you have to believe
in. That's how ideas become real. The important ones. The ones
that stay. The ones that are forever.

I wish Safiya could know how important her words were. How
she saved me. How she brought me home. How my parents who
are broken forever at least had me back in some way. At least they

got to bury me. To mourn me. I hope my parents can be happy again. I hope one day their smiles come back.

All those years ago, when I was little, Safiya gave me a gift. She gave me a little hope that I could hold in my hand. And she fought for me. That's not just an idea with a fancy name; that's something real. That day, in her store, meeting her; her talking to me was like the sun shining into a dark room.

Lately, I keep going back to the lake. Sitting there on the big rocks. Thinking of my parents and how we used to play on the shore when I was little. I can hear our laughter like it's almost real. I find myself there, again and again, the cold sun shining off the water like a million stars dancing on the waves. Then, one time, I saw it, felt it. I heard the quiet prayers. The end was right there. A rest, at last, after all the wandering.

I knew maybe I could step off the rocks and walk onto the water toward the horizon, where all the blues flow into each other. Be carried up into the clouds, past the sunrise, past the sunset, into the night sky.

High.

Higher.

A memory. A whisper. A wish.

A prayer.

A single star. Shining.

Verdict in People of the State of Illinois v. Nathaniel Chase Jr. and Richard Reynolds

May 30, 2023

Jury foreperson hands bailiff verdict. Bailiff hands it to the judge.

Judge: Ms. Foreperson, members of the jury, have you reached this verdict unanimously?

Jury: [*collectively*] Yes, Your Honor.

Judge: In the case of the People of the State of Illinois v. Nathaniel Chase Jr. and Richard Reynolds, in the first count, we the jury find the defendants Nathaniel Chase Jr. and Richard Reynolds guilty of murder in the first degree as charged in the indictment. In the second count, we the jury find Nathaniel Chase Jr. and Richard Reynolds guilty of aggravated assault as charged in the indictment. We further find the defendants Nathaniel Chase Jr. and Richard Reynolds guilty of a hate crime in accordance with Illinois Statute 720 ILCS 5/12-7.1.

Judge: Mr. Darrow do you wish for the jury to be polled?

Darrow: Yes, Your Honor.

Judge: [*to jury*] Beginning with the foreperson, please rise and answer as I ask you this question. Is this your individual verdict as well as the verdict of the jury as a whole?

Foreperson: Yes.

Juror 2: Yes.

Juror 3: Yes.

Juror 4: Yes.

Juror 5: Yes.

Juror 6: Yes.

Juror 7: Yes.

Juror 8: Yes.

Juror 9: Yes.

Juror 10: Yes.

Juror 11: Yes.

Juror 12: Yes.

Judge: Thank you, ladies and gentlemen of the jury.

Victim Impact Statement Transcript: Safiya Mirza

May 31, 2023

> **Safiya Mirza:** Your Honor, I would like to directly address Richard Reynolds for my statement.

> **Judge Majida Suman:** Understood. Please proceed, Ms. Mirza.

You have a killer smile.

I heard that about you so many times. That smile of yours drew everyone in. Everyone wanted you to be their friend. Your charm opened every door. I'm sure your family's money helped, too. It's something you could always count on. Here's what else you counted on: institutionalized racism, Islamophobia, patriarchy, misogyny. You counted on your word being believed. You counted on being innocent, even if proven guilty. You counted on everything working out your way. Of course you did, that's the story your parents raised you with. That's how this whole country operates. You counted on everyone being quiet because you are white and rich and male.

Here's what you didn't count on: me. And my anger. And my voice. You didn't count on people caring about Jawad. You didn't count on the strength and tenacity of Jawad's parents. You didn't count on a community that refused to give up. You didn't count on being told no. Of course you didn't. Your whole life is a testament to what it means to always be told yes. Yes, your bigotry is okay. Yes, this world belongs to you. Yes, you deserve every privilege you've ever been given, simply because you exist.

You know what really got me? That you smiled through this entire trial. Believing so much that you would win. You always won, didn't you? Until you didn't. Then your smile broke. I saw it. Was that fear that passed over your face when the jury read their verdict? I believe it was. Did your shoulders sag because you were scared? Is that why you couldn't face the jury as each of them confirmed their verdict when for the entire trial, you kept flashing that winning smile at the jury box? Did you feel a little terror in your heart when you finally realized you *weren't* going to get away with murder?

People say I should have mercy. I should forgive. But I can't. I hope you feel fear for a long, long time. I hope it haunts your dreams. Fills every waking moment. You loved scaring others. I saw your face when you attacked me. You *wanted* to hurt me. You *liked* seeing the terror in my eyes. That's why I hope fear will be part of your life forever, because I don't believe you'll ever feel regret. Or remorse. That's why you've been smiling almost this whole time, isn't it? That's why you've never apologized. Not once. To anyone.

You stole Jawad's life. Ended it. Brutally. Casually. Because you have so much hate in your heart. And honestly, I hope it rots you from the inside out. I didn't really know Jawad. I wish I had. He seemed like a great kid. He seemed like a bright light. He seemed like he was loved, and now that he's gone, there's a hole in the world in the shape of him. But I'll let those who knew him best, his parents, speak to what you so cruelly ripped away. The pain you caused them.

Right now, I want to tell you about the pain you caused me. Not because I think you'll feel bad. I think we've already established you won't. But because it's the truth I've been living with for sixteen months now and I deserve to speak it. I'm scared every day. And I'm so, so angry. All the time. You took a part of me. A trusting, understanding part of me and ripped it to shreds. I'm still working on piecing it back together. The relentless sting of what you did to me followed me from high school graduation into college. It's a permanent part of me now. Like a tattoo I never wanted. Like a brand burned into my skin. Months of not sleeping well. Of hearing the lies you told me in my mind, over and over. Of feeling your lips on my cheek, your hand on mine, the compliments, the sweet whispers of going to Winter Ball together. I want to erase those memories. I want to erase you. I wish I could.

Some of your fans on social media and in the right-wing press blamed me for bringing you down, even in the face of all the facts. Even when you confessed. They said I'd set you up. Sent me rape threats. Death threats. Painted me as some kind of seducer puppet master. My story wasn't believable they said. I was a liar. They didn't believe the facts. They didn't care about the truth. They refused to see it.

I kept thinking that maybe there was a sign I'd missed. How was I duped by you? How had I not seen through you? How could I let you gaslight me? It took me a long time to realize this, but the truth is, I didn't *let* you do anything. I didn't *choose* to be hurt by you, to be lied to, to be attacked. I didn't fall for anything. I was shoved. By you.

You're good at deceiving people. You're a pro. You practiced it more than swimming. Or lacrosse. None of the newspapers that described you as an honors student, as the varsity swim and lacrosse captain, printed your stats for cruelty. There's no real way to calculate those costs, I guess. Maybe that's why the press made sure to say you made swim captain two years in a row, that you hold the school's 100-meter freestyle record. That was their bias, to choose only the surface facts that were easiest to see and believe. It's the same reason you almost got away with it all.

You hate me because I'm Muslim. And brown. A child of immigrants. An upstart with too many opinions, right? Wrong opinions in your gross, distorted view of the world. That's why you wanted me dead. I know the verdict said it was assault. But let's not pretend. You and I know the truth of that night. You and I know about the rock in your hand. You and I know you lied and gaslit me. Know how you tried to manipulate me. *A game*, you called it on the night you attacked me. A game you were bored of. Are you bored now?

In the hospital, the police told me I was lucky because it could have been so much worse. Was I supposed to feel *lucky* that you didn't kill me? Was I supposed to feel lucky that all you did was assault me? That my injuries were "minor"? Was I supposed to feel lucky that the only reason you were prevented from crushing my skull like you did Jawad's was because Asma crashed her car into Nate's to stop you? It's a twisted way to ask someone to believe they're lucky. If anyone is lucky in this scenario it's you. Even here. Now. After a jury found you guilty. You're still lucky. Lucky you were born to a rich, white family. Lucky you get to have expensive lawyers who are going to be working overtime to try and get you out of this. Lucky you get to be alive. Unscathed. Without a broken bone or even the weight of remorse.

I'm going to get up out of this chair today and walk out of this courtroom, and you're not. You feeling a consequence—that's the only tiny solace I get.

I'm going to use whatever power I have, whatever voice I have, to make sure Jawad is remembered. To speak out against hate. To speak out against the unfairness of an entire system that kept giving you the benefit of the doubt. Those police who said I was lucky were right in a way. I am lucky to have the love of my friends and family, to have supporters who lifted me up, who lifted my voice, who amplified the truth. I don't know when I'll ever feel whole again, but one thing I can do is keep speaking up and speaking out. Keep shining the light on the truth.

That's one way I will be the change.

SAFIYA

POSTSCRIPT

Lie: Closure is an end.
Truth: It might be done, but it's never over.

Satisfied. That was what I was supposed to feel when the verdict came down.

Relieved. That was what I was supposed to feel when I read my victim impact statement.

Closure. That was what I was supposed to feel when the judge handed down a sentence of sixty years in prison for Richard and Nate.

I didn't feel any of that. I felt hollow.

As the judge read the jury's verdict, I stared at the back of Richard's head, saw his shoulders droop for the first time; it was so slight, but it was real. Nate yelled out, not words, but like a yelp. Like he'd been kicked in the gut. I wanted them both to feel so much worse than that.

Richard's father leaned over the banister that separated the defense table from the benches we were all sitting in. He clasped his hand on Richard's shoulder. He was saying something, whispering to the lawyers, but I couldn't hear him. The courtroom was in a bit of a frenzy for a minute. Judge Suman was banging her gavel telling people to come to order. I glanced over at Jawad's parents and nodded at them. His mom was crying. His dad was, too. I wondered if their pain would ever go away. I guessed it wouldn't. I don't know how anyone can live with a hole like that in their lives.

Right then, Richard glanced over his shoulder. He saw me. Caught my eye. At first I wasn't sure if I could face him, but then I couldn't take my eyes off him because there was something in his face I'd never seen before: fear. His smug smile had been erased. His family's wealth had always bought him everything, protected him. Then suddenly, it hadn't.

Immediately after the trial, attorneys from both sides held press conferences on the steps of the courthouse. The defense said they were going to appeal. They were hinting that the judge should maybe have recused herself, that there was bias in the case. I noticed that one of the defense attorneys kept emphasizing the judge's name when he said it. Said it over and over, Judge Majida Suman. And he mispronounced it, too. Even though inside the court he seemed to know how to say it perfectly fine.

Of course they're going to appeal. Rich white kids aren't supposed to be held accountable for their crimes, apparently. Richard did always act like he had a Get Out of Jail Free card up his sleeve. One of the newspapers reported that on his first night in jail he'd asked for a grass-fed steak for dinner. Of course he did. I wouldn't be surprised if he'd gotten it. The defense lawyers got Richard and Nate transferred to the cushiest jail there was, even with the verdict and the sentence. Money can buy comfort, I guess, if not always freedom.

The bruises and scrapes I'd gotten in my fight with Richard were gone but the memories were like scars on my body. Jawad was still dead. Murdered. Left alone in that cold, wet culvert until I found him. How could he ever have justice? There is no justice for murder and hate. Maybe even asking for justice, calling it justice in cases like this, is wrong. It's not like paying back money you stole. It's a life that was taken that can never be returned. It's all the lives that one life affects that can never be made whole again.

Jawad's voice, that woodsy musky incense smell I always sensed when I thought it was him around, his ghost, his presence, faded until a small part of me began to think it had all been a figment of my imagination. I think a lot about that afternoon years ago when Jawad and I were both little and he came into the store. Maybe that's why he chose me. Maybe I had a promise to keep. Maybe he needed my voice to speak because he couldn't. Even if I couldn't hear him anymore, he wasn't silenced. I carried a part of him with me now. That's how it would be, always.

I don't know how it's fair that I get a whole life ahead of me, I just know that I'm lucky to get it. Jawad's life is over, but his story hasn't ended. I won't let it be forgotten. Each one of us has stories that braid into other lives as those other lives weave into our own. The golden threads of Jawad's life are threaded through mine now. And looking up at the stars, I imagine him there. Shining.

HISTORICAL NOTE

The circumstances around Jawad's murder are based on the horrifying real-life slaying of fourteen-year-old Bobby Franks by Nathan Leopold and Richard Loeb in May 1924. Leopold and Loeb were obsessed with Nietzsche's Übermensch (superman) theory and believed themselves to be intellectually superior to others—above the law and society's norms. To prove that superiority, they decided to commit the perfect crime and spent months plotting a murder. Loeb knew Franks (they were second cousins), and Leopold and Loeb easily lured him into their car—rented under a false name—and killed him, dumping his body in a culvert.

At the time of the murder, Leopold and Loeb were nineteen and eighteen years old, respectively, and were from very wealthy, well-connected families. Loeb was affable and popular. Leopold was an introvert and avid bird watcher. After the murder, they left a ransom note for the Franks and even called, assuring them that their son was alive and that he was kidnapped, not murdered. The pair hoped to mislead both the parents and the police, but Bobby Franks' body was soon discovered with an incriminating piece of evidence—a pair of eyeglasses with a unique hinge, belonging to Leopold.

Leopold and Loeb confessed during interrogation, but each accused the other of being the mastermind and murderer. The murder called "the crime of the century" was met with a media frenzy, and the press often highlighted the wealth, family connections, and good looks of the accused alongside salacious details not always based in fact. The pair was defended by renowned attorney Clarence Darrow. In an unusual move for the time, Darrow employed an "affluenza" defense, along with claiming other mitigating factors, in hopes of preventing the death penalty for his clients. Leopold and Loeb were sentenced to life in prison plus ninety-nine years. Loeb was murdered in prison in 1936. Leopold was paroled in 1958 after serving thirty-three years in Illinois's Stateville Penitentiary.

To this day, we don't know the actual facts of what happened in that car. But here's a truth: Both Leopold and Loeb were murderers. Here's another truth: Bobby Franks has essentially become a footnote in the larger history of Leopold and Loeb. Bobby—an athletic kid who liked to play tennis and excelled on his school's debate team. He deserved a full life and now, at least, our remembrance.

To learn more about this case and get a look at primary sources, a good place to start is *The Leopold and Loeb Files: An Intimate Look at One of America's Most Infamous Crimes* by Nina Barrett.

AUTHOR'S NOTE

Dear Reader,

I wrote this book for a boy I knew who died too young.

I wrote this book for Our Three Winners, whose lives were ended by bigotry.

I wrote this book for an inventive kid whose world was turned upside down because he built a clock.

I wrote this book because we've lost too many people to hate and because so often we've witnessed the powerful and the privileged get away with murder.

I wrote this book to tell a truth.

In America, we tend to ignore an uncomfortable history—our history. We want our wrongs to stay in the past. We want to bury the truth and see history through rose-colored glasses.

But the thing about buried truths? They come back to haunt you.

For years, the ghosts of all those this nation has wronged have been rising up, clamoring for their stories to be recognized. It's up to us to give voice to those whose voices have been forcibly oppressed or forgotten. We might not be able to give them justice—because what is justice to the victims of racism, bigotry, misogyny?—but we can speak truth to power and insist on accountability.

When I started writing *Hollow Fires* in 2019, it was against the backdrop of years of toxic, damaging lies from our elected officials, from the highest offices of this country. It was in the midst of a societal upheaval, of people taking to the streets, demanding change so we could strive for that "more perfect union" politicians constantly laud. I wrote this book to ask uncomfortable questions and confront hard truths, because inside us, there's a small voice that says we can do better. We must. These voices need to be a chorus, a song we belt out, together.

And now, as *Hollow Fires* goes to print, I'm watching heartbreaking images on the news of Afghans trying to flee their country, fearful that the Taliban will retaliate against them—journalists, human rights workers, and interpreters, just like Jawad's father. Unfortunately, the United States has a terrible history of occupying other nations, asking those countries' citizens for help, and then all too often ignoring the pleas of local allies and leaving them behind to potentially face imprisonment or torture for aiding the United States. We've witnessed Afghans desperately handing their babies to American soldiers over airport barricades. We've seen images of people trying to jump onto departing US military planes, reviving painful memories of Saigon in 1975. Yet we hear a cacophony of hate from comfortably situated, xenophobic American pundits decrying the potential influx of Afghan refugees. Mind you, these refugees have been forcibly displaced, in part because of the actions of the United States. And the few who are lucky enough to make it to the United States and get visas, permanent residency, and citizenship (make no mistake, these are huge hurdles) are sometimes cruelly subjected to bigotry and hate in the communities they land in.

As Americans, shouldn't we ask more of ourselves? Isn't that what it means to call on the better angels of our nature?

The commentators who scream against allowing in refugees, the same talking heads who think the horrifyingly inhumane treatment of migrants at our border with Mexico is justified, buy into a deeply ingrained American myth—that there are always only "winners" and "losers." That war is a zero-sum game. That extending a helping hand to a displaced individual somehow means that somewhere, some American is getting less. But that binary is a lie. Here's a truth: Giving aid and comfort to a displaced person doesn't mean we can't also help Americans in need. We can and must do both.

We have choices to make. Important ones. About our future. About who we are as a nation, as a people, and as human beings. One of these choices is to live in a world where we call "alternative facts" what they really, truly are—lies that obfuscate, deceits that give cover to injustice, tools of cynical politicians. I'm asking us to speak tough truths out loud. To know we can do better and be better. I'm asking us to step forward, to face the truth of all we are, lanterns held high, illuminating the dark.

Warmly,

Samira Ahmed

ACKNOWLEDGMENTS

Hollow Fires was not an easy book to write—there were times when the weight of writing about the lives broken by bigotry and hate felt too real, too emotionally raw. Sometimes it felt like no matter what I attempted, I couldn't do Safiya's and Jawad's stories justice. And one of the things that kept me going was you, dear reader, knowing you would hold this book in your hands. Thank you for being a part of this journey.

Love and gratitude to my brilliant agent, Joanna Volpe, who always has my back even as she keeps a keen eye on the horizon. So much appreciation to the entire team at New Leaf Literary & Media. Heartfelt thanks to Jordan Hill for being a sounding board and for keeping me on track, to Kate Sullivan for the wisdom and encouragement, and to Abbie Donoghue and Jenniea Carter for their support. Thanks to Pouya Shahbazian for imagining a life for this story beyond the bookshelves.

I am over the moon that Alvina Ling was the editor for this book. She understood the heart of this story and encouraged me to put it on the page. My deep gratitude to the incredible team at Little, Brown Books for Young Readers that helped bring this story to shelves, especially Ruqayyah Daud for her wonderful insight, Emilie Polster, Bill Grace, Savannah Kennelly, Siena Koncsol, Barbara

Bakowski, Caroline Clouse, Victoria Stapleton, Christie Michel, Jake Regier, Patricia Alvarado, Andie Divelbiss, Shawn Foster, and Danielle Cantarella. A million high fives to Karina Granda, who designed the cover of my dreams, and Dana Lendl, whose beautiful illustration captured everything I wanted to say. Jackie Engel and Megan Tingley, I'm so proud and honored to be part of the LBYR family. Thank you all from the bottom of my heart for believing in my stories and bringing them into the world.

Independent bookstores have been huge supporters of mine since the very beginning, and I am so, so grateful to them. A special shout-out to the indie booksellers who embraced this story before there was even an ARC. I am so thankful to you, Cecilia Cackley, Joy Preble, Kathy Burnette, Samantha Hendricks, Jilleen Moore, and tee arnold.

I am grateful beyond words for friends and family, early readers and consultants, and delightful cheerleaders. Merci beaucoup to Pierre and Marie France Jonas, Sabaa Tahir, Karen McManus, Aisha Saeed, Stephanie Garber, Dhonielle Clayton, Tiffany Jackson, Sona Charaipotra, Amy Adams, Rena Barron, Ronni Davis, Gloria Chao, Lizzie Cooke, Kat Cho, Anna Waggener, Sajidah Ali, Amy Vidlak Girmscheid, Rachel Strolle, and Alison Siegler.

Shukria to my parents, Hamid and Mazher Ahmed, for their support and encouragement. And to Sara, Asra, Alia, Zayn, Nathan, Will, Raesh, Raj, Paul, and the Ahmed/Razvi cousins and fam for all the love and laughs.

To Thomas, Lena, and Noah, hearts of my heart, lights of my world, all my reasons for everything: I am endlessly grateful to live this life with you.

Erielle Bakkum

SAMIRA AHMED

is the *New York Times* bestselling author of *Love, Hate & Other Filters*; *Mad, Bad & Dangerous to Know*; *Internment*; and *Hollow Fires*. She was born in Bombay, India, and has lived in New York, Chicago, and Kauai, where she spent a year searching for the perfect mango. She invites you to visit her online at samiraahmed.com and on Twitter and Instagram @sam_aye_ahm.

SAMIRA AHMED